St. Helena Library
1492 Library Lane
St. Helena, CA 94574
(707) 963-5244

A Gift From
ST. HELENA PUBLIC LIBRARY
FRIENDS&FOUNDATION

ONE FOR THE BOOKS

ONE FOR THE BOOKS

Jenn McKinlay

BERKLEY PRIME CRIME
New York

BERKLEY PRIME CRIME
Published by Berkley
An imprint of Penguin Random House LLC
penguinrandomhouse.com

Copyright © 2020 by Jennifer McKinlay Orf
Excerpt from *Paris Is Always a Good Idea* by Jenn McKinlay copyright
© 2020 Jennifer McKinlay Orf
Penguin Random House supports copyright. Copyright fuels creativity,
encourages diverse voices, promotes free speech, and creates a vibrant culture.
Thank you for buying an authorized edition of this book and for complying
with copyright laws by not reproducing, scanning, or distributing any part of it
in any form without permission. You are supporting writers and allowing
Penguin Random House to continue to publish books for every reader.

BERKLEY and the BERKLEY & B colophon are registered trademarks and
BERKLEY PRIME CRIME is a trademark of
Penguin Random House LLC.

Library of Congress Cataloging-in-Publication Data

Names: McKinlay, Jenn, author.
Title: One for the books / Jenn McKinlay.
Description: First edition. | New York: Berkley Prime Crime, 2020. |
Series: A library lover's mystery; book 11
Identifiers: LCCN 2020019703 (print) | LCCN 2020019704 (ebook) |
ISBN 9780593101742 (hardcover) | ISBN 9780593101766 (ebook)
Subjects: GSAFD: Mystery fiction.
Classification: LCC PS3612.A948 O54 2020 (print) |
LCC PS3612.A948 (ebook) | DDC 813/.6—dc23
LC record available at https://lccn.loc.gov/2020019703
LC ebook record available at https://lccn.loc.gov/2020019704

Printed in the United States of America
1   3   5   7   9   10   8   6   4   2

Cover art by Julia Green
Cover design by Rita Frangie
Book design by Laura K. Corless

In loving memory of Jonathan Edwin McKinlay. You were our gentle giant, our fixer of all things, our true north, our hero. You loved deeply and truly with your whole heart, and we will miss you forever.

ONE FOR THE BOOKS

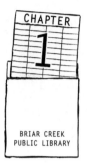

CHAPTER

1

BRIAR CREEK
PUBLIC LIBRARY

Why is everyone staring at us?" Lindsey Norris asked her fiancé, Mike Sullivan, known to everyone in their small Connecticut shoreline town as "Sully."

"Are they staring at us?" He looked up from his phone where he was scanning the news, which for him meant the current sports scores, and glanced around the shop.

"Yes," she confirmed. "And it's kind of creepy."

Having slept late that morning, they were in line at the bakery, which was tucked into the back corner of the town's lone grocery store. Their dog, Heathcliff, was sitting between their feet and behaving like a perfect gentleman, so Lindsey was certain he wasn't the one drawing the attention of every other customer in the bakery their way.

"You're right," he said. "They are staring."

"But why?" she asked. She gave each of their persons a

quick visual scan. They were both dressed with buttons aligned and zippers up and clothes right-side out. There were no spectacular bedhead or egregious stains to be seen. Having been the focus of unwanted attention a few months before, being stared at still gave Lindsey the odd twinge of anxiety.

Sully put his arm around her in a comforting gesture and pulled her close, kissing the top of her head. "Wild guess here, but I imagine it's because we're getting married in just over a week."

"Yes, but it's a tiny ceremony on Bell Island," she pointed out. "Just family and close friends, hardly an event worth noting."

"People like weddings." He shrugged.

"Sully, Lindsey, yoo-hoo!" A voice called, and Lindsey glanced past Sully to see Mrs. Housel, coming at them as fast as her short legs could carry her. Heathcliff hopped to his feet and began wagging his bushy black tail, looking for love from anyone willing to give it.

"Morning, Mrs. H," Sully said. "What can we do for you?"

"I just need to know where you're registered," she said. She was breathless, but still bent over to pat Heathcliff on the head before rising back up to smile at them.

"Registered?" Lindsey asked.

"Yes, you know, for a wedding gift," she explained. "I can't possibly show up at your wedding without a gift. It would be bad form."

"Uh." Lindsey glanced at Sully in a mild state of panic. Mrs. Housel was one of Lindsey's favorite patrons. They had bonded over a deep and abiding love of all things Agatha Christie. A tiny little bird of a thing, Mrs. Housel was the sweetest of the sweet. She lived on a fixed income in a modest cottage in the old part of town. Telling her the wedding was private and that she wasn't invited would be like punting a puppy into oncoming traffic. Everything inside Lindsey rebelled at the mere idea. Judging by the flicker of alarm in Sully's eyes, he was thinking the same thing.

"Mrs. H, Lindsey and I really appreciate the thought," he began, and then he stalled out. Sully's heart was as big as one of the tour boats he captained around the Thumb Islands in the bay, and Lindsey knew he was struggling to find the right words. She immediately decided having one more guest wasn't going to be a problem, especially one as tiny as Mrs. Housel.

"We haven't registered anywhere," Lindsey said. "In fact, we're asking anyone who attends our wedding to donate a book to the library instead of giving us gifts." This much was true, at least.

Mrs. Housel clasped her hands over her heart. "How wonderful. I just love you two. You're like family to me."

"And we love you, Mrs. H," Sully said. He looked oh-so relieved.

Mrs. Housel reached forward and squeezed their hands with hers. Then, with a wave, she fluttered out of the bakery as quickly as she'd arrived.

"That was nice of you, darlin'," Sully said.

Lindsey shrugged. "What's one more guest when it clearly means a lot to her? Besides, she's so tiny. How much could she possibly eat?"

"Yeah, it's like inviting a hummingbird to the wedding," he agreed.

Lindsey smiled, then she tipped her head back to meet his gaze. He was wearing his thick wool peacoat, a knit hat over his reddish brown curls and the scarf Lindsey had knit him last winter that matched his eyes perfectly. His cheeks were ruddy from the cold, making his bright blue eyes even more so. Lindsey felt her heart squeeze. He was going to be her husband in just a matter of days.

The thought never ceased to make her dizzy. She knew it was silly, that some would say marriage was just a piece of paper, but it felt like more to her. Much more. She was committing her life to his, a promise she didn't take lightly, and she found the thought alternately thrilling and terrifying, but definitely more thrilling.

"What are you grinning at?" he asked. A smile played on his lips, bracketed by deep dimples in each cheek.

"We're getting married," she whispered as if she was giving him brand-new information.

"Well, I, for one, can't wait," he said. "'Mrs. Mike Sullivan' has a nice ring to it."

"As does 'Mr. Lindsey Norris,'" she retorted.

"It does at that." He grinned and kissed her quickly before gently moving her up the line.

Brendan Taggert was working the counter. He grinned at the sight of them. "There's the bride and groom! Not much longer now, eh?"

Brendan was a big man in his mid-thirties. He was the chief baker and occasionally came out of the kitchen to lend a hand at the counter when the bakery was especially busy. He gave them each a large coffee in a thick paper to-go cup and pushed a bag of muffins at Lindsey while Sully paid. She glanced inside to find their usual, a lemon–poppy seed for Sully and a cranberry-walnut for her. The morning was looking up.

"Your wedding cake is going to be a thing of beauty," Brendan declared.

"Since you're baking it, I have no doubt," she said. Brendan was a wizard with fondant.

"I am a little worried, though." Brendan rubbed his jaw with the back of his hand.

"Oh?" Lindsey tried to keep the panic out of her voice, but the week before a wedding, a woman did not want to hear her cake baker expressing doubts. She knew she'd failed when Sully gave her shoulder a reassuring squeeze.

"Yeah, I don't think you ordered a big enough cake," Brendan said. "I hear people talking in the bakery all day long, and it sounds as if a lot of folks are planning to attend your big day."

Lindsey and Sully exchanged confused looks. Was Mrs. Housel not the only one planning to crash the wedding?

"But we're keeping it small," Sully said. "Just family and close friends." He frowned, clearly not understanding how it could be spiraling out of their control.

"I don't know what to tell you." Brendan shrugged. "You're the town boat captain, a native son no less, and she's the library director. Everyone knows you two, and they're very invested in your romance. Whether you invited them or not, it sounds like people are planning to attend. You're going to want a bigger cake. I'm just sayin'." Brendan raised his hands as if to signal that he'd done his part in warning them.

Lindsey felt her heart pound hard in her chest. Surely, he was overstating it. People didn't crash weddings en masse, did they? Then she thought of Mrs. Housel and her determination to be at their wedding, declaring that they were like family to her. How many other Briar Creek and Thumb Islands residents felt that way? Oh, no.

A puppy—not Heathcliff, who'd gone to work with Sully—romped past the circulation desk where Lindsey Norris stood. White, with floppy ears and a stubby tail, its coat was covered in bright spots of purple, green, yellow and all the other colors in the rainbow.

It was a big puppy, more like the size of a small horse. Lindsey squinted at it. Sure enough, a closer look identified the canine as being the Briar Creek Public Library's children's librarian, Beth Barker, wearing what looked like adult-size footie pajamas that she'd tailored to look like a dog by adding ears to the hood, a tail to the bottom and spots all over.

"Reading *Dog's Colorful Day* today?" Lindsey asked.

"Woof!" Beth barked. "Colors and counting, does it get any more fun?"

"It does not," Lindsey agreed. "Unless it's crafternoon Thursday and we're discussing *A Christmas Carol* by Dickens."

Beth stopped romping, and her eyes sparkled. A thick

thatch of black bangs stuck out from under her hood, giving her delicate features a mischievous air.

"Do you think Nancy made cookies?" she asked. She hugged her belly, where her new status as a mom-to-be was just beginning to show. "She's in charge of food this week, and baby and I are craving some of her Scottish shortbread."

"No." Lindsey shook her head, knowing full well that Nancy, who was her former landlord and a good friend, had surely made some. Then she teased, "But I'll bet she made you some dog biscuits."

"Woof, woof, so funny," Beth retorted. Then she looked thoughtful and scratched one of her dog ears. "Actually, if Nancy made them, they're probably pretty good."

"Fair point." Nancy was their local amateur baker extraordinaire and was known all over Briar Creek for her magical cookies.

"Whatever she brings, save some for me. I'm eating for two!" Beth cried, as she scampered off to the story time room in anticipation of the toddlers who would begin arriving in the next thirty minutes.

Petite in build and swallowed up by her slouchy dog outfit, Beth looked like a kid herself. Lindsey smiled. The town was very fortunate to have such a dedicated librarian. Beth's programs packed the house, making a delightful connection with the next generation of enthusiastic readers.

"Well, that should be quite a fun story time."

Lindsey turned to find Ms. Cole—nicknamed "the lemon" for her frequently sour disposition and old-school librarian ways—standing beside her.

Lindsey blinked. "Are you feeling all right, Ms. Cole?"

Today Ms. Cole was in her purple outfit. Purple tights with a dark purple wool skirt, matched—sort of—with a twilight-hued purple cardigan and a lavender silk top. It gave her an overall ombre effect that was actually rather appealing. Ms. Cole favored outfits that fell distinctly into one category on the color spectrum, so apple green was worn with chartreuse and forest green as if they all matched. They didn't. In fact, none of her outfits really matched, but neither Lindsey nor any of the other staff had the heart or nerve to tell her so.

"Yes, I'm fine. I'm trying to be less rigid," Ms. Cole said. She glanced at Lindsey over the tops of her reading glasses. "How am I doing?"

"Well, you didn't shush her," Lindsey said. "I'd call that a big improvement."

"I haven't shushed anyone in months," Ms. Cole said. She sounded forlorn. "My shusher has probably atrophied, but Milton told me that if I'm serious about running for mayor, I might want to be friendlier to my constituents."

Milton Duffy, town historian and president of the library board, was Ms. Cole's significant other. Ms. Cole had squashed any use of the word *boyfriend*, saying it sounded ridiculous to call a man in his eighties a boy, and she wouldn't tolerate being called his girlfriend either.

"He didn't tell you to smile more often, did he?" Lindsey teased. "Because that would be annoying."

Ms. Cole laughed, which was a rare occurrence, and it made Lindsey smile. "No, he didn't. He did say I needed to start attending all the town events so that I become more well known. I'm even going to the Briggses' Annual Christmas Bash this weekend."

"You are?" Lindsey could not have been more surprised if Ms. Cole had said she'd taken up exotic dancing for fitness.

"Yes," Ms. Cole sighed. "I've lived in Briar Creek my entire life, and I have never attended one of the famed Briggs Bashes. I thought I'd be shuffling off this mortal coil with my streak intact, but politics make strange bedfellows, as they say."

It was a wise political move. Steve Briggs was a corporate attorney, one of the wealthier residents of Briar Creek, and he was also the local justice of the peace. Ms. Cole needed to have his endorsement if she was to stand a chance against the incumbent, Mayor Hensen.

"Steve's not so bad," Lindsey said. "A little over-the-top in his enthusiasm for his parties, but during the holidays, that's not such a terrible thing."

The Briggses threw a holiday extravaganza every year. Lindsey and Sully always made an appearance because Sully and Steve had grown up together in Briar Creek and were, if not quite friends, then very warm acquaintances. While the parties were fun, Lindsey and Sully never lingered. Being an introvert at heart, Lindsey had a two-hour window for the overcrowded, loud sensory overload that was a Briggs party, and Sully was right there with her. If ever she needed proof that they were soul mates, that was it.

"Isn't he officiating your wedding?" Paula Turner, the library clerk, asked. She was working at the station on the other side of Ms. Cole, checking in the books from the book drop.

"Yes," Lindsey said. "Since we're getting married on Bell Island, where Sully grew up, and not in a church, we thought, being the local justice of the peace, he'd be the perfect choice."

The coastal town of Briar Creek overlooked an archipelago called the Thumb Islands, which had sported the summer homes of some of America's richest families during the height of the Gilded Age. A hurricane in 1938 had all but wiped out the old Victorian mansions that had once dominated the islands, and now the residences were smaller and more sustainable, mostly used as summer cottages. Only a few islands, like Sully's parents' Bell Island, were equipped with electricity, making them habitable year round.

Paula glanced at the calendar on the desk. "The wedding is in a little over a week. Are you ready for it?"

Lindsey blinked at her. Why was it so jarring when someone else told her the wedding was around the corner? It wasn't as if she wasn't aware. It just felt more significant when someone else said it. Her heart thumped hard in her chest, but she refused to freak out. This was why she and Sully had decided on the island. They wanted to keep their wedding small and simple, for friends and family only, in the Sullivans' large brick house on Bell Island.

"You look flushed, and not in a good way," Ms. Cole said. "Maybe you should sit down."

"Oh, no, I'm fine," Lindsey reassured them. She went to wave Ms. Cole's concern away and noticed that her hand was shaking.

"Uh-huh." Ms. Cole glanced from her hand to her face and frowned. "Sit."

"I'll get you a glass of water," Paula said. She slipped off her stool, moving it close so Lindsey could sit, before going into the workroom where there was a water cooler.

"You're not getting cold feet, are you?" Ms. Cole asked.

"Uh . . . I . . . ." Lindsey stammered.

"Cold feet? Who's getting cold feet?" Nancy Peyton and Violet La Rue appeared at the circulation counter.

They were carrying bags of food for the lunchtime craft-ernoon that met every Thursday at midday. Both women were wearing winter coats, hats and scarves, as the weather had turned decidedly wintry over the past few days and the temperature had plummeted.

"With this freeze snap, it's small wonder your feet are cold," Violet said.

"I think that was a metaphor," Nancy returned. Her bright blue eyes were filled with concern.

"Oh," Violet said. A former Broadway actress, she could convey more in one word than most people could in a whole sentence. She studied Lindsey. "You don't look well, dear."

"I'm fine," Lindsey protested.

"No, she isn't. She's freaking out," Paula said. She handed Lindsey a glass of water. They all stared at her as she took a sip.

"I'm not, really," Lindsey said on a swallow. The water went down hard. "It's just that the wedding is coming up so fast—"

"Isn't it thrilling?" Ferne Knauss, a patron and former

librarian, paused beside the desk on her way out. "Well, speaking for me and my quilting circle, we can't wait. Our group has made you a special surprise. Goodness knows you've given us plenty of time. It feels as if I've been waiting for you and Sully to tie the knot for years. And is there anything more romantic than a winter wedding? Maybe we'll get lucky and it will snow."

"Uh . . ." Lindsey's eyes went wide as Ferne waved the Nova Scotia quilting pattern book she'd just checked out as she strode to the door.

"I thought you said this was going to be a small friends-and-family-only wedding," Nancy said.

"It is," Lindsey said.

"Really?" Violet asked. "I didn't think you were that close to Ferne and her quilting circle."

"I'm not," she said. "I mean, I enjoy them all, but we're not best pals or anything."

"Well, you'd better make room for a few more at your wedding reception because it sounds like they're planning on being there," Ms. Cole said.

"Oh, man." Lindsey rubbed her temples with her fingers.

"Look on the bright side. Maybe they made you a nice quilt," Paula said.

Lindsey tried to smile, but given Brendan's warning about her cake being too small, Mrs. Housel's inquiry as to their registry and now Ferne Knauss's announcement that her quilting circle was coming, she couldn't help but think that something, somehow, had gone horribly awry.

"You all received invitations, correct?" she asked.

They all glanced at each other and then nodded.

"They were really beautiful, too," Paula said. "I especially liked the calligraphy."

"The woman at the stationery store specialized in that," Lindsey said. "And I had her mail the invitations for us."

Ms. Cole frowned. "There was no RSVP card included."

"Since we invited so few people," Lindsey said. "We knew we'd get verbal confirmations from everyone, and we have."

They were all silent, trying to puzzle out what could have happened that Lindsey's guest list seemed to have expanded without her knowing.

"When you made your guest list, did you start with a big number and then cut it down?" Nancy asked.

"Yes," Lindsey said. "We originally had over a hundred people on the list, but the island is so small, we decided to keep it to just our inner circle."

Violet gave her a shrewd glance. "Is there any chance you gave the stationer the wrong list?"

A cold knot of dread tightened inside Lindsey's chest. She stood and swayed on her feet. Given how crazy things had been at the time she'd hired the stationer, it was a distinct possibility.

Suddenly her intimate wedding for thirty-five was looking like it would be for three times that many. She thought she might be sick. She didn't even know if they could fit that many people on Bell Island. She glanced around at her friends in panic.

"What am I going to do?" she asked.

CHAPTER 2

BRIAR CREEK
PUBLIC LIBRARY

To start with, don't panic," Violet said. She was always fantastic in a crisis because, after a long and storied career as one of the first black actresses to win a Tony Award, there wasn't much that she considered impossible.

"Panic? Me?" Lindsey asked. "Why would I do that? Just because my tiny wedding that was supposed to be an intimate gathering is now a much bigger affair with a cake that's too small and not enough food and nowhere near enough tables and chairs to seat everyone on an island that probably can't have that many pe—"

"Breathe," Nancy interrupted her. Lindsey sucked in a great big gulp of air. She was feeling the tiniest bit woozy.

"I need to call Sully," she said. "How am I going to explain this? I'm a librarian. I'm supposed to be more organized than this."

"You were dealing with a stalker at the time when you

were arranging for your invitations to go out," Paula reminded her. "It was an easy mistake to make."

"Easy. Difficult. Stupid. Hard to tell the difference right now." Lindsey said. She couldn't even wrap her brain around this change of plans.

"Come on," Nancy said. "Let's go set up the crafternoon room for our meeting. We can discuss it while we work on your wedding favors, which we need to get going on, especially now that we're going to have to make a lot more of them."

"Wedding favors?" Lindsey asked. Since when was she having wedding favors?

"It was supposed to be a surprise," Paula said. She was their resident crafter. She tossed her seasonally dyed cranberry red braid over her shoulder. "Don't worry. I picked something so easy even you can do it. Pine cone fire starters. They're amazing."

In short order, a bewildered Lindsey found herself sitting at the table in the crafternoon room with her closest friends, discussing Dickens's *A Christmas Carol*, while dipping pine cones in melted colored wax. The lunch Nancy had provided was a typical British repast of hot tea and sandwiches, specifically curry chicken salad and cheese-and-pickle sandwiches, which Nancy had assured Beth, when she arrived, would be followed by Scottish shortbread and English thumbprint cookies.

"When did you decide to make wedding favors?" Beth asked Lindsey, as she dipped her pine cone into the peppermint-scented blue wax.

"I didn't," Lindsey said. "This is Paula's idea, and it's a

good thing, too, because apparently there are more guests coming to the wedding than I'd planned on."

"You sound stressed," Nancy said. "There's no need to be. We have everything under control."

"But how?" Lindsey asked. "I was planning on a tiny wedding, and now it looks like a good portion of the town is planning to come. How am I supposed to know how many people to provide for? This is a nightmare. And what if it's just the beginning of bad things happening to our wedding?"

"Easy, Lindsey," Mary Murphy said. She was Sully's sister and shared his reddish brown curls, deep dimples and unflappable disposition. Since she owned the local restaurant in town, she was excellent in a foodie crisis. "Ian and I are making the food, and we can adjust to whatever you need."

Since their restaurant, the Blue Anchor, was the only restaurant in town, it was a given that they would cater the wedding, but Lindsey hated that she had just tripled their workload.

"But I want you to enjoy the wedding," Lindsey protested.

"We will," Mary assured her. "That's why we have employees. It'll be fine. It's just as easy to cook for one hundred as it is for thirty."

Lindsey stared at her.

"It is," Mary insisted. Then she grinned. "Especially, when I'm not doing the cooking."

"I feel like an idiot," Lindsey said. "I don't even know how many people we should be cooking for. And your poor parents. They're opening up their home for our wedding, and I'm quite sure they didn't bargain on a wedding of this size. And around the holidays, too. Ugh."

Just before the crafternoon meeting had begun, she'd called the woman at the stationery store, who had confirmed Lindsey's fear that she'd left the wrong list. Lindsey had accidentally given the calligrapher their original guest list before they had decided to keep it small. Lindsey felt like a complete moron. How could she have messed up the invitations to her own wedding? It boggled. And because she hadn't included an RSVP, she really didn't know how many people were planning to show up, given that people tended to bring plus-ones and all.

"My parents won't care," Mary said. "They adore you. Don't you worry about it."

"I am worried," Lindsey said. "This is so unlike me, and I don't know how to fix it."

"Listen," Paula said. "There's no need to panic. The Briggses are having their annual party on Saturday, at which the entire town shows up. You and Sully could make an announcement at the party, letting people know that there was a mistake and invitations were sent to too many people and that you need to rescind some invitations. Sorry, not sorry."

"That doesn't seem like it would be incredibly rude?" Lindsey asked.

Paula shrugged. "Um, no. Rude is showing up at a wedding when there's been a mistake in the invites. It's your wedding. It should be the day that you want not what other people expect."

"She's right," Beth said. "And I am more than happy to go around town informing people that there was a mistake and they need to rethink their plans to attend your wedding."

Lindsey smiled. "Thank you, both. I appreciate the thought, I do, but I don't want to offend anyone. This was my mistake, and I need to own it." She sighed. "It's just that I'm not really into the whole princess-for-a-day thing. I'm an introvert, and speaking in public is not my bag. In fact, I hate it. I don't know how I'm going to get through the vows in front of the people I love and trust, never mind even more people."

"We know," Violet said. "We've seen your process for gearing up for the annual speech you give at the Dinner in the Stacks fund-raiser. It isn't pretty. But, somehow, we'll manage this, and you'll have a beautiful wedding."

Lindsey felt her shoulders drop. "Thank you."

The table fell silent as they all dipped their pine cones into the wax and let them set on the parchment paper Paula had set out. With each dip, the wax on the pine cones became thicker, and Lindsey could see that they would indeed make lovely mementos for her wedding. The best part was that they were useful and not something that would take up room or gather dust. In fact, she was going to take one home tonight and try it out in her fireplace.

"These really are lovely, Paula," she said.

"Thank you." Paula smiled, and then a teasing light lit her eyes and she said, "Since Lindsey is too preoccupied with her wedding to offer some Dickensian facts, I have a few items to share about *A Christmas Carol*."

"Do tell." Violet encouraged her with a wink.

"Did you know that it only took Dickens six weeks to write *A Christmas Carol*?" she asked. "He started in mid-October of eighteen forty-three and finished on December second."

"Six weeks? It's about thirty thousand words long, isn't it?" Nancy asked.

"Yes, and it was adapted to the stage by Edward Stirling six weeks after it was published," Violet added. "It came to New York shortly thereafter."

"Fascinating," Nancy said. She glanced at Lindsey. "Did you know all of this?"

Lindsey shook her head. "No, but I did know that he named Scrooge's sister Fan, or Fanny, after his own favorite sister."

"Aw, that's sweet," Beth said. She tied a cotton string, which would act as a wick, around another pine cone as she prepared to dip it. "I heard that Dickens did readings of *A Christmas Carol* right up until three months before he died. In fact, he used to drink a sherry with a raw egg beaten into it before his readings. Maybe you should do that before your vows."

Lindsey grimaced. "Thanks, but I don't think Sully wants me to throw up on his shoes mid-ceremony."

The others laughed, as she intended, and she was surprised to find she felt better. They would get a handle on the wedding. Maybe not everyone who got an invitation was planning to attend. It could be that there wouldn't even be that many people at her wedding. She could always hope. Right?

* * *

The Briggs party was well underway when Sully and Lindsey arrived. Parking was at a premium, so they left their car at the bottom of the hill and walked up the narrow street to the estate, which perched above the surrounding area like an osprey on its nest surveying the land around it for predators and prey alike.

Lindsey enjoyed the Briggses' mansion—as a guest. It was a modern, hurricane-proof glass structure that offered a 360-degree view of the islands in the bay and the town surrounding it. Steve and his wife, Jamie, lived alone in the eight-thousand-square-foot concrete, steel and glass structure, with hired help coming in daily to do the cooking, cleaning and yard work. With ten bedrooms and twelve bathrooms, it seemed like a ridiculous amount of space for just two people, but Lindsey supposed she shouldn't judge. Maybe they needed that much space to coexist.

She'd only seen Jamie Briggs at previous annual parties, as Jamie wasn't in residence very often in Briar Creek, preferring life in their Manhattan apartment to the small seaside town. The few times Lindsey had met her, Jamie had struck her as being a bit of a drama queen, but that could be because she was more high-maintenance than any person Lindsey had ever met—and being a public servant, she'd met her share.

"How long have Steve and Jamie been married?" she asked Sully.

They were halfway up the hill. Sully wasn't even breathing heavily, and Lindsey was mouth-breathing as she tried not to audibly pant and wheeze. Although she rode her bike to work every day, inclines were not her favorite thing, and this was a steep one.

"Seven years?" Sully said it as a question, making it clear he was guessing.

"Is she also from around here?"

Sully glanced at her, and Lindsey noted that he slowed his steps, clearly catching on to the fact that she was about to pass out. She would have continued trying to bluff, but to what purpose? She let her wheeze out as she paused and turned to him to hear his answer.

"No, Jamie is a Darien girl," he said.

Lindsey nodded. Darien was one of the many towns that made up the Gold Coast of Connecticut. It stretched from Greenwich to Fairfield and was inhabited by people who were known mostly for being loaded. Manhattan financial guys, Kennedys and celebrities like Robert Redford, Keith Richards and Martha Stewart resided in the area, making it extremely exclusive.

Briar Creek and the Thumb Islands did not have that sort of cachet. It suddenly made sense that Jamie Briggs was seldom seen there. The annual party was her one moment to acknowledge the people of her husband's hometown, which he loved so well, and then she could disappear back into her glam life in the city.

"Ah," Lindsey said.

Sully paused to look at her. She was wearing a green knit dress and black suede boots. Her curly blond hair was long and loose, and she wore a black wool pashmina over her dress for warmth. The wind coming in off the water was bitter, but she hadn't wanted to deal with a coat. Sully was wearing a black blazer over a white dress shirt and jeans, having also skipped wearing a coat. Given the workout they were getting walking up the hill, they really didn't need jackets to keep them warm.

"Have I told you how pretty you look tonight?" he asked her.

"Yes." She grinned. She sucked in a breath of cold air that burned her lungs. "And you look especially handsome." He smiled, and she narrowed her eyes. "Why do I get the feeling that you're stalling me with compliments so I can catch my breath?"

"That doesn't mean it isn't true. Is it working?" he asked.

"A little." She took in another deep breath. The sound of the party drifted down the hill. It was clearly in full swing. This was good. They could go in, say hello, and skedaddle. Sully took her elbow and helped her up the remaining climb, which included a wide stone staircase that led to the house.

It wasn't that Lindsey didn't enjoy parties, it was just that if she had her choice between going to a party or staying home, curled up by the fire with Sully and Heathcliff while reading a good book, well, the book and her boys won hands down. And right now, she was reading a really good one, the latest in the series by Deborah Crombie, a police procedural set in Notting Hill, and she really wanted to be with Gemma and Duncan solving a murder rather than trudging up a hill to a party that was going to be—

"There they are! Happy Christmas to the bride and groom!"

In the doorway stood a tall man wearing a bright green tunic over striped tights, pointy shoes and a hat that had a long curving point with a jingle bell attached to the end. Lindsey blinked. She had not expected an elf to greet them.

Sully broke into a grin at the sight of his friend. "Steve, you look . . . er . . . very merry."

"Right?" Steve Briggs asked, holding his arms wide. He reached forward and shook Sully's hand. "Jamie said I looked ridiculous, and she refuses to be seen with me, but I can't help it if I'm feeling extra festive this year. So many great things are happening. Like you two getting married."

"Well, I think you carry the outfit off really well. Not many men have the legs for tights," Lindsey said. She stepped forward and gave him a hug.

"Yeah, just me and Will Ferrell," Steve joked. He struck a pose, kicking up one foot behind him while framing his face with his hands. Lindsey and Sully laughed, and he straightened up with a twinkle in his eye. "And don't you worry, when I officiate your wedding, I promise to wear the requisite dark suit and tie and be appropriately somber."

"Maybe keep the hat," Sully suggested with a grin.

Steve laughed and clapped him on the back. "Only for you."

He moved aside and gestured for them to enter the house, turning to greet the next guests. Lindsey blinked as she took in the festive scene that opened up before them. A massive tree filled the center of the main room. It was covered in blue and silver ornaments and white twinkling lights. Giant silver snowflakes hung from the vaulted ceiling, giving the room a real winter wonderland feeling, accompanied by the holiday tunes that a DJ was cranking out from the high-tech sound system in the corner.

Food stations and several bars were located all around the room, which was particularly crowded. The large glass doors on the far side of the house were open, and Lindsey could see more food stations and a bar service out there under scattered heat lamps. Another massive tree and more decorations filled the yard, along with several bounce houses that had been set up on the lawn for all the children in attendance. Lindsey had a feeling that was where she'd find Beth, and she pointed in that direction to Sully, who nodded.

They had to navigate their way through the crush, greeting their friends and neighbors as they went through the great room. Several people mentioned their upcoming wedding, and by the time they got outside, Lindsey's face hurt from smiling. Still, it had given them the opportunity to talk about how it was a small ceremony, and no worries if people couldn't make it, given the busyness of the holidays and all. Lindsey didn't feel as if anyone was actually listening, but at least they'd tried.

"Drink?" Sully asked.

"Yes, please."

He squeezed her hand and stepped up to the bar while Lindsey stationed herself under one of the heaters. Shrieks and giggles sounded as the bounce houses wobbled under the weight of their very enthusiastic inhabitants. Lindsey's gaze swept over the lawn, and sure enough, there was Beth. She was sitting at a face painter's table, having a woman, who was dressed as an ice princess, paint what looked like holly leaves and berries on her cheek.

Beth caught her eye and waved. Lindsey waved back, noting that Beth's husband, Aidan, stood beside her with a matching holly leaf painted on his face. A fellow children's librarian, Aidan was Beth's perfect match. Lindsey had no doubt that their baby had won the parent lottery with those two and would probably come out of the womb with a board book clutched in its chubby fist.

At that moment, the contagious laugh of a young one sounded clear in the night air, and Lindsey glanced at the lawn to see Sully's sister, Mary, and her husband, Ian Murphy, with their toddler daughter, Josephine. Ian was tossing Josie up in the air and catching her, much to her laughing delight, while Mary stood beside him, looking alert and acting as a spotter.

"There is nothing in the world so irresistibly contagious as laughter and good humor," a deep British voice said from beside Lindsey.

She turned to find her friend Robbie Vine, a noted British actor, with his girlfriend, Emma Plewicki, who happened to be the Briar Creek chief of police.

"Quoting Dickens?" Lindsey asked him.

"British," Robbie said by way of explanation.

"He's been quoting *A Christmas Carol* for the past week," Emma confided. "It's kind of hot."

Lindsey burst out laughing as Robbie turned a wide-eyed look on his girlfriend, who grinned unabashedly at him.

"Bah, humbug," Sully said as he joined them and handed Lindsey a drink. He gave her a side-eye and asked, "Anything?"

"Sorry," she said.

"You have to be British, mate," Robbie said. He put an arm around Emma, nestling her close for warmth. Her dark head pressed against his reddish blond one, and it struck Lindsey anew that the two of them made for quite the good-looking couple, with Robbie's movie star good looks and Emma's delicate features and big brown eyes. She wondered if marriage was in their future, but knew better than to ask.

"It's a good thing I like the strong *silent* type," Lindsey teased.

"Silence?" Emma asked. "I'm sorry. What's that?"

"Oy, hey there," Robbie protested.

They all laughed at his mock offense.

"Are you two ready for your big day?" Emma asked.

"Yes, I think so," Lindsey said. She refused to dwell on the invitation kerfuffle. Emma and Robbie were close friends, so their attendance had been a given.

"You're tired of everyone asking about it, aren't you?" Emma surmised.

"What? Oh, no," Lindsey assured her, trying to look genuine.

Emma laughed. "I wish all criminals lied as badly as you."

"Really? Was I that bad?"

"Indeed," Robbie said. "It pains my actor's soul to watch. Have you learned nothing from our time together?"

Lindsey made a face at him. She glanced at Sully, who was trying not to laugh. She was about to chastise him, but whatever she was about to say was lost as Beth and Aidan joined them, along with Mary, Ian and baby Josie.

The baby was passed around, and she charmed whoever's arms she landed in but preferred her dad to all others. Beth and Aidan showed off their matching face paint, and Ian took off his Santa hat to reveal the reindeer face the artist had painted on his bald head.

Mary laughed at her husband, leaned close to Lindsey and asked, "Are you sure you want to marry into this crazy family? We come with Sully, you know."

Lindsey grinned at her. "I wouldn't have him any other way."

As if he heard her while he was busy chatting about football with Aidan and Ian, Sully squeezed her fingers tightly with his. She glanced at him out of the corner of her eye, marveling yet again that he was soon to be her husband. A giddy thrill thrummed through her.

"Lindsey, Sully, there you are," Nancy Peyton called to them as she strode through the crowd. Violet was right behind her. The two women were holding a plate of appetizers in one hand and a mug of some hot spiked cider in the other.

"Hello, ladies. Don't you look lovely," Sully said. Both Nancy and Violet took a moment to preen under his praise.

Violet was wearing one of her usual caftans, but this one was in a shimmering violet-silver that accentuated her tall, slim build and dark skin, while Nancy was wearing tailored black slacks and a snappy Christmas blazer in red-and-green plaid over a matching red turtleneck.

Violet looked at Nancy and then herself and said, "We do, don't we?"

"I think so," Nancy said. She turned back to Sully. "Nice of you to notice, however."

"My pleasure," he said.

"Now, down to business," Nancy said. She gestured for Sully and Lindsey to follow her and Violet away from the others. "We've been working the crowd since we got here, trying to get an idea of how many people invited to your wedding are planning to attend."

Lindsey had already explained the situation to Sully, and he'd taken it in stride as he did everything, assuring her that it would be just fine.

Violet found a vacant tall table, and she and Nancy unloaded their food and drinks onto it. "The good news is that some people have other plans, given that it's the holidays and all."

"But there are a few, mostly the older crowd, who feel as if it's their duty to be there," Nancy said.

Sully and Lindsey exchanged a look.

"This is what I get for marrying one of the town's favorite sons, isn't it?" she asked.

He shrugged. "It could be that you're the draw," he countered. "You're going to be a beautiful bride. Of course no one wants to miss that."

Lindsey shook her head at him and turned back to Nancy and Violet. "The man is a charmer. Small wonder I'm marrying him."

Both women sighed as they gazed at Sully, and Lindsey knew exactly how they felt. He was a keeper, no question.

Nancy blew the steam off the top of her cup and took a

sip of her cider. She peered into the mug. "Oh, this has got some kick."

Violet followed suit, and a slow smile spread across her lips. "Delicious. You should go get some. It'll cure what ails you."

"Right now, what ails me is not knowing how many people are going to pop up at my wedding," Lindsey said. "Did you get any sense of that?"

Nancy took another long sip from her mug. Then she closed one eye as she focused on Lindsey and said, "We tried to get a head count, but some people were rather cagey. Our best guess is that you may have a little less than a hundred people at your wedding."

"A hundred?" Lindsey gasped. "That's almost three times as many as I'm prepared for." She turned to Sully and said, "Let's elope."

He smiled. "Now, don't panic. We'll figure it out."

"But I don't want to have to speak in front of that many people even to say *I do*. Besides, I don't think we can fit that many people on the island," she said. "Elopement would solve all these problems."

"Except the problem of our parents never forgiving us," he said. "Bell Island is bigger than it looks. Tell you what, we'll go out there tomorrow and assess the situation. We can figure out how many people actually will fit and then work from there."

"We'll go with you and help," Nancy offered, and Violet nodded.

"Thank you." Lindsey didn't want to be a bridezilla, but she was having a really hard time accepting that her small wedding had morphed into something out of her control, even while knowing it was her own fault. Her librarian rage for order was making her bonkers.

"You okay?" Violet asked.

"No, I'm starting to freak out again," she said.

Sully kissed her head. "Don't. We've got this. Come on, let's get some of that punch. It'll make you feel better, at least temporarily."

He took her hand and led her to the food and beverage table. A big steaming vat of the hot spiked cider sat on the edge of the bar, and he grabbed two mugs and filled them. He handed one to Lindsey and tapped his cup to hers.

"To being mister and missus," he said.

She smiled and took a careful sip of the steaming beverage. The sweet tartness of the cider blended beautifully with the brandy, giving it a nice kick that mellowed under the influence of the ginger, cinnamon and cloves.

"You're going to need something a helluva lot stronger than that if you're getting married." A woman's voice spoke from behind Lindsey, and she turned around to find Jamie Briggs, Steve's wife, standing there. Jamie turned to the bartender and said, "I'll have a fifty-fifty dirty martini," before turning back to them. She leaned against the bar, resting her elbow on the edge, as she looked past Lindsey and stared at Sully with unabashed interest.

"Hello, Sully," she said. "It's been a long time."

She tipped her cheek in his direction, clearly expecting a kiss. Sully stepped forward and kissed the air near her, and Lindsey glanced down into her mug to hide her smile.

"It has," he agreed. He put his arm around Lindsey and drew her forward. "You remember my fiancée, Lindsey?"

"Of course," Jamie said, her voice a sultry low purr. Her gaze flicked over Lindsey dismissively. There was zero recognition in her eyes and even less interest. "All anyone is talking about is your wedding. So when's the big day?"

"Next Saturday," Sully said.

The bartender placed Jamie's martini in front of her, and she reached for it eagerly. The drink suited her. Her honey blond hair was up in a sleek French twist with precisely styled chin-length sections left loose to frame her delicate face. Emeralds sparkled at her ears and throat, and a diamond ring the size of a compact car weighed down her left ring finger. Her clothes, a backless print blouse and flared trousers over stiletto sandals, draped perfectly on her size-zero frame. She was stunningly beautiful in that untouchable way that wealthy women seemed to cultivate.

"Excellent, then you have plenty of time to change your mind." Her voice was flat as she sipped her beverage.

Lindsey blinked. She felt Sully stiffen beside her, but his voice was mild when he said, "I won't be changing my mind."

"I wasn't talking to you," Jamie retorted. She turned and looked at Lindsey, meeting her gaze with her caramel brown eyes for the first time. "Marriage isn't really in the best interests of a woman."

Lindsey glanced at Sully. What was she supposed to say? Was she supposed to say anything or just agree?

"In our case, I'd have to agree with you," Sully said smoothly. "I am definitely marrying up in this relationship."

"No," Lindsey said, shaking her head. "I think we're bringing equal strengths to our marriage."

Jamie scoffed. "Check back with me in a few years, and we'll see if you feel the same. Trust me, you marry a guy who you think is your Prince Charming, but it's only a matter of time before he turns into a frog." She glanced up at the house, where Steve's big booming laugh could be heard. He was still in costume, standing with his older brother, Nathan Briggs, who owned the local automotive repair shop. Jamie rolled her eyes. "Believe me when I tell you, it never lives up to what you imagined. Ever."

She downed the rest of her drink and put the glass back on the bar. Then she stepped away, pausing in front of Sully. She winked at him. "Same time next year?"

Before he could reply, she glided away on a cloud of expensive perfume that made Lindsey's throat itch. She sipped her cider, trying to wash it away.

"So that was fun," she said.

"Yeah, right up there with doing my taxes." Sully's voice was dry, and Lindsey smiled.

They watched as Jamie walked by Steve, leaning close to whisper something in his ear. He jerked away from her and gave her a dark look before turning his back on her and resuming his conversation with his brother, Nate. Even from across the terrace it was easy to feel the tension between them.

"Well," Sully said.

"Yeah," Lindsey agreed.

This was what she loved about their relationship. They had the couple mind meld going. Sully didn't have to speak his thoughts; she knew he was thinking the same thing she was: that the Briggs marriage was troubled. It was pretty obvious. She glanced around the terrace, taking in the opulent beauty of it all. It never ceased to amaze her that the people who seemed to have it all on the outside seldom actually did.

She finished her cider and put the mug on the bar. It had warmed her from the inside out, and she felt the tingle of the alcohol go right to her head, making everything that had been worrying her fall away. She and Sully would manage the wedding. After all, the important part was that she was marrying her best friend. Everything else was just details.

Suddenly, the desire to be at home with him, sitting by the fire with Heathcliff at their feet, overrode all others. She turned to Sully and said, "Hey, are you ready to go home?"

"I thought you'd never ask," he said. He put down his unfinished cider and took her hand to lead her through the crowd.

They were halfway across the crowded terrace when a man shoved past them, knocking Lindsey into Sully. With his quick reflexes, Sully managed to catch her before she fell. Sully would have started after him, but Lindsey grabbed his arm. She had smelled the fumes of alcohol coming off the man when he slammed into her. This was not a fight worth pursuing.

The man was clearly oblivious to the destruction he left in his wake. He knocked aside two other guests as he stormed the steps to the upper terrace. When he reached Steve, he tossed the contents of his rocks glass into Steve's face.

"You bastard!" the man cried.

CHAPTER
3

BRIAR CREEK
PUBLIC LIBRARY

The man, red in the face with fury, stood nose to nose with Steve, who was dripping wet and blinking.

"Hey!" Nate Briggs cried, and stepped in between his brother and the irate man.

"It's all right," Steve said. He put his hands on his older brother's shoulders and gently moved him aside.

The two brothers had similar features, seen in the blunt shape of their noses and their sharp jawlines, but not so much that you could tell they were brothers right away. Steve was clearly younger, with short-cropped dark hair and a slender build. Nate was shorter by a few inches and stockier, as if he'd been built to carry more than his fair share of life's burdens.

"If you could just get me a towel, that would be great," Steve said.

Nate didn't look like he wanted to move. He stepped

into the other man's space, crowding him. Then he reached out and swiftly patted the man down as if searching him for a weapon. In a low voice he growled, "Put one finger on him and I'll destroy you, Tony."

The man called Tony barked a laugh devoid of humor. "Your brother already did that."

Nate glanced between the two men, obviously unsure of what was happening. He reached behind him, grabbed a clean hand towel off of the bar and handed it to his brother. Steve patted dry his face and the front of his elf suit, taking his time, not rushing despite being on the receiving end of Tony's malevolent stare. When he was finished, he tossed the towel back on the bar and held out his hands in a placating gesture.

"Tony," Steve said. His voice was calm and cajoling. "Let's go somewhere and talk privately."

"Talk?" Tony cried. "You want to talk now? After you've kicked me out of the firm and ruined my life? I'd say it's a bit late for a talk, wouldn't you?"

"It's clear you're upset," Steve said. He looked and sounded perfectly calm and reasonable, even wearing his elf suit, which was no small feat. "Let's take a minute to calm down."

Steve went to take his arm, but Tony yanked it away. "Calm down? I've lost everything because of you! I'm not going to calm down. You've sent me to hell, and I plan to drag you down with me!"

He threw a punch at Steve, but it was a wild swing, sending him teetering to the side. Nate leaped into the fray, using Tony's own momentum to bring him to the ground.

He put his knee in the middle of Tony's back and held him there while Tony thrashed, trying to buck him off. He glanced up at his brother.

"What do you want me to do with him?"

"Walk him out," Steve said. He shook his head. "There's no reasoning with him when he's like this."

"Reason with me?" Tony howled. "You never even tried. You just ruined everything that was important to me—my wife, my career, my life. Well, now you're on notice, Briggs. I won't rest until I've taken everything from you. Don't forget. I know *everything* about you."

Steve's face became a cold, hard mask. Gone was the jovial host in the elf suit. Instead, his eyes frosted with a ruthlessness that was icy sharp, so much so that Lindsey was surprised it didn't cause Tony to spontaneously freeze. She shivered.

"I didn't ruin your life. You did," Steve said. "You're an alcoholic, Tony, whether you want to admit it or not. I've offered to help you time and again, and that offer still stands, but I won't let you destroy everything we've built. When you're ready to talk, I'll be here."

"You sanctimonious pr—" Nate hauled Tony to his feet, cutting off his ranting words. With a hand on the back of his neck, Nate half lifted and half dragged Tony toward the door.

"Sorry, but the party's over for you, Mancusi," he said.

Tony fought Nate's hold, trying to wriggle loose, but Nate held him without any visible effort. Sully leaned close to Lindsey and said, "Nate was All-State for wrestling. That guy's never going to shake him off."

"I'm going to have my driver take you home, Tony," Steve said. "We'll talk more tomorrow."

"There's nothing to talk—"

Whatever Tony had been about to say was cut off as Nate tightened his grip and pushed him through the crowded house and out the front door.

The partygoers were all silent as they processed the scene they'd just witnessed. Sensing the plummeting mood, Steve raised his hands wide and said, "Don't let that Ebenezer ruin the party, everyone! Eat, drink and be merry! DJ, hit us with some rockin' tunes!"

The DJ nodded, and upbeat holiday music swelled from the speakers all around. People began to chatter again, and the party atmosphere slowly returned, although a bit more subdued and with a ripple of gossipy whispers running through it.

Steve laughed with the people around him with a shrug that seemed to say, *What can you do?*

Lindsey noticed that the set of his shoulders was stiff and his good humor seemed forced. Not that she could blame him given what had just happened. She knew it was none of her business, but she wondered who Tony Mancusi was and why there was bad blood between him and Steve, especially as the Steve she knew was unfailingly thoughtful and kind.

"What do you suppose that was all about?" she asked Sully.

"I'm not sure," he said. "I do know that Tony and Steve have been partners in their law firm, Briggs and Mancusi, for years, but it sounds as if they've parted ways."

"Not by choice, at least on Tony's end," she observed. "He resembled a crazy ex-girlfriend there."

"He did, didn't he?" Sully agreed. "Still ready to leave?"

"More than ever," she said. "I don't like drama."

"Same."

They made their way through the crowd, pausing by Steve to say good night.

"I hope that scene Tony made isn't driving you out," Steve said. "There's plenty of life left in this party. We've only just begun. We're just about to start up the karaoke."

"Which is exactly why we're making our exit," Sully joked. "Seriously, we were on our way already. We have a dog who worries if we're not home by curfew."

Steve nodded with a small smile. "That must be nice, to have a furry buddy waiting for you." He glanced between the two of them and looked like he wanted to say something more but then changed his mind. "I'll see you kids at your wedding rehearsal, if not before."

"Sounds great," Sully said, and shook his hand.

Lindsey gave him a quick hug. "Thanks for a . . . er . . . festive party."

"Oh, yeah, it's been that," Steve said. He gave them a comical look, but the amusement didn't quite reach his eyes.

It struck Lindsey as they walked through the house that for a man who had a stunning home and a gorgeous wife and who, by all accounts, was successful and living his best life, Steve Briggs looked incredibly lonely, standing there in his elf suit with his pointed hat drooping a bit to one side.

Maybe she was wrong, but still, she couldn't shake the feeling that Steve Briggs's life was desperately unhappy.

The following morning was cold and crisp. It was Sunday, so the library was closed, giving Lindsey and Sully plenty of time to run out to Bell Island and assess the situation. Violet and Nancy were joining them, since they had volunteered to help manage what looked to be a much larger wedding celebration in any way they could. Lindsey was grateful for their support.

Bundled against the cold, they met at Sully's office on the town pier. His tour boats had been put up for winter, and he was operating just the water taxi for the island residents until spring, when the tours around the Thumb Islands would start back up.

They walked down the pier to the stairs that led to Sully's dock. His boat was bobbing on the water, waiting for them. Lindsey glanced across the bay and noted that the water looked choppy. She glanced up, wondering if the low-hanging thick gray clouds were going to give them a snowstorm.

Sully helped Violet and Nancy into the boat while Lindsey untied the lines. She tossed the rope to Sully, pushing off and jumping aboard like a regular sailor. She took her seat beside Sully's captain's chair while he fired up the engine and steered them away from the dock. The bay was a no-wake zone, which was fine with Lindsey because out on the open water, the air temperature dropped, and adding speed would only make it even colder.

The archipelago that made up the Thumb Islands included scores of very large rocks that lurked just beneath the surface. At low tide, they were easy to spot, but at high tide, it took someone who knew each and every island to be able to navigate through them without grounding their boat. Sully, having grown up on the islands, was that navigator.

He kept one hand on the wheel and turned it ever so slightly, adjusting the boat just enough to miss whatever lurked below. Lindsey, who was not a big fan of deep dark water, shivered in her puffy coat.

"You all right?" Sully asked.

The understanding in his eyes made it clear he knew she wasn't reacting to the cold.

"I'm fine," she said. She glanced around them at the relentless stretch of water, broken up only by the islands that jutted up out of its dark depths. "Is it just me, or is there an ominous feeling to the water today?"

Sully followed her gaze. Then he glanced up. A single snowflake drifted down and got stuck on his thick eyelashes. Lindsey smiled as she reached up with gloved fingers and wiped it away.

"It could be the change in weather that's spooking you," he said.

"Maybe." Except Lindsey liked snow. She loved the first snowfall of the season, mostly because it meant more indoor time spent reading by the fire, but also she loved how everything was coated in a pristine blanket of white. It felt as if the world had been tucked in and told that it was time to be still and silent. It was, in many ways, calming.

She also loved the crunch of it under her boots, the way Heathcliff romped around like a nut, trying to catch the snowballs she tossed into snowbanks. She liked sledding and building snowmen and walking until her feet throbbed from the cold and her nose felt as if it were going to fall off. So while she supposed the change in the barometric pressure could be what was making her edgy, she didn't think that was it.

Sully studied her closely. "It's not the weather, is it?"

"I just have this feeling of something not being right," she said. "I can't shake it."

He met her gaze. "This doesn't have to do with us getting married, does it?"

She shook her head. "No, not at all. I'd marry you right here, right now."

"Well, I could look into the maritime laws on weddings," he teased. "We've got two witnesses aboard."

"Don't tempt me," she said. She glanced out over the water. The persistent feeling that something was off wasn't going away. "Maybe I'm just overtired."

Sully tugged her out of her seat and pulled her close. He wrapped an arm around her and said, "Whatever is bothering you, we'll figure it out together."

Lindsey tipped her head back and studied him. This. This was why she was marrying him. There was no other person she'd ever met in life whom she could imagine sharing all of her burdens with—real or imagined—than him. He was her missing piece. He had been since the first time they'd met. She kissed him quickly, glancing over her shoulder to see Nancy and Violet pretending to look elsewhere while they covertly grinned at each other.

Their happiness for her and Sully dispelled Lindsey's gloom. As he cut the engine and slowed the boat, banking it against the Bell Island dock, Lindsey hopped out and tied the boat in place. In a few days, they'd be here for their wedding, and despite the current guest confusion, she couldn't wait.

Bell Island was one of the biggest of the Thumb Islands, and as such was one of the few that had electricity. There were four houses on it, one of which was the Sullivans'. Lindsey and Sully led Violet and Nancy up the stairs at the end of the dock to his parents' house above. A large grassy area and a small forest of trees separated the four homes, giving them each a quarter acre of privacy.

The sky was grayer than before, and another snowflake drifted down from above. A snowstorm was definitely on its way. The wind whipped across the island, darting through the branches of the trees that were leafless, making Lindsey hunker into her coat.

"Hello!" Sully's mother, Joan, called from the front porch of their house. "Come on up and get out of this weather."

They didn't need to be asked twice. Both Nancy and Violet led the way, darting inside the large brick house seeking warmth. Sully and Lindsey followed.

Sully's mother fussed over them as she took their coats and settled them into the front parlor, where a fire was crackling in the fireplace. She hugged Lindsey tightly and said, "You must be frozen. Mike is bringing tea."

Lindsey glanced at her future mother-in-law's face to see if there was any indicator that she was upset about Lindsey's mix-up with the invitations. But Joan Sullivan looked at her with the same affection as always. When she stepped away, Lindsey leaned close to Sully and said, "You did mention the situation with the invites to your parents, right?"

He turned and smiled at her. "Yup."

"And you're sure they're not mad?"

"Of course, not," he said. He took her hand in his. "They don't care. Ian and Mary had their wedding on the island, and it was easily twice as many people."

"Yes, but they also got married in the spring," Lindsey said. She glanced out the window at the center of the island, which was one large dried-up lawn surrounded by large trees. They had planned to have the wedding in the house, but now she suspected they were going to need a really big tent, the sort that could have heaters and side flaps to keep the wind out. What a disaster! How was she even going to arrange for that stuff on such short notice?

"You're fretting again," Sully said. "Don't worry. We'll figure it out. I promise."

Lindsey sighed and moved to stand by the fire, letting its heat wash over her.

The Sullivans' house was one of the oldest Thumb Islands houses and was registered as a historic landmark. As such, it retained its Victorian charm, meaning it was made up of many small rooms. There was no open floor plan here, keeping it cozy and full of old New England charm.

Violet and Nancy took seats in the cream-colored armchairs situated on each side of the fire while Sully joined Lindsey in front of the hearth. Sully's father, Mike, arrived in the room, bearing a fully loaded tea tray.

"This will help to warm you up," he said. He was big and broad like his son, but his hair was gray and he wore glasses, giving him a scholarly look. Lindsey knew that he and Joan had bought their island home when they were first married and had raised Sully and his sister, Mary, here. Sully's father had worked as an accountant, commuting off-island for years. With the rise of online business, he'd been able to stop commuting and now worked exclusively from home.

"Hot tea, how perfect," Nancy said. She'd brought a tin of cookies with her and handed them to Joan, who looked delighted.

She lifted off the lid and grinned. "Molasses cookies. My favorite."

Joan poured them all tea, and Lindsey gratefully took the thick ceramic mug in both hands, letting it warm her fingers.

"Looks like there's going to be some snowfall," Mike said. He and Joan sat on the sage green loveseat, leaving Lindsey and Sully to sit on the stone hearth facing them. The entire room was done in sage green and cream, with one wall full of books and a vintage acoustic guitar on a pedestal in the corner. Lindsey found it very soothing.

As everyone began to debate the incoming snow—weather watching being a daily pastime for New Englanders—the feeling of dread that had been swirling inside her began to abate. Sully's parents seemed not to be in a dither about the change in the wedding numbers, so she supposed she shouldn't be either. Still, she felt as if the upcoming wedding was the proverbial elephant in the room.

"Joan, Mike, I know Sully told you about the invitation mix-up, and I just want to apologize," she said. "I can't believe I made such a big mistake—huge, in fact—and if you no longer want the wedding to be on the island, I completely understand."

Mike and Joan exchanged a look, the sort that encapsulated an entire conversation without words, as only a couple who'd been married for forty years could have. Then Joan turned to Lindsey and said, "Oh, honey, it's okay. We can handle this. Truly, it's no problem."

"Absolutely," Mike chimed in. He grinned at her. "If we survived Mary and Ian's wedding, we can handle anything."

There was some good-natured laughter, and Lindsey glanced around the room. Both Violet and Nancy had been at Mary's wedding, which had been a few years before Lindsey had moved to Briar Creek, and they were chuckling as well. She suspected if Mary's husband, Ian, known for his gregarious personality, was involved, then it had been quite the shindig.

"It was that big?" she asked.

"It was over-the-top," Sully said. "Picture the annual Briggs Bash on steroids. And that's putting it nicely."

"Oh, wow," she said.

"Exactly," Nancy said. "It was all anyone talked about for months."

"Your wedding will be just as lovely. Don't you worry,"

Joan said. She reached across the space between them and patted Lindsey's knee.

"I don't need or want anything like that," she said. "As far as I'm concerned, the smaller and quieter the better."

Joan and Mike exchanged a smile, and then Mike turned to Sully and said, "She really is your soul mate."

Lindsey felt her face get warm, but Sully put his arm around her and pulled her close, kissing the top of her head. "Yes, she is."

"We will make sure you two have the perfect wedding," Joan said. "Don't you worry."

Lindsey sagged against Sully. She hadn't realized she'd been so tense about the whole wedding thing until she didn't have to be anymore. What a relief.

While they enjoyed the tea and cookies and the heat of the fire, the six of them began to plan how to handle the expanded guest list. Ideas for the wedding and how to host it were kicked around, and Lindsey felt her spirits lift. It was going to be okay. They'd figure it out. She could feel a surge of optimism that even though there would be more people than she had planned on for the wedding, at least it would still be on the island, and they could try and keep the intimate feeling she and Sully had hoped to achieve.

"Come on." Sully pulled Lindsey up to her feet and said, "Let's go take a walk and clear our heads."

Lindsey put down her teacup and nodded. "All right."

Violet, Nancy and the Sullivans smiled at them as they departed the room in that doting way people did when watching a future bride and groom. It made Lindsey self-conscious, but it also warmed her heart. Although being a bride had never been a do-or-die ambition for her, she was overjoyed to be Sully's bride. He had become her best friend over the past couple of years, and she loved him with more depth of feeling than she had ever thought possible.

They bundled up in their coats, hats and scarves and stepped out into the gray winter day. No snowflakes were falling, but the temperature had definitely dropped since they'd arrived. Lindsey huddled close to Sully as he led her from the house and down a path that circled the outer edge of the island.

The air was surprisingly still, and Lindsey squinted up at the heavy blanket of clouds above them. The atmosphere was thick, and she knew that the snow would come, and it would be heavy. It was just a matter of time.

"Your parents are being very understanding about the wedding," she said.

"Nothing ruffles their feathers," he said. "I think it's a perk of living a life on an island. They're always just a little bit removed from it all."

"I still don't see how we can have a hundred people show up," Lindsey said. "It's winter. Where are we going to put them all?"

"You heard the folks. We have some options. We'll figure it out. I promise," he said. He sounded as unflappable as his parents. Lindsey had never loved him more.

They hiked up to the highest point on the island, which overlooked the cove where there was a small sandy beach that was shared by all the residents. The frigid air hurt Lindsey's lungs, and she released her breath in a plume of steam. She watched it fade and then turned her head to take in the sight of the village on the shoreline across the bay. Bell Island wasn't that far out, and the view of Briar Creek was unencumbered by other islands.

She could just make out the steeple of the church in the center of town, and beside that the police station, the town hall and the stone facade of the library. The library had been built out of an old captain's house, so it sat prominently in the center of town and offered a spectacular view of their patch of Long Island Sound. As always, Lindsey felt a surge of pride for the place that felt like a second home to her.

A sudden breeze kicked up, and a hank of hair blew across her face. She went to brush it aside when, out of the corner of her eye, a splash of green against the beige sand caught her attention. She leaned forward and peered more closely. The shape took form, and she felt her stomach plummet.

With shaky fingers, she reached out and grabbed Sully's arm. He was gazing out at the horizon and when he turned to face her, his eyes narrowed in concern.

"What is it?"

"Over there," she pointed. "I think there's a body on the beach."

CHAPTER

4

BRIAR CREEK
PUBLIC LIBRARY

Sully's gaze followed the direction she pointed, and with a muttered oath, he broke into a run. Down the path, along the cliff's edge, he sprinted flat out to the wooden staircase that led to the beach below. Lindsey was right behind him. They pounded down the steps. The deep sand at the bottom slowed their progress, but Sully resumed his run, and Lindsey tried to keep up.

As they drew closer, it was easy to see from the muscular build that the body was a man's. He was facedown, wearing what looked like a green tunic over tights. Weird. Sully dropped to his knees beside him while Lindsey fumbled for the phone in her pocket. It was clear the man was in need of medical attention if not something more.

Sully gently shifted the body, easing him from his front to his back. As soon as his face was visible, Lindsey gasped. It was Steve Briggs, and he was still wearing his elf suit from the party the night before. His eyes were shut, but his mouth was slack. Sand was encrusted on his skin and in the blood surrounding the nasty gash on his head. More blood had soaked the collar of his costume. Sully ripped off his gloves and put his fingers on the pulse point beneath Steve's jaw. Steve didn't flinch at the contact. In fact, as Lindsey studied his chest, she couldn't detect any movement at all.

All too soon, Sully's hand fell away. He glanced up at Lindsey and said, "He's dead."

They stared at each other, their shock and confusion mirrored in each other's eyes. Lindsey didn't know what to say. She looked back down at the phone in her hand. "I'm calling Emma."

Sully nodded. He glanced back down at Steve with an expression of shock and horror. He looked gutted, and Lindsey had no idea what to say to him about the loss of his friend. She reached out and squeezed his shoulder while Emma's phone rang, and she willed the chief of police to pick up.

Twenty-five minutes later, Emma arrived on Bell Island with Officer Kirkland, a tall raw-boned redhead whom Lindsey had recently hooked into reading *Raven Black*, the first in Ann Cleeves's Shetland Island mysteries, featuring police detective Jimmy Perez. Kirkland had doubled back for book two and subsequently plowed through the series.

The two of them arrived on the beach, out of breath from their run from the Sullivans' dock. Wearing their winter uniforms, which included thick navy blue coats, they separated as Kirkland immediately began to mark off the area at the base of the stairs with yellow tape while Emma joined Sully and Lindsey where they were standing next to the body, not wanting to leave Steve in the cold all alone.

Sully had called his father and told him what was happening, but he'd asked them all to stay up at the house so that the scene of the accident wasn't contaminated by too many footprints. As they'd stood waiting for Emma, Lindsey had found it difficult to look at the face of the man who was supposed to marry them in just a week.

The gash on his left temple was deep, caked in blood and sand. There was nothing on the beach that appeared to have caused the head injury. She glanced at the water. There was no indication of how he had arrived on the beach. No boat or tracks of any kind. How did he get here? When? Late last night? Early this morning? Did he swim? His clothes were soaked. Lindsey suspected that if the blow to his head hadn't killed him, then hypothermia had. She wondered if he was alive when he arrived on the beach. Had he been too weak to climb the stairs and get help?

The thought of him dying on the beach alone was more distressing than she wanted to contemplate. She studied the sand at Steve's feet. A trail coming up from the water was evident, plowed into the sand. The high tide hadn't washed it away. The only question was, Had Steve managed to crawl up the beach by himself before collapsing, or had someone helped him? And whether he had been alone or with someone else, the bigger question was, How had he gotten here and why?

"Sully. Lindsey." That was the only greeting Emma offered before crouching beside Steve's body. Like Sully, she checked his pulse. Then she leaned back on her heels and studied the area. Her brown eyes narrowed as she took in the same markings in the sand Lindsey had noted.

"I don't see anything on the beach that could have caused that head trauma," she said. She glanced up at Sully and Lindsey. "I know the answer but have to ask anyway. You haven't touched anything on the beach, have you?"

"I rolled Steve over," Sully said. He swallowed as if the words were stuck in his throat. Lindsey put her hand on his back in a gesture of support. "He was facedown when we found him."

Emma nodded. "That explains the sand in the wound."

She carefully picked her way from the body, stepping in the same footprints that had brought her there. She pulled out her phone and started to take pictures. Lindsey noticed that she focused on the grooves in the sand that led to Steve's body from the water. She was frowning.

"I can't tell if he dragged himself up the beach or was carried," she said. "We're going to need some crime scene techs out here in case this proves not to have been an accident."

Sully nodded. His face was set in grim lines as if he'd already considered the same, even though he and Lindsey hadn't spoken of that possibility while they'd waited for Emma.

"Do you think it could have been . . . ?" Lindsey's voice trailed off. This was one of those moments in her life when she was concerned that because she read far too many murder mysteries, perhaps she saw foul play in things that were just horribly tragic accidents.

"Murder?" Emma asked. Her voice was flat, as if she'd seen so much darkness in her time as a cop that nothing surprised her anymore, except perhaps an absence of malice.

"Yes," Lindsey said. She felt Sully get tense beneath her hand, but she wanted to know what Emma was thinking.

"I hope I'm wrong," Emma said. "I really do, but what the hell is he doing here on Bell Island, on a deserted beach, in the dead of winter, still wearing his elf costume from the party last night? None of it makes sense unless you consider the possibility that someone caused this to happen. Someone who wanted him dead."

A snowflake fell, landing with a cold sting on Lindsey's cheek. She wiped it away, but it was swiftly replaced by another and another. She glanced up. The snowstorm had begun.

The Sullivans' house became an outpost while the police and the crime scene technicians struggled against the elements to gather all the evidence they could before the beach was covered in a thick blanket of snow. A temporary canopy had been put up over the body, and the team members took turns returning to the house to warm up with Joan's homemade clam chowder before going back out into the bitter cold.

Shock was the initial reaction to the news that Steve Briggs was dead. Both Violet and Nancy were undone by the tragedy. Nancy, because she had known Steve since he was born, and Violet, because Steve had been a regular performer in her community theater actors' troupe. The absence of his larger-than-life personality was going to be sorely felt in their small community.

No one spoke of contacting Nate, his brother, but it was on all their minds. Since their parents had passed away several years ago, Steve and Nate were the only Briggses left in Briar Creek. Lindsey didn't envy Emma the task of delivering the news. Of course, Emma was also going to have to break it to Jamie Briggs, Steve's wife. Given Jamie's propensity for high drama, Lindsey couldn't imagine how that was going to play out either.

It was a subdued group gathered at the Sullivans' house while they waited for the investigators to wrap up. Lindsey sat on the hearth in front of the fire. The chill in her bones from standing outside while keeping vigil over Steve's body wouldn't loosen its grip, and even the roaring fire couldn't warm her.

Steve was dead. It was incomprehensible. He was supposed to marry them. How could he be gone? Just like that? When she'd hugged him goodbye last night, it had been with the understanding that he'd see them at their rehearsal. Lindsey felt her throat get tight. She was nowhere near as close to Steve as Sully had been, but she'd liked him. She'd trusted him. She'd known he would treat their wedding with the respect and care that a lifetime commitment warranted.

When Sully had introduced her to Steve, she had known right away that he was the perfect one to marry them. He always had a twinkle in his eye, and he lived life on a large scale, but it was clear that he knew what mattered. He loved Briar Creek and had opted to never leave even though he had other homes in other places. This small shoreline town was where his heart had resided and so had he.

"Hey, you all right?" Sully asked as he sat down beside her.

"No, you?"

"No."

He put his arm around her and pulled her close. It was the first time all afternoon that Lindsey felt warm. She leaned her head on his shoulder, and he rested his chin on her hair.

"How is everyone else doing?" she asked.

"About as well as can be expected," he said. "Nancy and Violet are helping Mom feed the team. The temperature has dropped into the single digits, and it'll be getting dark soon. I think they're going to keep the area cordoned off, but with the six inches of snow that's predicted, half of which has already accumulated, I don't know what good it will do. Everything is going to be under a blanket of white."

"But when the snow melts . . ." Lindsey trailed off.

"Which may not be until spring," he said.

She glanced out the window. The snow was coming thick and fast, and the light was the pale gray half-light that came from the sun trying to shine through clouds that were too thick.

The back door to the kitchen blew open, letting in a swirl of snow as Emma Plewicki entered, followed by Officer Kirkland. They were both covered in snow, from their fleece-lined police hats all the way to their thick black boots.

They stamped their feet in the mudroom, trying to get

off as much as they could. Lindsey and Sully rose to their feet and moved aside as Joan ushered the two officers into the front parlor to stand in front of the fire.

"I don't want to get your carpet wet," Emma protested. The snow that covered her was already melting into a puddle at her feet.

Joan waved her hands in a dismissive gesture. "That carpet has seen plenty of snowmelt. Don't fret about it. I'll bring you both some hot coffee?"

Emma looked like she'd drop where she stood. "Thank you. That would be lovely."

Officer Kirkland nodded. "Yes, please, ma'am. I think I'm about frozen solid."

Joan retreated back to the kitchen, and Lindsey debated whether to say anything or not to Emma about Steve. Technically, she assumed that Emma couldn't answer any questions they might have, but it never hurt to ask, or so she told herself.

"Did you discover anything of interest on the beach?" she asked.

"Do you mean did we find whatever caused Steve's head trauma?" Emma clarified. Lindsey didn't say anything, just waited. "No."

"Any idea how he got there?" Sully asked.

"Judging by the drag marks up the beach, a completely unsubstantiated guess would be that he either crawled or was carried," she said. "But there are so many questions as to why he was here, how he got here, and what happened to him that anything I'm thinking about any of this is complete conjecture at this point."

Joan returned and handed Emma and Kirkland hot mugs of coffee. They both sighed as they inhaled the bitter steam coming off the tops of the cups. Nancy was right behind Joan, carrying a small tray with a pitcher of milk and a sugar bowl. Only Kirkland bothered to doctor his coffee. Emma drank hers black.

Joan and Nancy disappeared back into the kitchen, and Sully turned to Emma.

"I need to take both Nancy and Violet back to town, and it's getting dark," he said. "Is it all right if we leave soon?"

"Absolutely, the medical examiner has already left with . . . Steve's body," Emma said. She glanced down into her cup as if trying to avoid everyone's gaze. She winced as she sipped. Whether it was from the heat or the unfortunate circumstances, Lindsey couldn't tell. Emma glanced back up and met Sully's gaze. "If you and Lindsey could stop by the station and fill out a statement, that'd be great."

Sully turned to Lindsey, and she nodded. They could collect Heathcliff from home and bring him back to the station with them. He'd been cooped up much longer than she liked since they'd been gone most of the day. It was bad enough that he wasn't going to forgive them for going to Bell Island without him, and, yes, he'd know. That dog's olfactory senses were unparalleled. Plus, he loved boat rides, and Sully's parents were two of his most favorite people. The betrayal for him was going to run deep.

"We'll be there," Lindsey confirmed.

"Excellent," Emma said. She glanced at Sully. Her expression was concerned. "I'm trying to get your parents to consider going off-island for a few days."

Sully nodded. "Let me guess, they didn't go for it."

"Nope. They seem to think they're perfectly safe even though we have no idea how Briggs ended up here," she said. She looked grim. "We could be dealing with a murder, and I really don't like the idea of your parents and the other residents of Bell Island putting themselves in harm's way by staying here."

"Do you really think there's a murderer out there?" Lindsey asked. She desperately wanted Emma to say no, but she didn't.

Instead, she shrugged and said, "I don't know, but if there is and they're worried that someone saw them, where do you suppose they'd go?"

"Here," Sully said. "To make sure they didn't leave any loose ends."

"Precisely. Help me to convince your parents and the others to leave," Emma said.

"We can try," Sully said. "But they've ridden out hurricanes, nor'easters, and power outages that lasted weeks. This is their home, and they won't leave it easily."

"Damn."

They were all silent, contemplating the fire. Kirkland drained his coffee and said, "What if I stay?"

They all turned to look at him. He shrugged and said, "Someone has to keep an eye on the beach and make sure no one tampers with the scene until we can get a better look. I can stay out here tonight and keep an eye on everything. Wilcox can come out in the morning and take over if need be."

Emma gave him an approving glance. "Thanks for volunteering, Kirkland. With the storm, I expect things will be quiet in town, and having someone out here will ease my mind." She turned to Sully. "Do you think your parents would be willing to put up Kirkland for the night? He'll have to patrol, so he'll be coming and going all night."

"I'm sure they'll be fine with it," Sully said. "Anything to help the local law enforcement."

"All right," Emma said. She looked at her officer. "Let's go talk to them and make sure you have what you need. I'm going to want you to check in every hour on the hour so I know that things are okay out here."

"No problem, Chief," Kirkland said. "I wouldn't want you to worry."

Emma frowned. "I'm not worried."

"Whatever you say, Chief," he said. He glanced away before she caught him smiling.

Emma looked irritated, but no one said anything. They all knew she worried like a nervous mother hen over her officers, but she hated that everyone knew she worried. She tried to make it seem all business, but the truth was, she took it very seriously that she had men and women under her command who willingly put their lives on the line to keep their community safe. It was that concern and care that made her an excellent chief of police.

Sully's parents were happy to put Officer Kirkland up for the night. Mike even volunteered to join him on his rounds, an idea that was soundly discouraged. Sully didn't say as much when they climbed back onto the boat to head back to town, but Lindsey could tell he was relieved to have someone watching over his parents.

The ride back to shore was brutally cold. The snow was

coming in fast and thick, and visibility was reduced as they wound their way through the smaller islands to the pier. Lindsey jumped out and tied the boat while Sully cut the engine and then helped both Nancy and Violet up onto the pier before covering the boat for the night.

The ladies were headed to the Blue Anchor for an early dinner, and Nancy promised to tell Mary, Sully's sister, about the situation on the island. Sully and Lindsey hurried to get Heathcliff and double back to the police station to give their statements.

The restaurant sat at the base of the pier, and the smell of fried food filled the air as they got closer. A glass of wine and a plate full of fried clams with a baked potato on the side sure would hit the spot. Lindsey envied her friends their upcoming meal. With hugs and a promise to be in touch with any news, she left them at the front door and continued on to the parking lot with Sully.

His pickup truck was already covered in snow, and he reached into the cab and handed Lindsey a long-handled snow scraper with a brush on one side. She attacked one side of the truck while he cranked the engine to let it warm up before he worked on the other side.

The snow was light and fluffy and easy to dust off. In no time, they were climbing into the truck and setting out across town. The seats were icy cold, and the windows immediately began to fog. Sully put on the defrost, cranking cold air across the windows. Lindsey hunkered into her coat, trying to conserve her body heat.

"All right, darlin'?" Sully asked.

"As much as can be expected," she said. "You?"

"Same."

They were silent as he navigated the deserted streets. At the edge of town, they passed Nate's Garage, the auto repair shop owned by Nathan Briggs. It was closed for the day, the doors on the big bays pulled shut and the windows dark.

Lindsey thought about how Nate had defended his brother from Tony Mancusi the night before, and she felt her heart clench. She'd always been close to her brother, Jack, and she couldn't imagine getting the sort of news Nate was about to receive. She glanced at Sully. He was studying the building, too, and a heavy sigh left him as they continued past.

"Poor Nate," he said. "Steve is the only family he's got."

"Well, except for Naomi and the kids," Lindsey said. "He still has his family."

Naomi Briggs, Nate's wife, was one of Lindsey's favorite patrons. With their five children, all girls from ages six months to thirteen, she was one of the heaviest users of their children's section, and she was always happy and laughing, thoroughly enjoying her role as a wife and mother, despite the challenges.

"Thank goodness," Sully said. "He's going to need her now more than ever. I can't imagine how I'd feel if I lost Mary. I can't even think about it."

"I know. I feel the same way about my brother," she said.

Sully reached across the seat and squeezed her gloved hand with his. She studied his face and noted the tightness around his eyes and mouth. While Steve hadn't been one of Sully's closest friends, he was still an incredibly important part of his personal history. Both Briggs brothers were. Steve had been someone Sully respected and trusted enough to marry them, and now he was gone. Just like that.

Heathcliff was ecstatic to see them. When Lindsey opened the door, he dashed past them, out into the snow, running circles around the backyard at top speed, kicking up the snow as he went. When he finally wound down, they loaded him into the car and headed back into town to the police station.

The town was even quieter as they drove through the snow-covered streets. The snowfall was lessening, but it glittered in the overhead lights, giving the town the magical look of a storybook village under a blanket of white. Lindsey couldn't help but think that given the events of the day, this fairy tale was definitely more like one from the Brothers Grimm before they were rewritten and made nicer.

Sully pulled into the lot behind the police station, and they climbed out—well, Heathcliff jumped—before trudging into the building through the back door.

No one was there except Molly Hatcher, the station's desk clerk, coffee brewer, paper jockey and all around girl Friday. At the moment, the place was quiet, but Lindsey knew that wouldn't last for long once the news got out.

"Hey there, Heathcliff. Who's my good boy?" Molly said. She bent down, and a dog biscuit appeared in her hand. Heathcliff wagged and then sat, his eyes trained on the biscuit. Molly laughed. She was a robust brunette, all dimples and curves, who seemed to manage life with a big heart and a generous nature.

"Such good manners," she said. Molly gave Heathcliff

the biscuit, and he chomped it up and then nuzzled her hand in thank-you. She patted his head and then straightened up to look at Lindsey and Sully. The twinkle in her eye dimmed and her lower lip quivered.

It was then Lindsey knew that Molly had been told. She opened her arms and hugged Molly tightly. Lindsey wasn't a hugger by nature, but she and Molly had been through some stuff, and she felt a kinship with the woman that went beyond just having her work at the police station. When Lindsey released her, she held Molly's upper arms and studied her face.

"Are you all right?" she asked.

Molly nodded, even as a tear coursed down her cheek. She brushed it away with her fingertips. "Am *I* all right?" she asked. "It's me who should be asking you, since you found him." She blinked away her tears and focused on both of them. "How are you both? Can I do anything for you?"

"Thanks, Molly," Sully said. He stepped forward and hugged her just like Lindsey had. "I don't think there's anything that can fix this except finding out what happened, and even then . . ."

"It's a blow, a body blow," Molly said. "Steve was so much a part of life in Briar Creek. I mean just last night, he was standing right there in that ridiculous elf costume, and I . . . I . . ."

She broke down into shoulder-shaking sobs, and Lindsey patted her back while she cried it out. She knew exactly how Molly felt. It was hard to imagine never seeing their gregarious friend again.

"Did you stay at the party long?" Sully asked.

"Yes." Molly sniffed. She pressed the backs of her hands to her cheeks as if she could stop the flow of tears. She closed her eyes for a moment and took a deep breath, in and then out. When she opened her eyes, a small smile played on her lips. "You know me, I'm always the last to leave a good party. When my friends and I left, it was winding down, and it was just Steve, his wife, the DJ and a handful of other party guests, who were also headed to the door."

"Do you remember anything about the party that struck you as odd?" Lindsey asked.

"If you mean other than the altercation between Tony Mancusi and Steve, then no," she said. "That was the capper. Although there was one woman who struck me as being out of place."

"Really?" Sully's eyebrows went up, encouraging her to keep talking.

"Yes, I went to use one of the bathrooms on the first floor, but of course, they were clogged with lines that were at least five deep," Molly said. "Steve told me to go ahead upstairs and use one of those, so I did. When I reached the first one on the second floor, it was locked. I decided to wait. Finally, the door opened, and this woman came out. She was dressed all in black, including a dark veil, like some sort of ghoulish bride. She scared me so bad I yelped, and she hurried away down the hallway toward the bedrooms."

Sully and Lindsey both stared at her. Of all the things Lindsey had been expecting her to say, this was not it.

"What?" Molly asked. "It's true, I swear."

"How many glasses of that cider did you have?" Sully asked.

"Not so many that I'd imagine seeing a woman dressed all in black like that," she said. "Truly, I thought she was the Ghost of Christmas Future or something. Maybe Jamie has a crazy aunt that they keep in the attic. Wouldn't surprise me coming from that one."

"Did you mention her to Steve?" Lindsey asked.

"I did," Molly said. "When I got back downstairs, I told him he had a party guest leftover from Halloween. Then I described her, and he got the weirdest look on his face."

"Fear?" Sully asked.

"No," Molly said. "More like eagerness. Does that make sense?"

"None," Lindsey said. "But I assume he must have known her."

"I suppose," Molly said. She shrugged. "He certainly didn't seem alarmed. But still, that's weird, right? Being dressed all in black at a Christmas party?"

"Definitely," Lindsey said. She glanced at Sully, wondering what he made of this. He looked as bewildered as she felt.

"All right, Emma will have my head if I don't get your statements started," Molly said. "I put a pot of coffee on in the break room, and we also have some banana bread, homemade from Mrs. Redmond to thank us for finding her dog. Third time the little mongrel has taken off on her this month. I swear, it's a good thing her banana bread is so delicious, or I think the officers wouldn't look so hard for that sweater-wearing rat."

Lindsey glanced at her, and Molly had the grace to look abashed. "Sorry, but in my defense, it peed on the corner of my desk—twice." She glanced down at Heathcliff. "You would never do that to me, would you, handsome?"

He barked and wagged. Lindsey was sure he was just looking for another biscuit, but Molly seemed satisfied that he was agreeing with her.

Sully and Lindsey took seats at the scarred wooden table in the center of the break room while Molly poured two cups of coffee and plated two slices of banana bread. The room was warm, so they shed their coats before reaching for the pens and paper that had been left out for them. Lindsey had filled out more than her fair share of official statements, but she was dreading writing up this one.

There was no way to describe finding a man dressed in an elf suit dead on a beach with the severity it deserved. No matter how she thought to phrase it, it just sounded ridiculously comical when it was anything but.

She picked at her bread and drank a sip of coffee. She glanced at Sully and noticed he had yet to write down anything other than his name. Their eyes met, and his looked shadowed with sadness. It was the worst sort of grief, losing someone in the prime of their life like this. There really wasn't anything she could say, like at least he was no longer in pain or he was in a better place, because the truth was, Steve Briggs should not be dead. Period.

She opened her mouth to say something, anything, that might ease the look of grief on Sully's face when her words were interrupted by an ear-piercing shriek coming from the direction of the lobby.

CHAPTER

5

BRIAR CREEK
PUBLIC LIBRARY

G et that hairy mongrel, that rabies-infested monster, away from me!" a woman shouted.

Lindsey glanced around the room, looking for Heathcliff. He wasn't there!

She bolted up from her chair and ran from the break room, with Sully right on her heels, down the short hallway and into the reception area of the police station. Mayhem was ensuing, with Heathcliff barking and jumping on his hind legs, Molly trying to shush him, and the object of his attention shrieking.

"Heathcliff, sit," Lindsey ordered. He sat. He glanced back at her over his shoulder with his tongue hanging out and his tail sweeping the floor. He looked proud of himself, as if he'd treed a squirrel. Lindsey glanced at his quarry, and she had to admit, she could see his confusion.

There, with her pinched features and wearing her long camel coat with the thick rabbit fur trim and a cashmere plaid scarf in a beige, red, and black, and an air of privilege that one could only be born into, stood Jamie Briggs.

Her honey-colored hair was windblown, but it was the only disheveled part of her. Her makeup was perfection, and a faint scent of Joy perfume drifted off her skin. Aside from the curl of dislike on her lips, she looked incredibly well put together, right down to her black riding boots, for a woman whose husband had just been found dead on a beach with his head bashed in.

"He tried to bite my arm off," she snapped. She pointed at Heathcliff, her hands encased in black leather driving gloves. "That dog needs to be put down."

"Not on my watch," Sully said. He sounded furious, and Lindsey reached behind her to take his hand in hers. There was nothing to be gained by having a falling out with Jamie Briggs right now.

"I'm sorry if he startled you," Lindsey said. "He's been cooped up all day and didn't get his usual walk. I can assure you, he'd never harm anyone."

Jamie sniffed and glanced away. She didn't bother to greet either Lindsey or Sully, but instead turned to Molly. "I got a message that Chief Plewicki wanted to see me. Why?"

Molly's face went pale. She cleared her throat and said, "Why don't you have a seat in her office? She should be here in just a few minutes."

Jamie huffed a breath. "I don't have time for this. I'm on my way back to the city. I have so much shopping to do. I assume this has something to do with last night's party. Did we break a noise ordinance? Why doesn't she talk to Steve about it? It's his thing not mine."

"Can I bring you a cup of coffee while you wait?" Molly asked. Clearly choosing not to engage Jamie in conversation about why she was here.

Jamie pouted. "Fine."

Molly led her down the hall to Emma's office. Lindsey reached down and patted Heathcliff's head. She glanced at Sully and said, "Safe to assume she doesn't know?"

"Yeah," he said.

At that moment, the front doors banged open and Emma strode in. She looked cross and harried. Robbie Vine was right behind her.

"Aw, come on, love. Just tell me if you think it was foul play," he said.

"No," she said. She spun around to face him. "And stop asking because I'm not talking about this . . . er . . . situation with you."

"Case. You were about to say *case*, weren't you?"

"You really need to take another acting job," she said. "You have entirely too much time on your hands to play detective." He opened his mouth to speak, but she held up her hand. "Just because you played a detective inspector on television—"

"*Masterpiece Mystery*," he corrected her. "It's a cut above."

She rolled her eyes. "Whatever. Stop looking to reprise the role of DI Gordon."

Robbie huffed out an indignant breath, but Emma was

already in motion, striding across the lobby. Noticing Lindsey and Sully, Robbie perked up, but he didn't get a chance to say a word, as Heathcliff spotted him and charged his friend with ears perked up and tail wagging.

As Heathcliff held Robbie back, demanding pets, Emma smiled. "Good dog, Heathcliff." She turned to Lindsey and Sully, "Finished with your statements?"

"Not quite," Sully said. He met her gaze and held it. "Jamie Briggs arrived. Molly took her to your office."

"Oh." Emma nodded. Her face tightened. "She didn't mention . . ."

"She doesn't know," Lindsey said. "Or at least she didn't seem to."

"Right. Okay then." Emma stiffened her spine and headed to her office. "Finish up your statements, please. I may or may not have more questions for you."

"On it," Lindsey said. She patted her thigh, and Heathcliff abandoned Robbie for her.

"Faithless, that one is," Robbie muttered.

They were about to walk back to the break room when Jamie came out of Emma's office. She was lecturing someone, Emma presumably, over her shoulder as she strode toward the door as if preparing for a dramatic exit.

"Is this what we pay you for?" Jamie demanded. "To drag citizens into your office, where you interrogate them about their lives? I won't have it. I'm going to complain to Mayor Hensen about you. I'll have you fired!"

Emma was right behind Jamie. Her jaw was clenched, and she looked annoyed. Taking a deep breath, she said, "I wasn't finished."

At that, Jamie stopped and spun around. Her eyes were narrowed, and her chin was tilted up. She looked as if she couldn't believe Emma had the nerve to continue speaking to her. "I don't understand why you need to know my whereabouts from the end of the party until this morning. I told you, I went to bed and then I slept in this morning, like I always do. I require at least nine hours of beauty rest. This"—she paused to gesture in a circle around her face—"doesn't just happen, you know. You might consider upping your own sleep game."

Emma's eyebrows went up, but she didn't say a word. When it looked as if Robbie was going to protest, Emma shook her head at him. It was clear that Emma hadn't gotten a chance to tell Jamie about Steve, and she likely didn't want to have the conversation veer off into a spat before she did.

"If you could just come back to my office for a moment," Emma said in a gentle voice. "There was something else I'd like to talk to you about."

Jamie looked her over. She didn't move. Instead, she adjusted her scarf and said, "I am a very busy woman. Whatever you have to say to me, you can say right now."

Emma glanced at the rest of them. Molly had entered the room behind them and stood leaning in the doorway, looking as uncomfortable as everyone else felt.

"The thing is, I believe you'd be more comfortable hearing this is private," Emma said. "Also, you might want to sit down."

"Sit down?" Jamie snapped. "I don't have time to sit down. Honestly, just spit it out so I can leave this godforsaken little hamlet and go back to New York."

"I'm afraid you're not going to be able to do that," Emma said.

"What?" Jamie snapped. "Why not?"

"The reason I called you in here was because I have some bad news," Emma said.

Jamie blinked. "What sort of bad news? Has something happened? Have we been robbed? Was there a fire? My jewelry! No one stole my jewelry during the party, did they?"

"No, it's nothing like that," Emma said. "I'm afraid—that is, I'm very sorry to inform you that your husband, Steve Briggs, was found dead this morning on the beach at Bell Island."

As Lindsey watched, the color drained from Jamie's face. She wobbled on her boot heels, and then, almost in slow motion, she went limp, staggered a bit and with a coy look at the men, dropped to the floor.

"Whoa!" Sully yelled.

"Oy!" Robbie echoed.

The two men leaped forward, catching her before she hit the ground. Sully caught her around the shoulders, and Robbie caught her legs. Together they tried to carry her to the wheeled office chair that Molly was helpfully pushing forward.

"This way," Robbie ordered, leading with her feet.

"No," Sully disagreed. "Her head needs to go first."

They moved in an awkward, uncoordinated effort that made Jamie look like an inchworm trying to move across a leaf as her middle sagged toward the ground and was then stretched out. Jamie let out a feeble moan as the men turned and twisted, trying to figure out how to plop her gently into the chair.

"Good grief," Emma muttered. "This isn't brain surgery. Just put her down."

Sully angled Jamie's upper body over the seat and tried to lower her into it, but her hip hit the armrest, and the wheels spun. The chair moved, and the two men began to chase it, dragging Jamie's limp body. Molly stepped forward and grabbed the chair, holding it still so Sully could put Jamie in the seat while Robbie lowered her feet to the ground.

"That's the way, mate," Robbie said. He clapped Sully on the shoulder as if they'd just achieved the impossible.

Lindsey shook her head. A closer look at Jamie, and she noticed the woman had one eye closed and one eye slitted open as if she'd been watching the progress of her two rescuers with a wary glance at the floor. As soon as Sully stepped away from her, she let out another moan and put the back of her wrist to her forehead.

Emma stepped forward and said, "Mrs. Briggs—Jamie—are you all right? Can I get you anything?"

"You!" Jamie popped up to a seated position. Her eyes were wide, her cheeks flushed, and she pointed at Emma with a shaking finger. "How dare you say such a thing! I don't believe you. I refuse to believe such lies."

Emma stepped back in surprise. She steeled herself by straightening her spine and forcing her voice to be calm. "I'm sorry. I wish it weren't true, but Sully and Lindsey were the ones who found him. Your husband is dead."

"Noooo." Jamie went rigid as she let out a wail that was

little more than a high-pitched shriek. It was painful to see her agony, and Lindsey glanced away.

Molly patted her shoulder, and Lindsey was surprised to see Jamie turn and lean into Molly's warmth. Jamie clung to her, and Molly glanced over her head at Lindsey as if she didn't know what to do. She continued to pat Jamie's back, saying, "There, there. It'll be all right."

Several minutes passed before Jamie's sobs diminished and she wiped her eyes with the end of her scarf. Molly snatched a tissue from the box on her desk and handed it to her. Jamie dabbed her eyes gratefully. Remarkably, her makeup hadn't been smudged at all by her tears.

"Jamie, if you can manage it, I'd like to ask you a few questions," Emma said.

"What?" Jamie looked incredulous. "I have just been told that my beloved husband is dead, and now you want to ask me questions? Have you no heart?"

Emma pressed her lips together. She took a long breath in through her nose and let it out through her mouth. "I am sorry for your loss, truly," she said. "Steve was such a large part of this community . . ." She paused, clearing the catch in her throat. "It's going to be hard to imagine Briar Creek without him. However, there are certain realities in play here, one of which is the first forty-eight hours are critical to an investigation."

"Investigation?" Jamie asked.

"Yes," Emma said. "The manner of Steve's death requires an official investigation."

"I thought you said he was found on the beach," Jamie said.

"Yes," Emma said. She didn't elaborate.

"Wait . . ." Jamie blinked. She stared at Emma as if she might be able to read her mind. Then she asked, "Are you telling me that my husband was murdered?"

"We won't know for certain until we've completed our inquiry," Emma said. "But there is reason to consider the possibility that his death wasn't an accident."

Lindsey thought about the side of Steve's head. It certainly hadn't looked like an accident had caused the deep gash. Even if he had fallen off his boat and cracked his head on the way down, then where was the boat? How had he managed to swim to shore, and why was he still in his elf suit? So many questions. None of which Jamie seemed prepared to answer.

"I can't process this," Jamie said. Her voice quavered, and she looked to be on the brink of tears. "I need my Teddy."

Robbie's eyebrows shot up. He glanced at Sully, who looked equally as perplexed.

"Teddy?" Emma asked.

"Yes, he's my emotional support dog," Jamie said.

"Oh, *Teddy* not *teddy*," Robbie said. "Now it's all coming into focus."

Emma gave him a look, and he stopped talking.

"I can't possibly answer any questions without him," Jamie declared. "I'll unravel. I need him. He grounds me."

"All right, is he at the house?" Emma asked. She was very calm, and Lindsey marveled that she could keep her composure when she probably wanted to demand answers.

"Yes," Jamie said. "My housekeeper can bring him to

me." She glanced at Heathcliff with a dark look. "But that mongrel has to go."

"Hey," Sully protested at the same time that Robbie said, "Oy."

Lindsey shook her head. She didn't want them to antagonize Jamie. She had a feeling she was going to be difficult enough to interview without any additional upset.

"Why don't you take Heathcliff home?" Lindsey asked Robbie. "He could use a good run on the beach on the way there."

"But—" Robbie began to protest, but Emma cut him off. "Go."

Robbie glared at all of them. Then he patted his thigh and said, "Come here, boy. We know when we're not wanted, don't we?"

The doors shut behind him and Heathcliff as they left the building. Heathcliff romped ahead, but Robbie cast a forlorn look over his shoulder as he went. He really hated being out of the loop.

"Mrs. Briggs. Jamie," Emma said. "Would you like to return to my office while I have one of my officers go and fetch Teddy? We can talk about last night while we wait."

Jamie gave her a look of outrage. "I can't possibly." She sounded on the brink of hysterics. "Not without my Teddy." With that, she dissolved into tears and sobs that racked her thin frame.

Emma looked as if she was at a loss as to what to do. Molly stepped up and gently put her hand on Jamie's shoulder. "There, there. How about we make you a nice hot cup of tea. You can lie down on the sofa in the chief's office and await your Teddy. Does that sound all right?"

Jamie sniffed. She blinked at Molly and nodded, looking more like a child than a grown woman. Molly gently took her hand and led her away. She glanced back and nodded at Emma, signaling that she would stay with Jamie until her dog arrived.

Emma turned away from them and got on her radio. Lindsey and Sully listened while she called for one of her officers to swing by the Briggs house and pick up the dog. There was some pushback, as one of the officers was not a fan of dogs. In the end, Officer Wilcox agreed to get Teddy.

Lindsey and Sully went back to the break room to fill out their statements, and Emma followed. She said it was to pour herself a cup of coffee, but when she sat at the table with them and didn't drink, Lindsey suspected she was avoiding having to go and sit with Jamie Briggs.

"What does anyone know about Jamie other than she grew up in Darien and prefers life in New York?" Lindsey asked.

"Not much," Sully said. He glanced at Emma, and she shrugged, indicating that she knew as little as they did. "I know her maiden name is Gerbowski and her family made its fortune in the post-prohibition era, producing and distributing alcohol."

"Big family?" Lindsey asked.

Sully's brow furrowed as he tried to remember what he knew about his friend's wife. "I'm trying to remember. I was at their wedding."

"You were?" Emma asked.

"Steve and I go way back," Sully said. "I didn't stand up for him, but my whole family was invited. My parents might know more; my mother is very good at getting people to talk to her."

"I may have to call her in," Emma joked. "I have no idea how I'm going to question that one." She jerked her thumb in the direction of her office. "If there is a woman more opposite to me than her, I have yet to meet her."

"Hopefully her dog will calm her down enough to talk," Lindsey said.

"I can't help feeling like it was a ploy," Emma said. "Assuming the information that her husband was dead was news to her, don't you think she'd want to reach out to his family, or even her own, before demanding to see her dog? And she didn't ask any questions about him or the cause of death or even if she could see him, I mean—"

Emma glanced up at them and took a long sip of her hot coffee. She seemed to be reining herself in.

"Sorry about that," she said. "That was incredibly unprofessional. I shouldn't be talking about a case in front of civilians like that."

"Well, we're more than just civilians," Sully said.

"Yeah, we're your friends," Lindsey agreed.

"Doesn't make it okay," Emma said. "Please forget my random speculation."

"Already forgotten," Sully assured her. He glanced across the table at Lindsey and said, "Hypothetically speaking, if you were called to the police station because my body was found on the beach with a head trauma, what would your response be?"

Lindsey stared at him. "I don't like this hypothetical—at all."

Emma glanced between them. She tapped her chin with her forefinger and said, "For curiosity's sake, what would your response be?"

"I'd demand to see his body," Lindsey said. "I wouldn't believe it until I saw him with my own eyes, and then I'd have a million questions, and you'd better believe I'd want answers. I'd be on a mission to figure out what happened."

"I get that," Emma said. "I'd react the same."

"Me, too," Sully said.

"But people process bad news differently," Lindsey said. "Also, we don't know what their relationship was like. Remember what Jamie said at the party last night?"

"Oh, yeah, that was awkward," Sully said.

"What did she say?" Emma asked.

"She said, 'Trust me, you marry a guy who you think is your Prince Charming but it's only a matter of time before he turns into a frog,'" Lindsey answered. "I don't think it's a wild guess to say that she and Steve were unhappy in their marriage, or at least she was."

"Interesting," Emma said. "I suppose the question is, How unhappy was she? Enough to do something about it? And, if so, what?"

"She seems to have hired help for just about everything," Sully said.

He didn't elaborate. He didn't have to as both Lindsey and Emma knew what he was saying. If Jamie did have anything to do with her husband's death, she would have hired someone to do it for her. And if she had, then there was definitely going to be a trail of one sort or another.

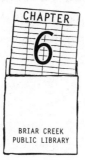

CHAPTER

6

BRIAR CREEK
PUBLIC LIBRARY

Officer Wilcox arrived within a half hour with a fluffy brown dog that looked unsurprisingly like a teddy bear. He was small and brown and groomed to look round in the face, like a baby bear. A middle-aged woman with short curly brown hair that was slowly fading to gray was carrying him in her arms. Beneath her long wool coat, she was wearing a black service dress with a white apron, and Lindsey recognized her as their neighbor Liz Lyons, who was employed as the Briggs's housekeeper.

"Liz, hi," Lindsey greeted her.

Liz glanced up from the dog. She looked wary until she recognized Lindsey and Sully, and then a smile broke across her lips. "Hey, you two. Fancy meeting you here."

"Hi, Liz," Sully said.

"I was just talking to Ray the other night about how

much I'm looking forward to your wedding," she said. "It is going to be the highlight of the month."

Lindsey forced herself to smile. It seemed weird to think about her wedding now. Given that Steve was a friend who would have been there. Heck, he was the one who was going to perform the ceremony. She froze. She felt like a jerk for thinking it, given the circumstances, but who was going to marry them now?

Teddy squirmed in her arms, and when Liz put the dog down, Lindsey noticed he was wearing a blue and white Fair Isle Christmas sweater that had a repeating pattern of snowflakes on it. He glanced up at her with his little tongue hanging out. He was ridiculously adorable.

"All right, your highness," Liz said. She glanced up at them. "He really is a love, but a bit spoiled. Have you seen Mrs. Briggs? Officer Kirkland wouldn't tell us why we were to meet her here."

"She's—" Emma began, but was interrupted.

"Teddy, is that you? Oh, my little sweet pea, come to Mommy. There's a good boy." Jamie's head appeared in Emma's doorway.

Teddy's ears perked up, and he bolted for her. Realizing that the conversation was over, Liz smiled at them as she hurried after the dog. Lindsey noted she was carrying a backpack with a pattern of dog paws all over it much like a new mother carries a diaper bag.

Jamie stepped out into the hallway and bent over. When Teddy reached her, she scooped him up and planted kisses all over his head. He licked her chin with his little pink tongue, and she gave him a weak smile.

Lindsey had always believed that dogs were a good judge of character. Assuming Teddy was like most dogs, then that was a point in Jamie's favor, which was good, because with her lack of interest in her husband's demise, she didn't have a lot going for her.

"All right, maybe now I can get her to talk," Emma said. She turned and followed Liz. She didn't get more than a few paces when Jamie held up her hand in a stop gesture.

"No," Jamie said. She gestured for Liz to open the bag. She pulled out a pair of very lethal looking shears. "Absolutely not. I need time to sit with Teddy, groom him, and meditate. Besides, I can't possibly talk to you until my attorney is present. Since it's Sunday, he won't be able to get here until later today or possibly tomorrow."

"Your attorney?" Emma gaped.

"Yes, I think that's best, don't you?" she asked. She held Teddy close to her face so that they were both looking at Emma. "Daddy always says, 'Never talk to an officer of the law without an attorney present.'"

"By all means, we can wait for your attorney to arrive," Emma said. She sounded very encouraging. "And I have a fabulous single room for you to occupy while you wait. Of course, it'll be awfully inconvenient for you to have to wait overnight, but hey, it's your call."

Jamie's eyes narrowed and her lips thinned. Lindsey felt as if this surly expression made her appear more than her actual age. Carrying Teddy under one arm, Jamie stepped forward and stared down at Emma as if she were a bug she'd found crawling in her dessert. "I may not have a law degree, but even I know that you can't keep me here unless you arrest me, and even then it's only for thirty-six hours until charges are made or you have to release me."

"Thirty-six hours can feel like an awfully long time in a cell," Emma observed. Her coolness under the fire of Jamie's ire was impressive.

"I'm going home," Jamie said. She tilted up her chin, but her voice wobbled. She was clearly rattled. She didn't move, and Lindsey wondered if she was afraid that Emma might tackle her to the ground.

"We'll go together," Emma said. "We need to conduct a search of the property." She paused to see what Jamie thought of that.

Jamie shrugged, putting the shears back in the bag Liz still held. "I don't care. The cleaning crew has been there all morning. There's not going to be anything worth finding." She looked smug.

"Maybe," Emma said.

Jamie looked less certain of herself and buried her nose in Teddy's fur.

"I'm sorry," Liz interrupted. "But what's going on?"

They all turned to look at her, and Lindsey felt her stomach drop. She didn't want to be the one who told her the news. She was still having a hard time coming to terms with it herself. Jamie didn't feel any such reluctance. She looked at Liz and said, "Steve is dead."

"What?" Liz rocked back on her heels. She looked shocked.

"I'm sorry," Emma said. Her voice was gentle, appreciating that he'd been Liz's boss and longtime friend. "But it's true. Steve Briggs was found dead this morning on one of the islands."

"This morning? On one of the islands?" Liz glanced at the window where she could see the bay through the snow that was still falling.

The storm made visibility impossible, and they could barely make out the islands. It would be fully dark soon, even though it was still afternoon, and Lindsey thought about the random happenstance that had caused them to go out to Bell Island today. If she hadn't messed up the invitations, they wouldn't have been there at all. And if they hadn't, would anyone have found Steve? The thought sent a shiver through Lindsey.

Sully put his hand on her back. "You all right?"

"Yeah, no, but I'm trying," she said.

He squeezed her shoulder and she took comfort in that. Liz glanced at them. "Is that why you're here?"

"Yeah," Sully said. "We were visiting my parents when we found him."

"But, I don't understand," Liz protested. Her voice was shaky and she looked rattled. "What happened to him? How could he be dead?"

Lindsey and Sully looked at Emma. This was her call since they had no idea how much information she wanted to give out.

"The medical examiner will determine the cause of death," she said. "Until he makes his report, we can't officially say anything."

"Oh my God," Liz gasped. "He was murdered." Then she rounded on Jamie. "You!"

Jamie reared back, holding Teddy in front of her as if he could protect her. "What?"

"You're the only one who would gain if Steve died," Liz said.

Jamie's eyebrows rose up to her hairline. "That's quite an assumption you're making."

"Is it, though?" Liz's eyes narrowed.

The two women stared at each other. The tension in the room was palpable, and Emma glanced between them, letting the moment unfold as it would.

Jamie straightened her spine and looked Liz over with a sneer. Very deliberately, she said, "You're fired."

"Too late," Liz shot back. "I quit." She reached under her coat and untied her apron. She flung it at Jamie, hitting her square in the belly with it. It fell to the floor, and no one bent to pick it up.

"Fine," Jamie said. She stepped over the apron and strode toward the door. "Don't bother calling me for a reference."

"As if I would," Liz grumbled.

With that, Jamie strode out the door. When it shut behind her, Emma turned to Wilcox and said, "Make sure she gets home okay. I'll be right behind you as soon as the warrant is ready."

"Roger that," he said. He took off after Jamie.

Liz was breathing hard. She looked rattled as she turned to them and said, "I can't believe I just quit my job a few weeks before Christmas."

They all watched her as if she might have an epic meltdown. She took a deep breath, trying to steady herself.

"And I really can't believe that Steve is dead," she said.

This time the tears did roll. "Is it true? Really? You're absolutely sure?"

Sully and Lindsey exchanged a look. Lindsey reached out and squeezed Liz's arm. "I'm so sorry. I know it's a shock."

"I just . . . last night . . ." Liz's voice trailed off. She looked at them with a worried expression. "Has anyone told Nate?"

Emma's phone chimed, and she glanced at the display. "I have to go pick up the warrant to search the Briggses' house. I'll talk to Nate on my way. And, Liz, I'll want to interview you, too, about the Briggses and last night when you're up to it."

Liz nodded. "I'll be home all evening."

Emma strode to the door, calling to Molly, "Call me if you need me."

"Will do," Molly said. She crossed the room and linked her arm with Liz's. "Come on, let's get you a hot cup of coffee and some banana bread." Then she looked at Sully and Lindsey and said, "And you two need to finish up your statements."

Like a mother hen, she led them all back to the break room. Lindsey dutifully resumed her seat and picked up her pen.

As she filled out her description of the events of the morning, she tried not to dwell on how Steve had arrived on Bell Island, still wearing his elf suit and with a head injury. What had happened to him? Horrible accident? Or intentional murder? She did not envy Emma having to figure this mess out.

*   *   *

Bam! A book was slammed down on the counter.

Lindsey glanced up and cringed. This was not how she wanted to spend her Monday afternoon. The morning had been rough, with everyone who came into the library talking about Steve Briggs. The sadness following the news of his death had left them all wrung out and weary. She'd hoped for a quiet afternoon where she could try to think about something else, something pleasant, at least for a little while. Clearly, it was not meant to be.

She turned and forced herself to smile, or at least not frown, at one of her most difficult patrons standing across the circulation desk from her. Karen Mallaber was always a pill, and judging by the cranky look on her face, today was going to be no exception. The staff had taken to calling her Ms. Malcontent, and while Lindsey didn't do that, as it was unprofessional and not a behavior she wanted to encourage, she certainly couldn't fault them for it. It took everything she had to keep her expression neutral under the glare that was being directed at her.

"Good morning, Ms. Mallaber. How are you today?" she asked. They'd never gotten friendly enough to be on a first name basis.

Ms. Mallaber ignored the greeting while she glowered at Lindsey as if she'd done something unforgivable. Lindsey scanned her brain. There'd been no changes in policy or hours, which was what usually kicked off public complaint. Still, there was no ignoring the way Ms. Mallaber's lips turned down at the corners. Lindsey braced herself for the complaining to start in three . . . two . . . one . . .

Ms. Mallaber jabbed the cover of the book on the counter in front of her with a bony finger and declared, "This is the very worst book I have ever read."

Lindsey glanced down at the mystery she was poking. Oh no. It was one of the books Lindsey had recommended to her last week. The series was one of Lindsey's favorites, and she'd hoped Ms. Mallaber would enjoy the feisty amateur sleuth, the humor and the quaint community full of quirky characters. Apparently she had not. Lindsey gently slid the book away from Ms. Mallaber before she could do it any harm.

"That's too bad," she said. "Fortunately, this author has other series—"

"No!" Ms. Mallaber snapped. She was short and stout, bundled in a thick, puffy gray coat with a beige knit hat and scarf. "This author is awful."

"And yet her books still land on the bestsellers' list," Lindsey said. She was feeling provoked into defending one of her favorite writers. Normally she could roll with a difference of opinion on a book, but Ms. Malcontent—okay fine, she *thought* it—wasn't one to have reasonable discussions. In fact, she was just a literary bully.

Ms. Mallaber sniffed in disdain, letting Lindsey know what she thought about bestsellers' lists. She yanked off her hat and untied her scarf. So she wasn't leaving any time soon. Okay, then.

"I can show you some other mysteries if you'd like,"

Lindsey offered. She hoped her voice didn't sound as half-hearted as she felt, but after the devastating day she'd had yesterday, she didn't have the reserves to pretend that she enjoyed Ms. Mallaber's company.

They'd done this reader-advisory dance so many times over the past few years, it was getting old. Lindsey suspected that Ms. Mallaber didn't care what book Lindsey recommended to her; she would hate it primarily so that she could then come back to the library and scold Lindsey for her dubious taste in reading material. Ms. Mallaber was borderline abusive in her contempt for the books and the authors, which caused Lindsey quite a bit of pain, since she tended to recommend books she loved. Maybe she'd start recommending books she couldn't stand, then when Ms. Mallaber trashed them, she could silently agree.

"No thank you," Ms. Mallaber said. She was so indignant that a few rogue dark hairs on her chin trembled along with the spiky gray hair on her head. She looked like a porcupine with quills out, except porcupines were cute. "I've given you plenty of chances. I just don't trust your judgment any longer. I don't see how you can call yourself a librarian when you can't even suggest a decent book to read."

Lindsey blinked. Even for notorious crabby appleton Ms. Malcontent, this seemed a bit over-the-top. She refused to let the woman hurt her feelings and tried to remember the wise words of one of her library professors when Lindsey told her she was going to work with the public. *Hurt people hurt people.* Clearly, there was something else going on in Ms. Mallaber's life that was making her lash out, and even though it felt personal, Lindsey was just a target and not the cause of her anger, and neither was her author.

"I'm sorry you feel that way," Lindsey said. "But, of course, I'm sure you can find plenty of books on your own."

"Obviously," Ms. Mallaber said. She turned on her heel and stormed away from the desk. Hurt or not, Lindsey was surprised to see that Ms. Malcontent's cold, cold heart hadn't caused icicles to form where she'd stood.

"What's got her in such a mood?"

Ms. Cole had come a long way in the years since Lindsey had become director of the small seaside library, and compared to Ms. Mallaber, she practically radiated sunshine and daisies.

"The usual," Lindsey said. "With an extra twist of mean."

"Such a sourpuss," Ms. Cole said. "She's always been like that, even when she was young. Reminds me of a lemon, all puckered up like that."

Lindsey's eyes went wide. "You don't say."

"I do say. She really needs to loosen up," Ms. Cole said.

When she went back to her stack of books for check-in, Lindsey turned her head away and smiled.

Thankfully, Ms. Mallaber left the library with a stack of books and her own personal black cloud shortly thereafter, and Lindsey settled in at the reference desk to read book reviews and work on her orders for next year. She was halfway through *Booklist*, by far her favorite book review source, when she saw Violet and Nancy enter the building.

Although, the crafternooners were all frequent users of the library, Lindsey had a feeling they were here for more than the usual library services of checking out books and movies or doing research that involved more in-depth knowledge than a Google search that may or may not give the correct answer.

"Good afternoon, ladies," Lindsey greeted them. "Any news?" She didn't have to explain about what. Steve's death had been the news of the town.

"Nothing as yet," Nancy said.

"Emma is staying very tight-lipped about Steve's death," Violet added.

They sat down in the two padded chairs opposite Lindsey's desk. This had been the traffic pattern all day. People coming into the library and, other than Ms. Mallaber, stopping by her desk, wanting to talk about Steve's death. There was much speculation, and the rumors were beginning to grow and warp with each telling.

One theory was he'd taken his boat out while drunk, as it had been discovered missing during Emma's search of the house and grounds. Another was that he had a side piece on one of the islands and had decided to go visit her but had crashed in the dark. A twist on that tale was that he'd been discovered by Jamie, who had clocked him on the head in a rage and set him out to sea. While that was wildly popular, since no one liked Jamie, most town residents had zeroed in on Tony Mancusi, Steve's former partner, as the person most likely to have caused Steve harm. Their fight at the party was proof enough in most people's minds that there was some serious bad blood there.

Variations of these theories had been offered up all morning, and Lindsey and her staff had listened, offering no opinions on what was an ongoing investigation. She knew that the library was the center point of the community, but she felt as if people were here for more than just the sense of connection. Everyone seemed to be looking to her for something, but she had no idea what.

"Why do I get the feeling you think I might know something?" Lindsey asked.

"Because you're you," Nancy said.

"Meaning?"

"Nosy," Violet said. "But in the nicest possible way."

Lindsey frowned. She wasn't sure how she felt about that. Sure, she had a librarian's keen interest in getting to the root of a question, but did that make her nosy or just really passionate about her job of gathering information? She preferred to think it was the latter.

"Well, I don't have any more information than anyone else." She shrugged.

"That disappoints," Nancy retorted.

"Until the medical examiner gives a cause of death," Lindsey said, "I don't think it's right to look for a murderer among us. It could have just been a terrible accident."

"Except." Violet raised a finger to show she had a point. "Steve grew up here. He knew the islands almost as well as Sully. There's no way he crashed his boat. Speaking of which, where is his boat?"

Lindsey sighed. Sully had made the same point over their morning coffee. He was struggling with the shocking death of his friend, and the fact that it appeared that Steve had crashed amid the islands he knew so well hadn't sat well with Sully. He didn't say he suspected foul play, but Lindsey knew him well enough to know he was thinking it.

"No one knows," she said. "Sully went looking for it out in the bay this morning, but there was no sign of it. Of course, he only had time for a cursory check of the islands. It could still be out there."

"Any word on how his brother is taking the news?" Nancy asked.

"No," Lindsey said. "I'm sure he's devastated."

Violet and Nancy exchanged a look. It was heavy with meaning, and Lindsey glanced between them. "What?"

"I heard that Emma questioned him about his whereabouts after the party," Nancy said. She kept her voice low, obviously not wanting anyone to overhear her.

"That seems like a procedural sort of thing, doesn't it?" Lindsey asked. "I mean, he's Steve's brother, and he was a part of the altercation with Tony Mancusi. She might have been trying to determine whether the brothers had another argument with Mancusi, which, judging by how furious he was, seems highly likely."

"That makes sense," Violet said. "I can't see Nate Briggs being involved in anything criminal. He's the nicest man. Why, I remember when my car broke down on the Post Road. He was already there to tow another car, but he came right over and changed my tire for me so I could drive back to the garage on the spare."

"Isn't that just like him?" Violet agreed. "I think everyone in town has a Nate Briggs story. For me, it was a hot summer day, and my car overheated in the middle of nowhere. Like a knight on a white stallion, he appeared out of the waves of heat and got my baby cooled off and running again. Of course, his stallion was his beat-up white tow truck, but I might have had a touch of heatstroke."

Lindsey smiled. "I remember there was this time that Sully dropped a tiny screwdriver down into the truck's engine when he was fiddling with it and trying to fix it himself." She paused to shake her head. "Nate told him not to do that again but then managed to fish the screwdriver out and fix the problem."

"He's just a good man," Nancy said.

"One of the best," Violet agreed.

"Which is why I'm certain Emma talking to him was just a formality," Lindsey said. "Poor Nate is probably desperate to know what happened to his brother."

"I know I would be," Nancy said. "I can't even picture this town without Steve Briggs in it."

The three of them were silent for a moment, trying to come to terms with the loss of such a larger-than-life personality.

"I'm sure you've thought of this," Violet said. "And I hate to bring it up and cause you any added stress, but it needs to be dealt with." She leaned over the desk and said, "Who are you and Sully going to get to marry you? You have less than a week to find someone. Pastor Williams is celebrating his thirtieth wedding anniversary and won't be returning to Briar Creek until the week before Christmas."

Lindsey felt her insides twist into a knot. She hadn't wanted to say anything, but there it was. Briar Creek was a small town. There weren't a lot of options if they wanted an official-type person to perform the service with the same panache that Steve would have brought to the ceremony with his deep voice and charming grin.

She nodded. "I know, I know. I've been trying not to freak out, but I have no idea what we're going to do. I don't even know if Emma is going to let us have the ceremony on the island. As of this morning, the residents were asked to vacate to allow the investigators the run of it now that the snow has stopped. They are crawling all over the place, looking for clues as to what happened and how Steve got there."

Both women looked at her, and Violet issued a stern warning, "No fretting. It gives you wrinkles. The wedding is in five days. Surely we can find someone in that time who can perform the ceremony."

"Would you consider it?" Lindsey asked. It had just hit her that Violet would be perfect. She was a brilliant actress, elegant and beautiful, and carried herself with such an air of authority that she would give the ceremony the gravitas it warranted. Also, she loved Lindsey and Sully, so it would have the same feeling of longtime friendship that Steve would have given them.

To Lindsey's surprise, Violet burst into tears, and not delicate little sniffles either. Oh, no. Enormous drops of water coursed down her brown skin, over her jutting cheekbones, to drip off her chin. Nancy opened her purse and pulled out a pack of tissues. She handed one to Violet.

"She can't," Nancy said. "Violet is a crier. She can't get through a wedding, even a stranger's wedding, without sobbing herself dry."

"I'm sorry, but it's true." Violet blew her nose. "But how

lovely of you . . . to ask me . . . for your special day . . ." She stopped, dissolving into sobs and tears again.

"See?" Nancy asked. "I always tell her she could be rented out for weddings and funerals."

Lindsey reached across the desk and patted Violet's hand. "Don't worry. We'll find someone. We have five days. It'll be fine. Totally fine."

When Violet and Nancy departed, Lindsey went back to her review reading. There had been a new resurgence in romantic comedies, and she found a title about a young woman revisiting her gap year, including Paris, that she knew she had to order multiple copies of because, as the title suggested, Paris was always a good idea. Maybe she and Sully should elope to Paris.

"Hi, Lindsey."

Lindsey glanced up and grinned. One of her favorite patrons, Kathi McIntyre, a retired science teacher, was walking past her desk. She had a stack of books in her arms and Lindsey spied a mystery by Deborah Crombie and a thriller by Hank Phillippi Ryan.

"Excellent choices," she said.

"Thanks." Kathi smiled. She surreptitiously took a sip of the Coca-Cola she clutched in her free hand. Lindsey raised an eyebrow and Kathi shrugged. "I know, I know, no beverages in the library, but it's my one weakness."

"I won't tell," Lindsey said. She raised the coffee cup she had hidden on the shelf under her desk and Kathi blinked at her from behind her glasses, tossed her light brown hair back, and laughed.

"You're a rebel, Lindsey Norris," she said.

"Takes one to know one." Lindsey toasted her with her mug and Kathi returned it with her soda can before heading to the checkout desk.

When Ann Marie, the library's adult services librarian, came to relieve Lindsey from the desk, she was ready for the break. Her book orders were done, she'd given plenty of reader's advisory, and the two reference questions she'd gotten had been asked and answered. In giving Ann Marie a rundown on the state of the service desk, she was pleased that she didn't have any questions to roll over. Ann Marie looked relieved as well.

Lindsey glanced at the stack of papers in her hand. "Programming?"

"Yes," Ann Marie said. "I'm already booking the guest speakers for spring. Can you believe it? The year isn't even over yet, and I'm booking for March. Speaking of which, how would you feel about a baking program? Any chance we could commandeer the staff kitchen for a visiting chef?"

"Before I hastily say yes and live to regret it, can you send me a description of the program, including the cost?" Lindsey asked.

Ann Marie handed her a sheet of paper. "I anticipated that reaction. Here's the presenter's credentials and requirements."

"Excellent. I'll have an answer for you by tomorrow."

"Thanks," Ann Marie said. "Not to show my hand, but I'm thinking I'd like to do a series of programs with visiting chefs. Just think how it could help showcase our cookbook collection."

Lindsey smiled. "I like the way you're thinking."

Ann Marie grinned, and Lindsey left the floor, thinking how lucky she was to have such a crackerjack staff. Their commitment to their community was unparalleled.

When she arrived at her office, it was to find Robbie Vine waiting for her. As was their habit, he stopped by the library every now and then in the afternoon to share a spot of tea. A pot covered with a knit cozy in the shape of a Santa Claus head sat on the corner of her desk with two cups beside it.

"You are wasting your time," Lindsey said. "I don't know anything about what happened to Steve Briggs. If your chief of police girlfriend isn't telling you, she certainly isn't telling me."

"Now, is that nice?" Robbie asked. He rose to his feet and shoved his phone into his pocket when she entered. "Here I go to all the trouble to brew a pot of tea and bring some of your favorite biscuits and you accuse me of being here just to get the goss. The cheek!"

Lindsey burst out laughing. She couldn't help it. No one could feign innocent chagrin like Robbie. His strawberry-blond hair was ruffled, and his pale green eyes twinkled with mirth.

Lindsey glanced down at the package of Biscoff biscuits. Okay, he had her there. Those Belgian cookies were a weakness, especially when paired with a hot cup of tea. She circled her desk and sat down while Robbie poured their tea and plated some cookies.

"I apologize," Lindsey said, "if I misread your intentions."

"No need." Robbie waved away her apology. "As it turns out, I am here to talk about one of the Briggses."

Lindsey paused with her delicate china cup halfway to her lips. "*One* of the Briggses? Not Steve?"

"Not directly," he said. He gave her a considering glance. "It just so happens that at the party, I overheard a heated discussion between the two brothers."

"Really?" Lindsey asked. She frowned. She thought about how Nate had been beside Steve, defending him from Tony Mancusi. She'd always thought the Briggs brothers were close. She had a hard time believing that any discord between them was anything more than the normal sibling-type stuff. Even she and her brother, Jack, were known to rile each other every now and again.

"You doubt me?" he asked.

Lindsey took a sip. The Earl Grey was divine, warming her up against the cold day.

"No, I can understand that the two brothers might have not always gotten on," she said. "But enough for Nate to have harmed Steve? No, I just don't see it."

"Not even with the disparity in their incomes?" Robbie asked. "Steve lives in a glass mansion on the water while Nate . . ."

"Lives in a three-bedroom single-story house on the edge of town with his wife and five children," Lindsey finished. "Do you really think that would give him reason to harm his brother?"

"Maybe he asked for a loan and Steve said no," Robbie suggested. Lindsey made a face, and he shrugged. "I don't like it either, but I know what I heard."

"What exactly did you hear? And how?"

"I had left the party to use the loo," he said. "I was

waiting for my turn, but the line was long, so I thought I'd kill some time in the library while I waited."

"Steve has a library?"

"Huge one," Robbie said. "I didn't realize anyone was in there, as the room is shaped in an L, and they were around the corner from me. When I heard the voices, I thought about leaving, but they sounded as if they might come to blows at any moment, so I thought I should stay just in case it got ugly."

"What were they saying?" she asked.

"That's the tricky part, isn't it?" he asked. "I couldn't see them, and their voices are as similar as their faces. The only reason I even know it was them is because they used each other's names."

"Have you told Emma about this?"

"Of course," he said. "I told her first thing."

"What did she say?"

"She was going to interview Nate about it."

"I heard that she already talked to him about his whereabouts after the party."

"Where'd you hear that? You really are dialed in, aren't you?"

"Yes, I am. Won't it be awkward if Nate asks who overheard him?"

Robbie chewed his lower lip. "It's fine. I could take him."

Lindsey shook her head. Nate was a mechanic who picked up and tossed spare tires like they were softballs. If provoked, he could pound Robbie into the ground like a hammer on a spike.

"All right, fine. So the strapping young lad could thrash me," he said. "What do I care? I have one thing he'll never have."

"What's that?"

"The chief of police as my backup."

CHAPTER

7

BRIAR CREEK
PUBLIC LIBRARY

nless she gives you up for being the meddlesome boyfriend you are," Lindsey said.

Robbie grinned. "She'd never. She's too smitten."

Lindsey rolled her eyes. "Okay, spill it. What did you hear?"

Robbie leaned forward and set his cup on the desk, then he rubbed his hands together as if he were trying to get warm.

"All right, so there I was, perusing the titles in the library—quite the eclectic reading taste, I might add," he began. Lindsey rolled her hand at him to indicate he should move it along, and he sighed. "Fine. Once I heard them talking and noticed that their voices were heated, I began to back out of the room, but then I heard one of them say, 'If you go through with this, you'll be dead to me.'"

Robbie's imitation of the American accent was spot-on,

and Lindsey was enthralled. She could just imagine over-hearing such a conversation, and she didn't fault Robbie a bit for loitering. She sipped her tea while he continued.

"Naturally, I froze. I wondered what might happen if the two came to blows. I didn't want to just walk away."

"Could you tell which brother said, 'You'll be dead to me'?" she asked.

Robbie shook his head. "No, blast it. Emma asked me the same thing."

"What do you suppose they were talking about?" Lindsey asked.

"Not *what*. *Who*," Robbie said. "After that dramatic de-clarative statement, the conversation continued, and it be-came clear that the Briggs brothers were arguing over a woman."

"Whoa," Lindsey said. She sank back in her seat. That was the very last thing she'd expected. "Are you sure? What did they say? Who is the woman?"

"Well, if I knew that, I'd have told Emma, wouldn't I? And she'd be questioning her," he said. "But they never mentioned a name."

Lindsey tapped her chin with her forefinger. Judging by Jamie's reaction to the news of Steve's death, she had the feeling that there wasn't a lot of love between the two. Per-haps it was just on Jamie's side, but it was hard for her to imagine the wealthy Jamie, who didn't like Briar Creek, having an affair with local boy Nate.

Besides, everyone knew that Nate was crazy about his wife, Naomi. They were high school sweethearts, both born and raised in Briar Creek, and they had five adorable daughters. No, Lindsey couldn't see Nate cheating on his wife.

"What about the woman in black?" Lindsey asked. It occurred to her that whomever Molly had seen dressed in disguise might be the woman in question.

"Woman in black?" Robbie asked. "I think you've got your mystery novels mixed up. It's *The Woman in White* by Wilkie Collins, and what does that book have to do with anything?"

"No, I'm not talking about a novel," Lindsey said. She waved her hand at him. "Molly at the police station told Sully and me that she bumped into a woman dressed all in black, including a heavy black veil, when she was upstairs using the restroom. Don't you think it's likely that she was the woman they were fighting about?"

"Do you suppose they were having an affair with the same woman?" Robbie asked. "The scandal!"

"No, I don't see Nate cheating," Lindsey said. On this she was absolute. "What else did they say? Try to remember it exactly."

"One of them said, 'She's not yours,' and the other said, 'She is for the right price,' and that's when one of them made the death declaration, perhaps meaning it literally."

Lindsey stared down into her teacup.

"I'll admit it sounds bad," she said, "but there are certain realities in this conversation."

"Such as?"

"Well, for one thing, only one of the brothers has money," she said. "So that would indicate that whoever said, 'she is for the right price' had the money to back up his claim."

"Hold it." Robbie sat up straight. "I've been going at this all wrong."

"What do you mean?"

"I assumed they were talking about a woman but what else is usually ascribed a female gender?"

"You lost me."

"We're taking *her* out for a drive," Robbie said. He wagged his eyebrows at her, trying to get her to catch his meaning.

"Cars, boats, planes! Ah, of course!" Lindsey cried. "They could have been talking about something other than a woman. That makes so much more sense, especially since Nate is a mechanic."

"Any idea how we can find out what he's been working on?" Robbie asked.

"Naomi, his wife, is in here all the time with their girls," Lindsey said. "I could try and find out if she knows anything about a disagreement between the brothers." She sighed and leaned back in her chair, feeling relieved. "It could be as simple as Nate advising his brother away from a bad purchase, couldn't it?"

Robbie's face grew serious. "No, we have to remember that whatever he was suggesting was very serious to Nate. Otherwise, why say, 'You'll be dead to me'?"

"Oh, right." Lindsey took another biscuit and bit it in half. "So it could have been a car he was working on, maybe a car he wanted to invest in, or possibly a boat, although I don't think Nate did much work on boats."

"Steve's boat is still missing," Robbie observed. "And it's a top-of-the-line craft, easily worth a couple hundred thousand."

"It could be he was thrown overboard," Lindsey said. "He might have bashed his head on a rock in the bay and had to swim for it."

Robbie refreshed their tea and said, "Doesn't it seem awfully odd that he would have been joyriding on his boat in the middle of the night when it was bitterly cold wearing only his elf suit?"

"That had occurred to me," Lindsey said. "I'm sure Emma has thought the same."

Robbie nodded. "She won't discuss it, but I know it bothered her, too."

"So that makes it seem more likely that it was murder," Lindsey said.

He shrugged. "How drunk was he when he left the party?"

"I can't say for sure, but it's well known that Steve doesn't drink. He's been sober for as long as I've lived in Briar Creek. Unless, of course, he had a relapse . . ."

"It would explain a lot," Robbie said. "Some of my worst decisions were made when I was tanked. Then again, some of my best decisions came from the same place."

Lindsey gave him a look, but he made a scale with his hands and pretended to weigh the good versus the bad.

"Be that as it may," she said, "it doesn't seem likely that Steve got drunk and decided to go joyriding in his boat, does it?"

"Maybe the argument with Mancusi or his brother set him off on a bender," Robbie offered.

"I feel like we're reaching," Lindsey said. "We have to leave it to Emma to figure this out. I don't have time, and with Steve, well, gone, I have to find someone who can perform our wedding ceremony in just a few days. Not to mention the fiasco of having three times as many people in attendance than I had planned."

Lindsey pushed aside her cup and rested her head on her desk. She was not overwhelmed. She was not. Just because the island where she planned to get married was off-limits due to an investigation, her family was arriving in a matter of days, she had no one to perform the ceremony, and one of her future husband's lifelong friends had been found dead under mysterious circumstances, there was no reason to be riddled with doubt and anxiety.

"Chin up, love," Robbie said. "Surely it can't be that hard to find someone who is already ordained and has a certificate from the county clerk as well as a letter of good standing. I mean, that's the easy part. What you really want is a person who can deliver a bang-up service. This is your big day, after all."

"I'll settle for someone who can 'mawwage' their way through the service," she said.

Robbie burst out laughing. "Like in *The Princess Bride*?"

"Exactly," she said. "Beggars not being choosey and all."

"I bet you'll find just the right person," Robbie said. He gestured to the library around them. "Why, they're likely right under your nose."

"You're probably right," she said. She rose up from the desk, retrieving her cup and finishing her tea. "I just feel as if Steve's death has cast a pall over the whole thing. I mean, he was our friend, and he was a cornerstone of the community. It feels so wrong to continue with the ceremony without him, but I feel like if we don't get married this weekend, we never will."

"Ask yourself this, what would Steve want you to do?"

"Get married," she said. She knew it as surely as if he was standing there saying it to her. Steve had been thrilled when they asked him to perform the ceremony. During their conversation about the service, he'd confided to them that he was a sucker for weddings and considered them the highlight of his position as a justice of the peace.

It was one more reason that Lindsey had never understood his relationship with Jamie. It was so clear that Steve loved Briar Creek and was happy here while Jamie could barely stand it. What sort of marriage was that? Had Steve been happy? Jamie clearly hadn't been. What did it all mean in regard to Steve's death? She didn't know.

"What are you thinking?" Robbie asked.

"That I have a lot of questions about Steve's death," she said. "But Emma would probably say—"

"Leave it to the police," Robbie finished for her with a sigh.

"And she'd be right," Lindsey said.

"That's never stopped us before," Robbie said.

"We had reasons before," Lindsey said. "People we cared about were being wrongly accused or were in danger."

"I fail so see your point," he said.

"We have no reason to think Steve was murdered as yet," Lindsey said. "Also, I have a wedding that I need to be thinking about. I can't be getting all caught up in some possible investigation."

"Of course, you're right," Robbie said. "It'd be bad form

of us to assume the worst and then start looking for a murderer in our midst. Besides, even if there is a culpable party, my money is on that Mancusi fellow. He clearly had a beef with Briggs that had been festering for some time."

"And if he is the responsible party, Emma will no doubt be on top of it," Lindsey said.

"So, is this how it's going to be now?" Robbie asked.

"How what's going to be?"

"This. Us. Me, the fabulous yet out-of-commission undercover operative, and you, the good-hearted librarian who no longer sticks her nose where it doesn't belong?"

"I'm not sure I like that description of me," Lindsey retorted.

"Sorry," Robbie said. "I just felt like we were a team, taking on the bad guys and all."

"We were," she said. "I just think we need to join a volleyball league or something, as our time as sleuths has obviously come to a close. No more bad guys should be a good thing."

"Meh. Volleyball?" Robbie made a face of disgust.

Lindsey laughed. "Fine, you pick our new hobby, but, yes, I do think those days are done. I hope so, at least. Wouldn't life be better if there were no more murders in Briar Creek?"

"Well, yeah, but . . ."

"No buts," Lindsey said. She glanced at the clock on her computer. "And I have to get back to work."

"Why is teatime always the shortest part of the day?" Robbie asked. He stood and began gathering their things, loading up the tray he'd used. Lindsey helped, and when he lifted the tray, he stared over it at her with a considering look.

"What?" she asked.

"I was just thinking," he said.

Lindsey waited. She knew Robbie. She knew how his brain worked. He had an angle he was working. She perched a *no* on the tip of her tongue, getting it ready.

"You said that we don't have a reason to investigate this situation," he said. "But I'd argue that as long as your wedding is swinging in the balance, we very much have a reason to find out what happened to Steve Briggs, because the sooner we know, the sooner the island will be available for you to get married. And the clock is ticking."

Lindsey exited the library, leaving Beth in charge for the evening. Sully's parents were still staying at the bed-and-breakfast while the police finished up on the island, so Lindsey and Sully were meeting them for dinner at the Blue Anchor.

Mike and Joan were already seated in a booth with Sully when Lindsey arrived. She hung up her coat on the rack at the end of the booth, draping her scarf over her wool coat. Sully and Mike both stood, and Sully hugged her and gestured for her to go ahead into the booth. She sank gratefully onto the dark brown vinyl seat, already thinking about what she wanted for dinner.

The biscuits she'd had with Robbie at tea a few hours

ago were history, and her stomach was ready for more. The smell coming from the kitchen was a combination of lobster bisque and clam fritters, and she was torn between the two and debating ordering both.

"Lindsey, I'm so glad you're here," Joan said. "I had an idea about your wedding."

"You did?" Lindsey asked. With only a few days to go, she'd thought the time for ideas was done, but she was willing to listen.

"Yes," Joan hesitated. "I hate to even mention this because it seems cold, but you still need someone to marry you, yes?"

Lindsey glanced at Sully. Unless he'd pulled off a miracle of which she was unaware, they still needed someone to perform the service.

"Do we?" she asked. He nodded. So no miracle then. She turned back to Joan. "Yes, it appears we do still need someone."

"Okay, then, I was thinking about my uncle Carl," she said. "He's retired, but he was a minister in Durham for years."

"Oh, Mom, no," Sully said. He shook his head. Lindsey glanced at his face. He looked pained, as if he didn't want to reject her suggestion but felt he had no alternative.

"Why? What's wrong with Uncle Carl?" she asked.

A waitress came by and delivered a glass of wine to Lindsey. She glanced at the bar and saw Ian. He waved, and she smiled. He was going to be her brother-in-law in just a few days, and she knew she couldn't ask for a better one.

"Dad, help me out," Sully said to his father.

Mike's gray eyebrows rose up to his hairline. "Sorry, son, you're on your own."

"Well?" Joan persisted.

"Mom, the last time he was assigned grace at Thanksgiving, he went on for five minutes and then fell asleep," he said. "He almost did a face-plant into the mashed potatoes."

Mike burst out laughing and clapped Sully on the shoulder. "And he would have if Ian hadn't scooped them out of the way in time."

"Not a surprise. You know how Ian feels about his taters," Sully said.

"It was a very busy day, and he was tired," Joan said. She gave them both a reproving glance and then turned to Lindsey. "He's a very nice man."

"He is," Sully conceded. "He's also ninety-six and hasn't left his assisted-care facility in the middle of winter in years. The shock might do him in."

"Sully!" Joan frowned.

"I'm sorry, Mom, I love Uncle Carl, too, and if he was a decade or two younger, I would absolutely consider him, but this day is going to be too much for him, and you know it," he said.

Joan sighed. "I know. I'm just afraid if we don't find someone . . ."

"We'll find someone," Lindsey said. "I'm sure of it. I have everyone I know looking. It'll be okay." She wasn't sure of anything of the sort, but she must have sounded more confident than she felt, because Joan looked reassured.

"I think we need to consider the possibility that we won't be able to get married on the island," Lindsey said. "Maybe we should find a place in town to have the wedding."

Sully nodded. "I was thinking the same thing." He turned to his parents. "Has Emma said when you'll be able to go home?"

"She said they'd be done with their investigation by tomorrow," Mike said. "Don't worry. The island will be in perfect shape for the wedding."

Joan nodded. "It'll be lovely, you'll see."

Lindsey felt herself relax. If Mike and Joan felt this confident, then surely she should, too. Her parents and her brother were arriving in a few days. They were all staying at the Sullivans' house on the island, and the wedding would be a simple ceremony with a reception to follow. Thankfully, they'd managed to rent a large tent with side flaps that closed and portable heaters so that they could accommodate everyone who was planning to come. She tried not to think about the invitation debacle. On the scale of bad things that had happened lately, this certainly seemed rather insignificant in the grand scheme.

She looked at Sully. "If it's too hard for you to get married without Steve, we could postpone."

He turned to face her. His blue eyes were warm, and his mouth curved up on one side, deepening a dimple in his cheek. His expression was a mix of gratitude and grief.

"Thank you for saying that. I appreciate it. But Steve would have been the first one to tell us to carry on without him."

Lindsey nodded. She could see that. Steve had been a big believer in living life to the fullest.

"Talk about carrying on," Joan said. "Isn't that his wife, Jamie, eating dinner with a strange man?"

CHAPTER
8

BRIAR CREEK
PUBLIC LIBRARY

Lindsey turned and glanced in the direction Joan indicated with a tip of her chin. On the far side of the restaurant, tucked into a booth, was Jamie Briggs. Across the table from her was a man in a suit. They were both leaning in, meeting halfway across the table, while they had what appeared to be a very intense discussion.

"That's her," Sully confirmed. He frowned.

"He might be just a friend," Lindsey said. "Maybe he's here to comfort her after her loss."

"That's no friend," Ian said as he stopped by their table. "That's her attorney."

"That explains his shiny suit and pointy shoes," Mike said.

"I'm surprised they're meeting here," Lindsey said. "Wouldn't she want to do this in the privacy of her own home?"

"She would, but given that all of her household staff has quit, she has to eat somehow, doesn't she?" Ian asked. "I doubt that girl knows how to boil a pot of water."

"They all quit?" Lindsey asked. She knew about Liz, but she couldn't believe they'd all left their jobs, and right before the holiday.

"Every one of them," he said. "Apparently, she got home from the police station and held a meeting. She told them that since Steve was gone, there would be no end of the year bonuses for anyone since she didn't know how the finances were going to work without Steve. They all quit on the spot."

"But she just lost her husband," Lindsey said. "Maybe she's not thinking straight."

Ian shook his head at her. "Steve paid their staff very well to put up with her. By all accounts she was a misery to work for and always has been. She genuinely felt that their domestic staff were at her beck and call twenty-four seven and should be happy to be so. When Liz Lyons had to have her appendix out, Jamie thought she should be back at work the next day. She even called her and chewed her out, accusing her of being lazy."

"Not to pile on with the gossip," Joan said, "but I did hear that she fired one of her cleaning people for refusing to give her a pedicure."

"Ew," Mary said as she joined them. She leaned over to kiss her mother's cheek and then her father's. She ruffled Sully's hair affectionately and then draped an arm around her husband's shoulders. Ian beamed at her.

"I take it they're filling you in on Jamie Briggs," she said to Lindsey.

"And how," Lindsey said. "Is she really that awful?"

"Well the pedicure story ranks right up there," Mary said. "But that's just one story of many. I think the only reason Steve was able to keep the staff here in Briar Creek as long as he did was because she was gone most of the time, preferring the city. It'd be interesting to hear what the city domestic staff think of her."

"Maybe she was just super mean because she didn't want to live here," Lindsey said.

"No, she's just a horrible person," Ian said. "You know, she doesn't drive. Apparently . . ." He pantomimed chugging a drink before he continued. "There were some issues. When her driver was off and she wanted to go somewhere, she paid her next-door neighbor's kid, a sixteen-year-old, to drive her to a bar in New Haven on a weeknight, and then she had him sit in the car and wait for her for three hours. The kid was scared to death, didn't know how to get out of the city, and was out well past curfew. His parents threatened to sue, but Steve settled the dispute with a nice cash payout."

"Oh, that is bad," Lindsey said. Liz's abrupt departure from her job, despite the holidays, suddenly made a lot more sense.

"Quite. Without Steve to rein her in, the staff knows she's going to make their lives a misery. I think they all decided to get out while the getting was good."

"You don't think it makes them look like they know something about Steve's death and they're trying to hide it?" Lindsey asked. "Like, maybe Jamie is buying them off."

"Nah. Believe me, if they knew Jamie had done something, they wouldn't hesitate to turn her in," Ian said.

Lindsey glanced back at the table where Jamie sat with her presumed attorney. Whatever they were talking about, Jamie was clearly fired up. Her face was flushed, and she was tapping the table with her forefinger as if driving home her point. Her lawyer nodded as if he was taking in everything she said, but there was a distracted air about him as if he'd rather be anywhere but there.

"What about Tony Mancusi?" Lindsey asked. "I would think if the police believed it was foul play that caused Steve's death, that Mancusi would be at the top of the list."

"He is," Ian said. "At least, that's what I gathered from what I overheard when the officers were here for their dinner break. Unfortunately, he's also gone missing."

"Overheard?" Sully asked.

"Overheard. Eavesdropped." Ian shrugged. "Same thing."

"Oh, Ian," Joan said. "Do be careful. If this Mancusi is dangerous, you want to stay out of it." She glanced at Lindsey and Sully. "That goes for you two as well. You're to be married in a matter of days. You can't risk it all by getting mixed up in something potentially dangerous."

"We won't," Sully said. "But if Steve Briggs was murdered, I'm not going to turn my back on finding out who did it."

"*If* he was murdered?" Ian asked. He glanced at Sully with a sympathetic look. "You haven't heard then."

"Heard what?" Lindsey asked. Her heart dropped into her feet. She could tell from the expression on Ian's face that the news was bad.

"The same officers that were in here talking about Mancusi mentioned that the medical examiner has ruled Steve Briggs's death a homicide."

Lindsey and Joan gasped at the same time. Sully reached across the space between them and squeezed Lindsey's fingers with his.

This was a devastating blow. It was bad enough that Steve was dead, but to know that someone had intentionally taken his life? It was just too much.

"Do the police think it was Tony Mancusi then?" Mike asked.

Ian shrugged. "It seems likely after that nasty scene at the party, and he is missing, so it looks bad for him, but it could be someone else. I mean, they were in a law firm together. It could be someone who was out to get the both of them."

"You mean a case they worked on together?" Joan asked.

"It's possible," Ian said. "It could be there is a disgruntled client in their past."

"Who would know?" Lindsey asked. "Jamie?"

They all looked back at her booth. She and her attorney were still deep in discussion. She looked angry and frazzled while he looked nervous. Lindsey didn't think that spoke well for their professional relationship.

"Nah, I doubt she knew much of what went on in Steve's office," Ian said. "I think it would have to be someone closer to him."

"Like Nate?" Sully asked.

"Yeah, he'd know if someone was threatening Steve," Ian said.

Lindsey glanced at Sully, wondering if he was thinking the same thing she was.

"Isn't it weird how your truck is making such a strange noise all of a sudden?" Lindsey asked him. "I suppose you'll have to take it in to Nate just to be on the safe side."

Sully looked at her with a gleam of appreciation in his eyes. "Yeah, it's the craziest thing."

"No, no, no," Joan shook her head. "You have to stay focused on your wedding. No chasing down murderers, no getting into harm's way, none of that. Save it for the police."

"We will," Sully said. "I'm sure Emma has everything under control."

"Absolutely," Lindsey agreed. "She's the best."

"But since the investigation could shut down the island indefinitely and we still don't have someone to marry us, we do need to pay attention to what's happening, don't you think?" Sully asked. His expression was one of such innocence, Lindsey had no doubt that this was exactly how he had looked when he was a boy trying to get something by his parents.

"The sooner the case is solved, the more likely our wedding is to go off without a hitch," Lindsey agreed.

Joan looked from Sully to Lindsey and then to her husband and said, "Soul mates. I always hoped he'd find his. And clearly he has."

Mike nodded. He pointed to Ian and Mary and said, "Just like these two."

Ian and Mary exchanged a grin and she said, "We just followed your example, Mom and Dad."

Joan lifted up her napkin and dabbed at her eyes. "We're not even at the wedding, and I'm beginning to cry." She sighed and then looked at Sully and Lindsey with a sternness that only a mother could harness. "All right, you two, do what you have to do, but be careful."

"Of course," Sully said. "Nothing is going to get in the way of our wedding. We promise."

The next morning Sully and Lindsey arrived bright and early at Nate's Garage. Situated on the edge of town, Nate's Garage was housed in an old gas station. Behind it, down a winding dirt road, was a small ranch house where he and his wife, Naomi, lived with their five girls.

Everyone in town had a story about Nate saving the day. Everyone except Lindsey. Since she didn't have a car, she hadn't needed him to rescue her as yet. But he'd long ago won her over with his exceptional skills as a dad.

Last year, Beth had decided to have a crafternoon for some of the tweens who liked to hang out in the children's area. She'd wanted to teach them to knit and invited parents to come along and help. Lindsey had stopped by the tween crafternoon to see how it was going. They were discussing *Black Beauty*, one of her favorite books, while they knitted and snacked on lemonade and cupcakes. Much to Lindsey's surprise, there was only one parent in attendance. Nate.

Sitting in the middle of a circle of eleven-year-old girls, wearing his mechanic's uniform, he'd clutched a pair of knitting needles in his scarred and calloused hands, breaking only to eat a cupcake while listening to his daughter gush about her love for *Black Beauty*. Lindsey had decided that he was a perfect dad right then and there. When another father came into the room with his son, looking for books about fishing, Nate had nodded a greeting at the man without dropping a stitch or looking embarrassed.

Sully opened the door to the office and held it for Lindsey. She walked into the garage and waited for him to join her. Beyond the office were two bays where Nate's three employees were busy working on cars. Ahead of them was one customer, and they waited while Nate talked to her. It was Kerry Tomlinson, and she was asking about her SUV. Apparently, her son, Lucas, had taken it for a ride and managed to break an axle and a torque mount.

"How does a teenage boy manage to break an axle and trust mount?" Kerry asked.

"Torque mount," Nate corrected her.

Kerry waved her hand. "Just tell me."

Nate put his hand on the back of his neck. He looked uncomfortable. He also looked tired, as if he hadn't slept in days. Lindsey felt for him. She couldn't even imagine how she'd feel if anything happened to her brother, never mind the horror of having him be the victim of a murder.

"It's pure speculation, Kerry," he said. "Without being there . . ."

Kerry shook her head as if to say *out with it*.

"My guess would be he was attempting to do burnouts, donuts, or something like that," Nate said.

"So this is not something that would occur when one swerved to avoid hitting a stray cat?" she asked.

"It seems unlikely," he said. "But again, without being there, I can't swear to it."

"You don't need to swear to it," she said. She adjusted the strap of her purse on her shoulder as if she was putting on a shield and preparing for battle. "Lucas and I are going to be having a long chat about how driving is a privilege and perhaps it's time he got a job."

Nate nodded. He looked pained, as if he felt bad for causing the teen in question the trouble that was headed his way.

"I'll call you when the work is done. Should be by the end of the day," Nate said.

"Thank you." Kerry turned to leave but then swung back. She reached across the counter and patted his arm. "I'm sorry. I was so caught up in my own drama that I neglected to mention how very sorry I am about your brother, Steve. Please take your time on the repairs. Your family is the most important thing right now. Besides, it will be an excellent lesson for Lucas to be without a car for a while."

"Thank you," Nate said. His voice was gruff, and Lindsey could hear the struggle to keep his voice even.

Kerry nodded at them as she passed, and Lindsey shared a look of acknowledgment with her. Kerry was a preschool teacher, and she used the library's collection of picture books to supplement her own collection. She'd even had Beth out to her classroom to do story time at her school. She was usually quick with a smile and a funny kid-related tale, but not today. Oh, Lucas was in big trouble.

"Sully, Lindsey," Nate greeted them. "What can I do for you?"

Sully gave Lindsey a long look. She knew without him saying anything that he wanted to play it straight. He wanted to tell Nate why they were really there, and he wanted her agreement. Lindsey nodded. Sully had known Nate and Steve Briggs all their lives. If he thought this was how they should approach it, then she trusted his judgment.

"How are you holding up, Nate?" Sully asked.

"Better when no one asks me how I'm holding up," Nate said. His tone was rueful.

Sully held out his hand, and Nate returned the handshake. Sully pulled him in close for a quick hug and let him go.

"Is there anything we can do for you?" Sully asked. "Anything you need?"

Nate shook his head. He looked haggard, as if the grief he was feeling was leaving its mark upon him. "I feel bad that I'm at work, but if I'm not here, I don't know what to do with myself. I drove Naomi crazy all day yesterday. I couldn't sit still. I just kept tinkering with things around the house. I'd be fine one minute and then just undone the next." He looked at Sully and Lindsey through narrowed eyes as if he were staring at the sun and it hurt. "I just can't believe he's gone."

"I know," Sully said. "He's been a part of my life for as long as I can remember, but I'm not his brother. I can't imagine how it feels to lose someone who's been with you for your entire life journey."

Nate's eyes filled with tears. He blinked, forcing them away. His voice, when he spoke, was gruff. "We're only eighteen months apart. I'm older than him, but you'd never know it. I was the quiet one. I just wanted a simple life here in Briar Creek with Naomi, but Steve always wanted more."

Sensing he had more to say, both Sully and Lindsey were quiet.

Nate ran a hand through his dark, close-cropped hair, leaving finger trails in it. He glanced past them out the doors to the small parking lot beyond. He seemed to be somewhere else entirely.

"He was my first best friend," he said. "I remember when my mom was walking me to preschool when I was four, it's one of my earliest memories, and she sensed my lack of interest in school, even at such a young age, and she was trying to talk me into it. She said, 'It's going to be so great. You're going to make new friends.' I stopped walking, looked at her and said, 'I don't need friends, I have Stevie.'"

Lindsey let out a soft chuckle. She could just picture a very earnest Nate saying exactly that. Sully smiled as if he could, too.

"And I meant it. We did everything together, fishing, camping, boating, heck, we were inseparable. But then after middle school, we started to drift apart. I wasn't interested in school, and he was an academic whiz kid. It seemed like all of a sudden, we didn't have anything in common anymore.

"His friends were all the brainiacs, and my friends were the townies. I spent my time ditching school to hang out at the garage, and he took on AP classes. Then I met Naomi my senior year, and that was it for me. I knew she was the one."

"I remember when you two were made prom king and queen," Sully said. "Wasn't the theme song 'Wonderwall'?"

Nate nodded. "Yeah, Oasis." He threw up a rock-and-roll sign and then sighed. "Steve skipped going to that prom so he could study for the SATs. At the time, I didn't care. Whatever, you know? But looking back, I realize it was kind of a big deal, and he wasn't there. Oh, he was best man at my wedding, but he had to fly down from Cornell to do it, and I remember it felt like I was inconveniencing him."

Lindsey felt her heart squeeze. She couldn't imagine having Jack feel that way about her wedding. Life moments were so important to share with family, and if your family didn't care, then what was the point of even having one? There was a world of pain in Nate's words, as if it was just beginning to hit him that he'd lost his brother totally and completely with no chance to ever have the connection they'd once shared. She felt her own eyes well, and she glanced away.

"It was a beautiful wedding," Sully said. "I remember thinking we were entirely too young to be getting married, and I'm a few months older than you, but then Naomi arrived, and she was so lovely and perfect, I thought, 'That Nate Briggs is a lucky man.'"

Nate nodded and the memory of his bride pushed away the sadness in his eyes for a moment. "I am."

"With Steve living here in town, did you reconnect at all?" Lindsey asked. She could hear the hopeful note in her voice and wished she could erase it, but she couldn't help it. She was invested.

"You'd think so, wouldn't you?" Nate said. "But he only started living here full-time about five years ago. Before that, I was so busy getting the garage off the ground. It took every second of every day for years. In all honesty, I wasn't there for him either. Did you know for the first two years of our marriage, Naomi and I lived above the garage?"

He pointed up, and Lindsey glanced at the second floor. Her eyes went wide. The old building did not have much of an attic in its triangular space. Interpreting her look, Nate nodded. "A mattress on the floor, a microwave and mini refrigerator. We had to use the bathroom down here and go to my parents' house for showers."

"Wow," Sully said.

"Yeah," Nate agreed. "Crazily enough, those were some of the happiest days of our marriage. We were living on dreams and love, and it was more than enough."

The romance of it all was too much for Lindsey, and she sighed.

"When the girls started arriving, I thought Steve would be the cool uncle, you know? But he wasn't around enough to really connect with them, and when he was around, he was always studying. Not his fault. His dream was just as all-consuming as mine. I was so proud of him when he got into Yale Law School, but it was such a different life. When my oldest, Maddie, asked me why we never saw Uncle Steve even though he lived in town, it hit me that he and I really didn't have anything in common anymore except our last name. We both made mistakes, but now they can never be fixed."

Nate's hurt was so raw it left Lindsey wishing she could say something, anything, to ease his pain. There was nothing.

"He was your only family?" she asked, hoping that maybe there was another sibling out there.

"Yeah, our folks passed away about ten years ago. Mom first and then Dad followed right after her, as if he couldn't figure out how to go on without her. You'd think that would have brought us closer, but after the estate was settled, he was off doing his corporate law thing in Manhattan while pursuing Jamie." He paused. "I was not the best man at his wedding."

"That's okay," Sully said. "We suffered through the wedding together."

At that, Nate cracked a smile, and they exchanged a knuckle bump. Sully glanced at Lindsey and said, "Over-the-top would be putting it mildly."

She pondered Jamie as a bride and then nodded. "Got it."

Nate glanced between them as if realizing he was over-sharing and was horrified. "Oh, hey, you two have your own wedding coming up this weekend. I am so sorry. I didn't mean to go on and on about me and Steve. It's just . . . well . . ."

"It's all right," Lindsey said. "We're all processing."

He gave her a grateful smile. "So, what brings you two in here for real? Is it the truck?"

"No," Sully said. He gave his friend a direct look. "I'm going to be straight with you. The police have Bell Island closed off for the investigation, and we don't know if we'll be able to have our ceremony there until the mystery surrounding Steve's death is solved. I hate to intrude on your grief, but we need answers, and we were wondering if you knew of anyone who had an issue with him. An issue that would have driven them to murder him."

CHAPTER

9

BRIAR CREEK
PUBLIC LIBRARY

Nate blinked. "Well, that's a lot to take in. Not the murder part so much. Emma told me about that." He took a deep breath. "She wouldn't give me specifics, but apparently the ME said that the head injury he sustained was caused by a blunt object and not something that he would have come into contact with by falling off his boat."

"Assuming it was his boat, since that is still missing," Sully said.

"You think someone stole his boat?" Nate asked. His gaze was sharp.

Sully shrugged. "Until it's found, we won't know."

Nate shook his head. "I've thought of nothing but who could have wanted him dead since Emma told me. My first thought was Mancusi. He was angry enough over being kicked out of their law practice. Or Jamie, since she was clearly unhappy in their marriage."

"Not a lot of love lost there?"

Nate just looked at him, and Sully nodded. "Understood."

Lindsey took this to mean no. She couldn't really see Nate and Jamie having anything in common. She wondered if this was the time to mention what Robbie had told her about overhearing the two brothers argue. Knowing that Robbie had already mentioned it to Emma, she decided that she would err on the side of discretion and leave that information for the police to deal with. Nate had been very up front about he and his brother not being close, and with Steve's boat missing, and boats being referred to as "she," maybe it was the boat they'd been arguing about.

"I wish I knew more of what was happening in Steve's life," Nate said. "But as I mentioned, we just weren't as close as we used to be. If he had enemies, he never mentioned them to me. Other than Mancusi, who I saw at the party, I didn't know of anyone who wanted to do him harm."

"You were very protective of Steve at the party," Lindsey said.

"We may have grown apart, but he was always my older brother."

"Nate, if you don't mind my asking, what time did you and Naomi leave the party?" Sully asked.

Nate shrugged. "It's no secret. We said goodbye to Steve and Jamie at about nine, shortly after I hustled Mancusi out. Our littlest one has been sick, so we didn't want to keep her up too late, knowing that she was probably going to wake up with croup and have to be driven around, which she did."

Lindsey looked at the dark circles beneath his eyes. This was definitely someone who was lacking in sleep.

"She had it last night, too?" she asked.

"Oh yeah. It'll last for a week or two," he said. "We have a very specific croup loop that we drive, usually about midnight. We take the road out of town, hit the Post Road all the way to Madison and then double back along the shoreline. Windows cracked, heat blasting, radio on jazz, she usually conks out about halfway and then is deeply asleep with her cough eased by the time I get her home, where I roll her back into bed for the night."

Nate ran a hand over his face, as if he could wipe away his fatigue.

"Unfortunately, I don't fall back asleep so easily, but what can you do?"

"You're a good dad," Sully said.

"Maybe. I wish I'd been a better brother."

"Why do you say that?" Lindsey asked.

Nate looked uncomfortable. "It's nothing. I just . . . the last conversation I had with Steve wasn't great. We argued, and now that will forever be our last conversation."

"That's rough," Sully said. "What did you fight about?"

"Nothing much. It was just a brotherly disagreement, but still . . ." Nate didn't offer any more information, and Lindsey tried not to feel frustrated. The man had lost his brother, after all.

"Word of advice?" Sully asked.

"Sure."

"Be prepared for the police to ask about it," he said.

Nate looked alarmed.

"In a town this size, someone will know about it," Sully said. "And they will tell the police. You want to be ready."

Nate looked wary. "Do I need a lawyer?"

"It wouldn't hurt."

Nate put a hand on the back of his neck. "I don't think I can swing that. The girls . . . Our oldest has a rare condition that our insurance is refusing to cover. Just paying for her upcoming surgery is keeping me strapped."

Sully studied his friend. "I might know someone who can help. An old navy buddy who just got his law degree and owes me a few favors."

Nate sagged with relief. "Anything you can do. I'd be forever grateful."

Sully held out his hand. The men shook, and Lindsey impulsively stepped forward and hugged Nate. "I'm so sorry about Steve."

He hugged her back and then let her go with a sad smile. His voice was tight when he said, "Me, too. I really don't know what I'm going to do without him."

His voice cracked when he said it. It made Lindsey think, again, about her brother, Jack. She couldn't bear the thought of anything happening to him, and she felt such deep empathy for Nate at the loss of his brother. It was a crusher.

"He is going to be sorely missed," Sully said.

He and Lindsey turned to go when Nate called them back.

"Hey, wait," he said. "Wasn't Steve supposed to marry you two this weekend?"

They exchanged a glance, and Sully said, "Yeah. We weren't sure we were going to go through with it—"

"You have to," Nate interrupted. "Steve would have wanted you to. He was a big believer in happy ever after, even if he never managed to find his own."

Lindsey felt her heart squeeze. She and Sully had thought as much, but it was nice to hear it confirmed by the person who knew him best.

"That's what we thought, too," Sully said. "But thanks, it's good to hear you say so."

Nate nodded. He looked as if he was about to say something, but a shout sounded from the garage behind him, and he glanced over his shoulder. One of his mechanics was waving to him, and he signaled that he'd be right there.

"Sorry, I have to go," he said. "Listen, I know you're tight with Emma and the police. If you hear anything about what happened, loop me in?"

"Of course," Sully said.

"Thanks." A look of sadness passed over Nate's face, and he turned and left, striding back into the garage with an air of relief that at least broken cars were something he understood and could fix, unlike the mystery surrounding his brother's death.

Sully and Lindsey left the garage. The cold winter air was like a punch in the face after the toasty office. Lindsey burrowed into her coat, trying not to think about Steve during his final hours, freezing to death on the beach in that ridiculous elf suit. The thought of it made her sad, and she reached for Sully's hand.

His response was immediate, as if he had been just about to reach for her, too. His gloved fingers wrapped around hers, letting go when he opened the truck's door for her. She shivered against the cold seats while he walked around the front and climbed into the driver's seat. Thankfully, the truck heated up quickly, and they were halfway through town when Lindsey felt a stream of warmth glide over her cold toes.

"What do you think about Nate's story?" she asked.

"I believe him," Sully said. "I can't picture him harming Steve no matter how at odds they were."

"Agreed," Lindsey said. "But I'm worried about his alibi. I doubt if anyone saw him driving the baby around in the middle of the night other than Naomi."

"Does he really need an alibi?" Sully asked.

"Robbie heard the brothers arguing," Lindsey said. "Just like you told Nate someone would, and he's told Emma, so she knows, too. It may have just been brother stuff, but since the medical examiner declared this a murder, everyone is a suspect."

"I just can't see Nate having anything to do with Steve's death," Sully said. His tone was stubborn, and Lindsey knew that he was digging in his heels where his friend was concerned. He simply refused to consider Nate capable of harming Steve. Lindsey thought his loyalty spoke well of him.

"I can't see it either," she agreed. "But we have no idea what was happening between the two brothers. They were estranged, they did argue, and none of that is helping Nate."

"But Mancusi actually threatened Steve," Sully said. "And he's missing. Plus, Jamie."

"What about her?" Lindsey asked.

"Don't they always look at a spouse first?" Sully asked. "She stands to inherit millions."

"Which is undoubtedly why she was talking to a lawyer at the Blue Anchor last night," Lindsey said. "She has to know she's a suspect."

"And she was very open about not being happy in her marriage," Sully said.

"She was," Lindsey agreed. She pursed her lips, thinking about their conversation with Jamie on the night of the party.

Sully steered the truck into the library parking lot and pulled up to the back of the building by the staff entrance. He put the truck in park and turned to face her. "What are you thinking?"

"That her obvious unhappiness makes her seem like less of a murderess," she said.

Sully frowned. "How do you figure that?"

"If she was plotting his death, she would have been much more careful with what she said, don't you think? She wouldn't want to bring suspicion upon herself."

"Fair point," he agreed. "Unless it was a crime of passion and she didn't think it through."

"Nate said she's not one to get her hands dirty," she reminded him.

"In a rage, she might not have noticed," he countered.

They sat quietly for a moment.

"We still need someone to marry us."

"We'll find someone," he said. "Even if it is my ancient uncle Carl."

Lindsey leaned across the seat and kissed his cheek. "I don't care who marries us as long as I'm Mrs. Sullivan at the end of the day."

Sully grinned. It was the first real smile she'd seen out of him since they'd found Steve's body.

"I like the sound of that," he said. "Pick you up after work?"

"Yes, please," she said. She opened the door and stepped out of the warm cab and back into the cold. The chill went right into her bones, and she hurriedly shut the door and sent Sully a quick wave before racing up the walkway to the back door.

She tapped in the key code on the number pad, and when the lock clicked open, she slipped into the library. The building was already bustling with staff and patrons. Lindsey pulled off her gloves and unwound her scarf as she walked down the short hallway and into the workroom. It was empty as she passed through to her office.

The door was ajar, and she could see someone was inside waiting for her. A quick glance at the fiery head of hair, and she recognized Robbie Vine. He was reading a magazine with a pot of hot tea steeping beside him. Lindsey would have been annoyed, but the tea was too inviting to pass up.

"It's a bit early in the day for tea, isn't it?" she asked. She strode into the room, hanging up her coat on the rack inside the door, along with her scarf. Then she dumped her handbag in one of the lower drawers of her desk before taking her seat.

"Once the temperature drops and stays in the thirties, it's teatime anytime you have a chill in your bones," Robbie said. He flipped another page in the gossip magazine, not looking up at her.

"What are you reading?" she asked.

"The latest scandal involving the royals," he said.

"Do they have scandals still? I thought it was all beautiful weddings and adorable babies," she said.

"There's tension betwixt the brothers," Robbie said, his accent making it sound more serious than it was. "Whose wife has the queen's favor. You know, that sort of rubbish."

"Hmm, brothers." Lindsey sat in her seat and swiveled to face him. "Funny you should mention brothers."

Robbie tossed aside the magazine and reached for the teapot. "This is about the Briggses, isn't it? What did you learn?"

"Nothing absolute, except that Nate admitted that he did argue with his brother," she said. "Also that he left the party early because their youngest was sick. He drove her around in the middle of the night so that she could sleep."

"A baby is not the world's greatest alibi," Robbie said.

"No, but there might be another way to prove it if it becomes necessary, which I doubt it will, because neither Sully nor I believe he harmed his brother."

"I like Nate," Robbie said. "It seems unlikely to me, too, but that doesn't mean he didn't do it. We have no idea what skeletons are lurking in their family closet."

Lindsey hated that he was right. "Has Emma had any luck finding Mancusi?"

"Not that she's shared with me," he said. "Actually, if she had found him, I think she would have told me, so I believe that's a solid no. Given that he's missing after threatening Briggs, he does seem like the more likely suspect, doesn't he?"

"Yes, although Jamie Briggs appears to be the one with the most to gain," Lindsey said. "So that makes her very suspicious to me."

"Any chance the two of them could have been working together?" Robbie asked. "What sort of relationship did Mancusi and Jamie have?"

"No idea, but she must have known him somewhat if he was partners with her husband, right?"

Robbie handed her a cup of tea. Lindsey took a sip of the steaming brew. It was almost too hot to drink. Almost. The heat poured into her, and she sighed, feeling warm for the first time all morning.

"Any luck finding someone to perform the ceremony?" he asked.

"Not yet," she said. "But we have Sully's uncle Carl, a pastor, as a backup plan."

"Why a backup?"

"He's in his nineties and tends to nod off in the middle of sermons," Lindsey said.

Robbie tried not to laugh. Obviously not hard enough, as he tipped his head back and hooted. Lindsey waited it out. "I really don't think it should be that hard for you to find a person who could stay awake."

She shrugged. "It'll work out. I hope. In the meantime, we have permission to get married on the island, so I've got a list of things to do on my lunch hour that could make me cry if I had time." She glanced at the clock. "But I don't have time. And now Sully is determined to find out who murdered his friend. I think he doesn't feel as if he can get married with a clear conscience if he doesn't discover what happened. Does that make sense?"

"Yes. He doesn't want anything to taint your very special day, and having a murderer on the loose could definitely damage the day. In fact, given that you don't have someone to marry you, one could argue that it already has."

"I suppose," she agreed. She bit her lip, trying not to think about what a catastrophe her wedding was turning into right before her very eyes. Of course, she immediately felt terrible for even thinking of the wedding. Steve's death was a real tragedy, whereas her wedding . . . Well, it wasn't something that couldn't be fixed, even if she wasn't quite sure how at the moment.

"Everything will be fine," Robbie said. "You have a bride, you have a groom, the rest is just details."

"Says the man who is no longer married," she retorted.

"That doesn't mean I'm wrong," he said. He leaned back with his own mug of tea, and they drank in companionable silence. Lindsey wondered if most brides spent the week before their wedding trying to solve a murder. Somehow she doubted it.

A commotion from the library turned her attention to the window in her office that overlooked the main floor. A horde of children raced by, looking as if they were fleeing from a monster or possibly trying to run down an ice cream truck. Hard to say. Shrieks and squeals sounded from the floor, and Lindsey knew that there would be a knock on her door in five, four, three . . .

"I am trying to be better, really I am, but this is just too much." Ms. Cole stood in the doorway with her index finger jammed into her eyelid, as if applying pressure would stop it from twitching.

"Problem, Ms. Cole?" Lindsey asked. She took a sip of her tea, bracing herself for the tirade that she was certain would follow.

"*She* has set up a scavenger hunt," Ms. Cole said. "And she did not contain it to the children's area. I don't think I'm overstating it to say the entire building is under siege."

CHAPTER

10

BRIAR CREEK
PUBLIC LIBRARY

Lindsey pressed her lips together trying not to laugh. She didn't dare glance at Robbie for fear of bursting out with a guffaw and offending Ms. Cole. It had taken her long enough to win over the traditional librarian.

"Ms. Cole, why don't you sit and have a calming cup of tea," Lindsey suggested. "I'll go out and deal with the . . . situation."

"That's not necessary," Ms. Cole demurred.

"I insist," she said.

Robbie was already pouring Ms. Cole a cup. He gestured to the empty seat beside his and asked, "How do you take your tea, Ms. Cole?"

His manner was so charming that she couldn't refuse, and so she sat down and let him fix her a cuppa. Lindsey winked at Robbie before she slipped out of the office to survey the scene outside.

She found that for once, Ms. Cole wasn't exaggerating. The library was in chaos. Kids were running everywhere at top volume. Utter mayhem ensued. She found two of her staff members, Paula and Ann Marie, hunkered behind the checkout desk.

"I think I'm actually in agreement with Ms. Cole for the first time in our collective history," Lindsey said. She glanced at her staff, who both nodded.

"Agreed," Ann Marie said. "These wildings are even making my two boys look tame, and that's saying something."

"What's the haps?" a voice asked from behind them. They all whirled around to find a pleased-looking Beth standing there. "Isn't this great?" she shouted over the yelling kids. "A scavenger hunt, celebrating all the holidays! I have them searching for Hanukkah dreidels, Diwali candles, Kwanzaa flags, Ramadan lanterns and Christmas stars. Genius, right?"

"It's something, all right," Paula muttered.

"I'm not going back out there unless I get hazard pay," Ann Marie said.

Her eyes went wide as the notorious Collins cousins, Alexandra, Mackenzie, Jared and Shane, went hurtling past the service desk, looking like they were on a seek-and-destroy mission, with their amused fathers, Brad and Greg, hot on their heels. Even though they were all grown up and had left their mischief-making days behind them—mostly—Brad and Greg were still known locally as "those Collins twins." That just showed how long the memory of a small New England town could be for twin boys who were known for their ability to bounce back up after a fall, especially on the local tennis courts.

"Hold the fort," Lindsey said to her staff. She looked at Beth and jerked her head in the direction of the library. "We need to contain this."

"Aw, why?" Beth asked. "Everyone's having so much fun."

"You're giving Ms. Cole an eye twitch."

"Better than a nervous tic," she said. Lindsey gave her side-eye, and she sighed. "Fine."

Beth stepped into the middle of the library and began to clap her hands in a rhythm. She repeated it a couple of times, and slowly but surely, the kids started to pick up on it. Pausing what they were doing, the kids began to echo her clap, even the little ones. Once everyone was watching her, Beth announced that the remainder of the treasure hunt had to be done in absolute silence, otherwise the prizes would be forfeit.

Immediately, the kids became as quiet as whispers. On tiptoes and using hand signals instead of words, they finished searching the library. Lindsey glanced over to where "those Collins twins" stood, leaning against each other as if plotting some mischief of their own. Catching her eye, Greg sent her an impudent grin while Brad offered a sly wink. Incorrigible! She had no doubt that the Collins cousins had learned their shenanigans from their fathers.

As the horde of children and teens made their way back to the story time room, which was command central, Lindsey saw Naomi Briggs with three of her daughters. Two of them were happily following the rest of the kids, but one, the youngest, was looking devastated. As Lindsey watched, Naomi planted a small dreidel on the shelf behind her, then she maneuvered her preschooler right in front of it until the girl saw it and snatched it up in a chubby fist. She skipped off to join her big sisters, and Naomi watched her go with a smile.

"Clever move, Mom," Lindsey said as she approached her.

Naomi glanced up and smiled with a shrug. "I just hid it in plain sight. You do what you've got to do for your babies."

"I get that," Lindsey said. She studied Naomi's face, trying to determine whether she was up to talking, but Naomi's expression was closed. She decided to err on the side of being polite. "How are you holding up?"

Naomi's gaze met hers and then slid away. She began to walk to the story time room, and Lindsey fell in beside her. They passed through the tables and chairs where people were studying alone or meeting in small groups. The low hum of voices filled the space again as normal activity resumed.

"I'm fine," Naomi said. "It's Nate who I worry about. He loved his brother so much. I don't know how he's going to get over this."

"I know," Lindsey said. "I saw him this morning."

Naomi turned to look at her. Although Lindsey knew Naomi from her years of bringing the girls into the library to check out books, she realized she didn't really *know her* know her. Oh, she knew that she was a good mom, attentive and kind and encouraging. Naomi was always checking out books of science experiments, crafting, astronomy and whatever else the girls were interested in. She also read to the younger ones every night, fully utilizing the picture book collection.

When Naomi came into the building, she greeted everyone with a smile and a kind word. Because of this, Lindsey had always felt as if there was a closeness between them, but now, she didn't feel close at all. She felt like an interloper, and Naomi was looking at her as if she expected Lindsey to say or do something that might hurt her or her family.

"You were at the garage with Sully," Naomi said. "Nate told me. He also told me that Sully thinks he should get a lawyer."

"Only if he is asked questions by the police," Lindsey said. "It's just a precaution."

"If you're guilty of something," Naomi said. She sounded angry. Lindsey looked at her in surprise. Naomi glanced away. Her voice was softer when she spoke again, as if she was trying to sound more reasonable but it was an effort. "We don't have the money to hire expensive attorneys 'just in case.'"

"That's why Sully is contacting a friend of his from the navy to see if he can help Nate out if need be," Lindsey said.

Naomi sagged a bit at that. "I know, and I appreciate it, I do, but I don't understand why he would need an attorney at all. Everyone knows how close he was to Steve. My God, it's killing him to have lost his brother."

"I know," Lindsey said. "But he doesn't have an alibi for that night, and if someone wants to make things difficult for him, she could, because his whereabouts aren't accounted for."

"He was driving Matilda, the baby, around, trying to get her croup under control," Naomi said. "I can vouch for him. I packed her up in her car seat before they left."

"And he was gone for how long?" Lindsey asked.

"A little over an hour," she said. "He drives the same route. There have to be security cameras out there that picked him up in the minivan."

"Maybe," Lindsey said. "What about the rest of the girls and you?"

"All asleep," she said. They reached the story time room, where the children were inside, singing a song about Diwali. "No one heard him come home. When I got up in the morning, he was asleep beside me, and the baby was in her crib in the corner of our room just like always."

Lindsey nodded. "I'm sure it's going to get sorted out, and Nate won't be under any sort of suspicion."

"And yet you still suggested he get a lawyer," Naomi said.

"Just to be on the safe side."

"I can't believe that Steve is making our lives more difficult in death than in life," she said. The words were barely out when she glanced at Lindsey and said, "Sorry, I didn't mean that the way it sounded."

"It's okay. I'm sure this is a difficult time," Lindsey said.

"Yes, it is. Nate loved his little brother so much, but it was such a complicated relationship," Naomi said. She glanced in through the window of the story time room. "Sorry, I just have to make sure my girls are okay. Madison, our oldest, stayed home with the baby, so it's just me and the three middles. You'd think it would be easier to keep track of three instead of five." She watched the sisters where they shared a story time cushion as they listened to Beth read to them about Hanukkah. Satisfied, she turned back to Lindsey. "What were we talking about?"

"The complicated relationship between the brothers," Lindsey said.

"Oh, right," Naomi sighed. "Steve was just so jealous of Nate. It made things very awkward, and I don't think Nate knew how to deal with it."

Lindsey blinked. This was not what she had expected. "Steve was jealous of Nate?"

Naomi nodded. "I know it sounds crazy. Nate and I struggle financially, there is no question about that. We have an awful lot of mouths to feed and bodies to clothe and little ones to love on, and it can be scary and frustrating, and sometimes I worry that we're failing, but I can't imagine living my life any other way."

"You have a beautiful family," Lindsey said.

Naomi shot her a grateful glance before she continued. "I suppose it would seem, from the outside looking in, that Steve, with his law practice, oodles of money, multiple homes, beautiful wife, exotic vacations and so forth, is the one who has it all. But the truth is, the one thing Steve has always wanted above all else is a family, and Jamie has made it perfectly plain that she will not be having any children, ever. So Steve lives in the cold comfort of everything his money can buy, but no family of his own. Or, rather, he *lived*. I'm still having a very hard time accepting that he's gone."

"Me, too," Lindsey said. She shook her head. She glanced at Naomi and asked, "This is none of my business, and maybe you don't know, but didn't the subject of children come up before Steve and Jamie got married? I can't believe they had such an elemental difference and didn't talk about it."

"According to Nate, Steve was positive that he could get Jamie to change her mind," Naomi said.

"Oh."

"Exactly. They fought about it a lot, more and more each year. It didn't help that every time Nate brushed by me, I got pregnant."

"Do you think Steve was going to divorce Jamie?" Lindsey asked. This would certainly tip the scale in favor of Jamie having a motive to murder her husband.

"Nate never mentioned that as an option," she said. "I think there were financial concerns that kept Steve from wanting a divorce."

"She would wipe him out," Lindsey said.

"And enjoy every second of it," Naomi agreed. She reached for the doorknob on the story time room. "I'd better get in there. The girls have been good far too long, and I don't want to push it."

"One more question," Lindsey said. "If you don't mind."

"Sure, what is it?"

"Do you think Steve might have been having an affair?" Naomi looked shocked. "Steve?"

"I only ask because I've had a few people tell me about a mysterious woman in black who was at the Christmas party."

"Woman in black?" Naomi repeated. She looked bewildered. "I don't understand. She was wearing a black outfit?"

"Topped off by a dark veil," Lindsey said.

"Well, that seems a tad dramatic."

"I think she was trying to conceal her identity," Lindsey said. "Which, given that no one knows who she was, was well done."

"But an affair? That's not like Steve."

"No, I didn't think so either, but Jamie made it pretty clear that she was unhappy in the marriage, and now it sounds as if Steve was as well." Lindsey shrugged.

"I guess it could be someone from his law office," Naomi said. She looked uncomfortable even thinking it. "I mean, it would have to be someone from somewhere else, don't you think? Briar Creek is just too small; everyone would know if he was having an affair."

"You're right," Lindsey said. Her voice was rueful. "Not much happens in this town without everyone finding out or wanting to be a part of it, be it a funeral or a wedding."

"Speaking of weddings, shouldn't you be preparing for your own?" Naomi asked. "I know Steve was supposed to marry you, and I know that Sully is probably devastated by his friend's death, but Steve would want you to forge on. He adored you two, and I know he'd want you to have a long and happy life together."

Naomi's voice broke on the words, and Lindsey impulsively reached forward and gave her a quick hug, feeling her own throat get tight as she did so.

"You're right," Lindsey said. "There's an awful lot to be done in not much time."

"Think about that then," Naomi said. "Forget about what happened to Steve. He wouldn't want your special day overshadowed by his death. He'd be the first to say the party must go on."

With a sad smile, Naomi slipped into the story time room, and Lindsey headed back to her office. She spent the rest of the morning clearing her desk of her to-dos and then spent her lunch hour finalizing wedding plans. Her parents and her brother were arriving in a few days, and she wanted to be able to spend time with them without being a crazed bride. Her mother had already talked her off the ledge from the invitation debacle—twice.

Lindsey hadn't had the heart to call and tell them about Steve Briggs. She didn't want her parents to start worrying that the wedding might not happen. It would happen even if Lindsey had to host the wedding in her own home. To that end, she called all her wedding vendors and finalized food counts and paid her bills until her lunch hour was over and she was back on the clock.

Her cell phone rang, and she snatched it up, happy to see Sully's name on the display. "Hello, husband-to-be," she answered.

"Afternoon, wife-to-be, what are you doing after work?"

"No plans," she said. "Other than to take my dog for a walk and eat my body weight in chicken pot pies as I read my book and pretend it's just another day."

"That works," he said with a laugh. "Or you could come with me to interview Donna Dimovski, an ordained minister who might be the answer to the who-is-going-to-marry-us dilemma."

"Donna Dimovski?" Lindsey asked. "Do I know her?"

"Doubtful," he said. "She used to live out on the islands but moved inland a few years ago. One of my pickups in the water taxi reminded me about her, so I called her, and she's willing to meet with us after you get off work."

"A woman officiating?" Lindsey asked. "I like that."

"More important, let's see if we like her," he said. "I never met her when she lived on the islands, as she was a bit reclusive."

"Meaning she was odd," Lindsey said. "Is that what you're not saying? She was odd? As in, she's going to perform some sort of ritualistic marriage ceremony that's going to make my mother faint and cause my dad to have heart palpitations."

"Easy there, darlin', you're getting way ahead of the crazy train."

"Sorry," she said. "Who knew wedding planning could take a perfectly reasonable, mature woman and turn her into a paranoid disaster?"

"In your defense, most brides don't find the justice of the peace who was about to marry them dead on a beach wearing an elf suit."

"I'll take that pass," she said.

"Pick you up out front at six?"

"I'll be there," she said. "One question, any idea what sort of ordained minister she is?"

"I believe she belongs to the Church of One Truth."

"Is it local?"

"Online."

"Oh."

"Desperate times," he said.

"Oh, yeah, we're there all right," she agreed. "But that doesn't mean I want to be married by a cult leader."

"It's not a cult . . . er, I don't think," he said. "Also, she's not the leader, just a disciple."

"And I'm liking it less and less," she said.

"Let's just meet her. Then we'll have a better idea."

"All right," she agreed. "If you're willing, I am, too."

"That's the spirit," he said.

"Have you heard anything from your lawyer friend?" she asked.

"Yes, he's agreed to meet with Nate."

"Good. I just had a long talk with Naomi," Lindsey said. "Did you know Steve wanted kids and Jamie didn't?"

Sully was quiet for a moment. "I do remember him saying something about it a while ago. He seemed convinced she'd change her mind."

"She didn't."

"So the marriage was not what either of them wanted," he said.

"Apparently." Then in a moment of pre-wedding panic, Lindsey said, "I know we've talked about this before, but—"

"I don't want kids," Sully interrupted. "And I'm not going to change my mind. How about you? Now that Beth is expecting, are you feeling any sudden pangs of wanting to have a baby?"

"Well . . ."

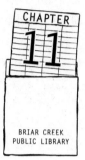

CHAPTER

11

BRIAR CREEK
PUBLIC LIBRARY

O h, boy. Go ahead, you can tell me," he said.

"Nope. Not even a flutter," she admitted.

"So we're good?" he asked.

"Totally."

"Phew, you had me nervous there for a second," he said. "I mean, I love kids. Other people's kids. You know, the kind you get to play with and give back after you've spoiled them completely rotten."

Lindsey laughed. "I feel exactly the same. Does this make us defective?"

"No, it makes us honest," he said. "I can love kids and not feel the need to have any of my own, and so can you."

"I love you," she said.

"I love you more," he replied.

"Not possible," she argued.

He laughed, sounding pleased. "See you in a few hours."

"Can't wait," she said.

Lindsey ended the call and glanced at the clock. It was just a few hours until he'd be there, and she discovered she really couldn't wait. She missed him. Was this how their marriage would be? Always looking forward to the end of the day when they could be together? She certainly hoped so.

Lindsey was out front on the curb when Sully pulled up in his truck. She yanked the door open and climbed in, letting the heat wash over her from the vent in the floor. The temperature had dropped when the sun set, and now it was bitterly cold. She leaned across the seat to give Sully a quick kiss before buckling herself in while he merged with the traffic onto the main road.

Neither of them had learned anything more about Steve Briggs's death or the people in his life. Emma had stopped by the pier to talk to Sully about Steve's boat, what it might have been worth, and where a person who had stolen it might take it. It was off-season, so if they'd stolen it to sell it, it was going to be noticed. Marinas all up and down the Connecticut shoreline had been alerted to its possible theft.

Lindsey shared her conversation with Naomi and mentioned her thought that Steve might have been having an affair. Sully seemed to reject that theory, but Lindsey wasn't sure if it was because he was defending his friend's honor or if Steve really wasn't the sort to cheat, even in an unhappy marriage.

They reached the outskirts of town, and Sully turned

onto a narrow back road that was poorly lit and jutted with potholes. The truck bounced and crunched over the uneven pavement until, mercifully, an old single-story ranch house came into view. A large conversion van sporting a vibrant flowery paint job was parked out front on the circular gravel driveway, and Sully parked behind it.

Lights were on in the short stone house, which gave it a welcoming feeling, despite being surrounded by deep dark woods. It was quiet, the slamming of the truck doors the only sound to be heard as they climbed out. No dogs barked, no birds chirped. It was a winter night, and anyone, person or animal, with a lick of sense was snuggled up somewhere, keeping warm.

Sully took Lindsey's hand in his and led the way up the steps to the front porch. He knocked on the door with a gloved fist, and they waited. Just when he was getting ready to knock again, the door swung inward, and there stood a tiny woman, dressed in a burgundy velvet robe with angel sleeves, a dropped waist with a gold rope tie and a hood. Her long gray hair was curly and had bold streaks of blue. She looked like a pagan wisewoman.

Before either Lindsey or Sully could utter a greeting, she began to chant, *"Sage and sweetgrass burning free, as the sun returns, so shall it be."* She then held up a burning bundle of sage, which she waved in front of them as if fumigating them.

Lindsey leaned close to Sully and said, "I'm going to go ahead and say no."

He turned to look at her, laughter in his bright blue eyes. "She is a bit more than we bargained on."

"With her, our wedding will be like dinner and a show," she said.

The woman hushed them, and Lindsey pressed her lips together and tried to look contrite. It was difficult since this was dinnertime and she was missing it to be brushed down with sage smoke by a woman who looked like she'd just walked out of George R. R. Martin's A Game of Thrones series.

Finally, the woman stopped chanting and extinguished the sage smudging stick by sticking it, smoking side down, into a snowdrift. She inclined her head and gestured for them to enter. Lindsey half expected the house to be full of medieval sword-and-sorcerer-type artifacts, at the very least a gargoyle or two, but instead the front parlor that she led them into was painted a cheerful butter yellow color with dark blue upholstered furniture, a crackling fire in the fireplace and one—no, two . . . wait, make that three, four, five—cats all reclined on various pieces of furniture in the room.

"Good evening, Ms. Dimovski," Sully said. "I'm—"

"I know, Captain," she interrupted. "Come in and sit. We'll talk."

She crossed the room to the fireplace, where a squashy sofa and two matching armchairs were arranged for optimum heat. There was also a huge mural painted on the wall, depicting their hostess in the center of the woods with her arms raised high and the sun perched on her open palms. Huh. Lindsey tightened her fingers around Sully's hand, but she wasn't certain whether it was for courage or to keep it together. The urge to laugh kept bubbling up inside of her.

"To answer your unasked question, I am an ordained pagan," Ms. Dimovski said. "Winter solstice is coming, so I am preparing."

"Ah," Sully said. One syllable, and yet it spoke volumes. He and Lindsey sat on the sofa, which had a fat gray tabby draped across the back of it, while Ms. Dimovski took one of the chairs.

"You were looking for something a bit more traditional for your marriage ceremony?" she asked.

"Well, um, Ms.—" Lindsey began, but was interrupted.

"Don't worry, you won't offend me. And call me Donna, please." She pushed back the hood of her gown, revealing the rest of her long gray hair and her amazingly wrinkle-free face. She looked much younger than the gray hair would indicate, but it could be a dye job, or maybe she was prematurely gray. Donna turned to Sully. "Well?"

"Traditional," he said. "We were definitely looking for traditional."

"And you?" Donna turned to Lindsey.

"Er, we just need someone who is ordained to read the ceremony to us," she said. "Honestly, I think we might be too tame for you."

"Really? No drinking a goblet of each other's blood then?" Donna asked.

"No!" they said together with a note of panic.

"No binding your legs before having you walk across hot coals as one?"

"Definitely not," Sully said. This was good, since Lindsey found herself incapable of speech. Did people really do that?

"No public consummation of the marriage vows?" she asked.

"Oh, hell to the no," Lindsey said. Her voice came back with force.

"Pity."

Sully started to rise. He glanced at Donna with a look that was apologetic, and yet not so much. "I'm sorry. I think we've got the wrong address."

"Relax, big guy," Donna said. "I'm just messing with you." She waved a hand for him to sit as she laughed. It sounded like more of a cackle, high-pitched and coming from her throat. It made the hair on the back of Lindsey's neck stand on end.

"About the hot coals, drinking of blood or public consummation?" he asked.

"All of it," she laughed harder. "That being said, I'm not really who you need for this ceremony. First of all, you need someone who believes in the sanctity of marriage. I don't. And second, Saturday is college football, and I can't miss it. You'd have to reschedule the time of the ceremony or, even better, the date of the ceremony if you want me there."

"College football?" Sully asked. He glanced at Lindsey. "Didn't see that coming."

"It's my one true love," Donna said. "Well, besides my cats, but they're named for our teams, aren't you, cuties?" She gestured to one cat and said, "That's Tiger, there's Wolverine, this one's Ducks—it's all right, sweetie, the name will grow on you—over there is Gator and, last but not least, the one with the stripe down his back is Sun Devil."

Sully took in all the cats with a grin. "Clever."

Donna shrugged.

"Well, we can't change the date and time of the wedding. We're down to just a few days as it is," Lindsey said.

"Then I can't help you."

"I don't suppose you know of anyone else who is ordained to marry people?" Sully asked.

"Other than the guy you had originally, Steve Briggs, no. Those straightlaced types don't really run in my circle," she said. "It doesn't take much to get ordained online. You could ask a friend to do that for you with the Universal Life Church."

Sully and Lindsey exchanged a glance. Who could they possibly ask? Ian was already Sully's best man, and Beth was Lindsey's matron of honor, and being pregnant, she really had a lot on her plate as it was. The names of their family members flitted through Lindsey's mind, but it seemed like an awful imposition to ask someone at the eleventh hour. Plus, it would require someone who was okay with being in front of a crowd. Given her own dislike of public speaking, Lindsey couldn't imagine asking someone to do the same for her.

"Thank you for the suggestion," Sully said. He started to rise, pulling Lindsey up with him. "We won't take up any more of your time."

"That's all right," Donna said. "It's always a pleasure having visitors. Usually, it's just me and the kitties until the longest night of the year. That's when we have a houseful.

Lots of folks needing to cast out the old negative energy as we welcome back the sun."

She grabbed a small cloth string bag and handed it to Lindsey, tucking her fingers around it.

Lindsey glanced at the cloth sack and then up at Donna. "Am I supposed to burn this?"

Donna laughed. "No, it's lavender. Getting married is stressful. Smell that when you're going sideways, it'll calm you down."

"Thank you," Lindsey said. She was genuinely touched.

Donna nodded. "Don't fret about your wedding. Much as I dislike any sort of negative energy, including gossip, I don't think I'm speaking out of turn to say Steve Briggs would not have been a good choice for your ceremony."

Sully went very still. "Why do you say that?"

"He had some demons about him," she said.

"Did you know Steve?" Sully asked. His voice was tight, as if he'd defend his friend's honor if required.

Donna tipped her head to the side. She looked like she was considering what to say. "He wasn't the same man you remember him to be."

Sully's jaw stuck out a fraction of an inch, just enough to let Lindsey know he was planning to take on this woman who was speaking poorly of his friend.

"You didn't answer my question," Sully said. "Did you know him?"

Donna considered him, then she nodded slowly, as if accepting that she was going to have to say things she didn't like. "Yes, I did. I was at his Christmas party, in fact."

"So he was a friend of yours?" Lindsey asked. The tension was thickening, and she lifted her sachet up to her nose and took a gentle huff. The smell of the lavender was lovely.

"I wouldn't call us friends, but we were acquainted," she said. "He came to me once, looking for assistance."

"In what way?" Sully asked.

"He wanted me to cast a spell on his wife to make her want to have a baby," she said. She gave them a look. "I'm a pagan priestess, not a Wiccan, and even if I was, I wouldn't have done such a thing."

Lindsey frowned. This was the second time today that she'd heard of Steve's desire for a family. "It sounds like he was desperate for a child."

Sully glanced at her but she kept her gaze on Donna. "Sometimes people become consumed with a desire that they believe will fulfill them. Generally, it doesn't. Contentment has to come from within, but when you are a person who has been able to achieve everything you have ever set out to do, being thwarted doesn't sit very well."

"You're saying that Steve was obsessed with having a child," Sully said.

"Yes," she said. "But even more than that, he was trying to coerce his wife into having a child. Meanwhile, she was busy with her sidepiece. It really isn't a surprise that there was a tragedy in that marriage."

"You think Jamie killed him?" Sully said. His jaw was clenching, and Lindsey debated holding the lavender up to his nose, too.

Donna shrugged. "That I can't say, but I did walk in on her and a man—tall, thin, slicked-back hair and wearing a shiny suit—canoodling in the gazebo the night of the holiday bash."

"That sounds like the man she was eating dinner with last night," Lindsey said. "That's pretty bold to invite your . . . sidepiece . . . to your annual party with your husband right there. Do you suppose he's living with her now?"

"Maybe that's why she announced to the staff that there would be no Christmas bonuses," Sully said. "She must have known they'd all quit, and then who would be there to see her with her new man?"

"That sounds likely," Lindsey said. She turned to Donna. "Are you planning to tell the chief of police what you saw?"

"Er." Donna glanced away, looking uncomfortable. "I'm not on Chief Plewicki's favorite-resident list."

"Oh?" Sully asked.

"There might be a few parking tickets that have gone unpaid," Donna said. "Why don't you tell her what I told you? But don't tell her who told you. That way she'll know, but I don't have to get another lecture."

"Or pay your fines," Sully said.

"That, too."

"Donna, you're missing a fabulous opportunity here," Lindsey said.

"How do you figure?"

"You have information—the canoodling—that the chief will definitely want to hear. Presented correctly, I'll bet you can get her to waive those parking tickets for the information."

Donna studied her. "You think?"

"I do."

"Might be worth a try," Donna said. "I'll think it over. Maybe call her and feel her out first."

"Excellent idea," Lindsey said.

Donna turned to Sully. "You'd better marry this one quick. Smart girls like this are hard to find."

"Don't I know it," Sully said. "I've looked for a girl like her my whole life."

Donna grinned at them and then stood back with her arms held wide. "May the blessings of the crone and the maiden be upon you," she said.

She put her hands over her heart and gave a gentle bow as they stepped out into the cold. Sully swiftly pulled the door closed behind them.

The thin layer of snow crunched under their feet as they strode to the truck. The sky was a deep velvet purple with pinpricks of stars shining overhead. Lindsey watched her breath mist on the air, and she pulled her coat more tightly about her.

Sully opened her door, and she climbed in. She stuffed the lavender into her pocket before buckling her seat belt.

A draft of cold air entered the truck cab with Sully, and Lindsey shivered against it. He turned the key, and the old engine sputtered to life. They rocketed out of the driveway and back along the road to town. There was only a sliver of a moon, but still the snow on the ground glowed in the darkness.

"I have no idea what to make of that," Sully said.

"Me either," Lindsey agreed. "Except that perhaps there was more going on with Steve than we were aware."

"I just don't get it," Sully said. "Why not get a divorce? Why try to force your wife to have a kid?"

"I'm guessing he'd lose a lot financially," Lindsey said. "Connecticut is an equitable-distribution state."

"But if he wanted a family, wouldn't it be worth it to take the financial hit and then go find someone to have a family with?"

"Maybe he wanted it all," she said. "Or maybe he really loved Jamie."

"Did he, though?" Sully asked. "He lived here, and she lived there. They were seldom together. I would be miserable if, when we're married, you lived in another city or state."

"Same," Lindsey said. "Luckily, we only have the one home with no pesky choices to make about where we live."

Sully grinned. "Yeah."

"So, what do we do now? Tell Emma about Jamie's extracurricular activities or leave that to Donna?"

"Let's give Donna the opportunity to do the right thing," Sully said. "We can tell Emma what we found out tomorrow at the town's tree-lighting ceremony. In the meantime, we are getting down to the wire in finding someone to marry us."

Lindsey felt her heartbeat kick up a notch. Everything would be all right. Surely, there had to be someone.

Sully was quiet, and she sensed that he was struggling with all that had been revealed about his friend.

"When do you suppose everything changed for Steve?" Lindsey asked. "It seems like he went from being on top of the world to having his life slowly unravel. A nasty split from his partner, estranged from his wife, at odds with his brother. What do you think caused it?"

Sully sighed. He glanced from the road to her and back to the road. "I think Donna was onto something with him getting everything he ever wanted and not being able to handle it when he was thwarted."

"It hurts you to even think it, huh?" she asked.

"Yeah, and now we need to find out who the guy in the suit is," he said. "As far as I'm concerned, Jamie having an affair right in front of Steve means she has an even bigger motive than Tony to murder Steve."

Lindsey shook her head. The thought of a marriage going so horribly awry was not something she wanted to be thinking about just days before her wedding. And yet, here she was. She studied Sully's profile by the light of the dashboard. He looked grimly determined, and she knew that he would have no peace until he found out what had happened to his friend and why.

CHAPTER

12

BRIAR CREEK
PUBLIC LIBRARY

Lindsey spent the day finalizing her wedding details. Weirdly, the fact that everything was going perfectly made her even more nervous. She was certain she must be forgetting something, but then she remembered that they had no one to marry them, and her panic resumed, making her feel more normal.

She was meeting Sully on the town green for the town's tree-lighting ceremony. It was a Briar Creek tradition, and everyone would be there. Lindsey knew Sully was hoping they'd see or hear something that would help them discover what had happened to Steve. It was a long shot, since they had no idea who had attacked him, and at this point, it could be anyone.

The library closed early, and the staff walked to the park together. Since Ms. Cole had announced her intention to run for mayor in the upcoming election, she had taken to attending all the town functions so that she could see firsthand how the mayor handled these situations. It was a pretty steep learning curve for a person who generally tolerated no nonsense and wasn't prone to overblown flattery.

Beth was going mostly so she could help Ms. Cole take it all in. Beth had appointed herself "the lemon's" unofficial campaign manager. Ms. Cole had resisted her at first, but Beth had the ability to wear a person down if she felt they desperately needed her expertise. It was her superpower, and Ms. Cole was helpless in the face of it.

"Now, Mayor Hensen knows you're running against him," Beth said, "so it's very important that you look fearless."

Ms. Cole gave her a steely glance through her glasses.

"But look friendly so that people think you're likable."

"Likable?" Ms. Cole asked. "What does likability have to do with competency?"

"Well, there's a question," Paula said from the other side of Lindsey.

"I mean, honestly, shouldn't the only criteria be that I'm more suited to the job than he is? I know how to get things done. I have an institutional memory of the town and a clear idea of how to keep our town prosperous and safe for all of the residents," Ms. Cole declared.

"Spoken like a true mayor," Ann Marie chimed in. "You've got my vote."

"Well, I should hope so," Ms. Cole said. "Truly, the only thing Mayor Hensen has going for him is a brilliant set of very white teeth and a nice head of hair."

Lindsey tried not to laugh but failed miserably. If Ms.

Cole won the election next fall, she was going to be a force of nature. It was about time. While Mayor Hensen enjoyed riding in the convertible on parade day, Ms. Cole would actually make sure the town had something to be proud of come parade season.

"Lindsey!"

She turned and saw Sully waving at her from where he stood with Mary, Ian and Josie. His parents were with them, and Lindsey realized as she excused herself to her colleagues and crossed the green, winding her way through the crowd, that in a few days, they would all be her family, too. She felt her heart lift in her chest. Tomorrow, her parents; her brother, Jack; and his girlfriend arrived, and she couldn't wait to have them all together to celebrate their big day, assuming they actually found someone to help them tie the knot. She pushed the thought aside. A panic episode would not be helpful at the moment.

The enormous evergreen tree that stood at the edge of the park, the same tree that the ladies from the local women's league decorated every year, was all ready to be lit. All they needed was the local high school band to finish playing, and then the mayor would give his speech and turn the lights on. Following that, the children's choir would sing a song and they'd all race to the Blue Anchor to warm up with a pint or a hot chocolate.

Sully hugged her close, and she folded herself into his warmth, hugging the rest of his family, one after the other, with her available arm. The sounds of people talking and laughing while children raced in and around their legs made for a festive atmosphere, and Lindsey found herself grinning as she looked forward to seeing what sort of magic the women's league had pulled off this year.

"Nate, how are you?" Sully called to Nate Briggs, who was standing a few feet away with his wife, Naomi, and all five of their girls.

Nate turned around and shook Sully's hand. He shrugged, looking even more tired than he had the day before. "I'm doing all right, I guess. Had to come for the girls, you know. They love it so much."

The oldest daughter, Maddie, was holding the baby, Matilda, while the three middles were chasing each other in a tight circle. Naomi was doing what she could to manage the chaos, but the girls were excited and not listening. When the youngest of the three tried to tag the oldest, the lid on her hot chocolate flew off, and she doused herself, soaking her coat through.

As soon as she realized what had happened, the tears started, and Naomi looked at her with genuine sympathy. Nate immediately pulled a wad of paper napkins from his pocket and handed them to Naomi.

"Ha, I knew these were going to come in handy. Go ahead and dry her off while I contain the other two." And just like that, the parents were on a mission to save the moment. Nate snatched up the other girls, tickling them into submission, while Naomi gently dabbed at the chocolate on the little one's coat.

"It'll be all right, Maggie," she said. "I'll wash your coat as soon as we get home, and it'll be like brand-new."

Big tear-filled eyes met hers as Maggie asked, "Are you

sure, Mama? Because I do not want to get on the naughty list. Not this close to Christmas."

"It was an accident," Naomi said. "You don't get put on the naughty list for accidents, especially if you feel bad about it."

"I do," she said. "I really, really do."

"Okay, then help me throw these napkins out, and I'm sure you'll be just fine." Naomi took her daughter's hand and led her to the garbage can at the edge of the park.

Lindsey glanced up at Sully, but he was talking to Nate in low tones, and she had a feeling it was about Steve. How awful for Nate to have to muscle his way through the holidays, trying to keep it light and happy for his girls, when inside he must be heartbroken. Lindsey glanced around the park. For that matter, how many people here were struggling to find the joy of the holiday season because of loss or illness or hardship? And yet they were here and they were trying. That had to count for something, surely.

She turned back to Sully and noticed that he and Nate were looking at the trash can where Naomi had taken Maggie just a few feet from where they stood. Naomi was standing beside the trash can, waving frantically for Nate to join her.

"Excuse me," Nate said. "Do you mind keeping an eye on my girls for a sec?"

"Not at all," Sully said. He turned and tapped Ian's shoulder and gestured for him to keep an eye, too. Ian nodded.

Nate hurried to Naomi's side. What could be happening? Was her daughter sick? The band stopped playing, and the mayor climbed the steps to the stage, waving to the crowd despite the fact that most people were ignoring him.

Lindsey saw Ms. Cole standing off to the side with her beau, Milton, on one side and Beth and her husband, Aidan, on the other. Judging by the frozen smile Ms. Cole was wearing, she had taken Beth up on her advice. It would have been great advice if Ms. Cole didn't look positively pained.

A shout brought Lindsey's attention back around to Nate and Naomi. As she watched, Nate reached into the garbage can. He pulled out a long black wig and a veil.

Lindsey gasped. Those items had to belong to the mystery woman in black! Was she here? Had she thrown away her wig and veil, hoping no one would find it in the park? She felt her heart hammer in her chest, and she scanned the crowd. If the woman in black was here, where was she? Who was she?

But Lindsey wasn't the only one who saw the veil and knew what it was. A low murmur started to ripple through the crowd as they all looked toward Nate and Naomi. Nate wasn't having it. He balled up the wig and veil like he was going to pitch it into the sea.

"What do you have there, Nate?"

Just like that, the crowd parted, and Emma plowed through the bodies to reach Nate. She was in street clothes, which meant she'd been off duty, and Robbie was right behind her. He caught Lindsey's eye as he followed and wagged his eyebrows as if to say, *Look at me!*

At Naomi's urging, Nate handed Emma the bundle, and

she immediately took out her phone and started to clear the area.

The mayor, oblivious to anything that was happening around him, continued his long-winded speech about peace on earth and goodwill toward all men, but no one was listening. Most were actively trying to eavesdrop on Nate's conversation with Emma. Naomi filled in her part while Emma nodded. She questioned the people in the surrounding area, but no one had seen anyone dump the wig and veil in the garbage. When a squad car arrived with its lights off, Emma took the items and excused herself. It was obvious she wanted this evidence under lock and key as soon as possible.

Having been left behind, Robbie followed Nate and Naomi back to their girls, who were oblivious to anything that was going on except a countdown until Santa Claus's appearance in their lives.

Nate and Naomi looked rattled, but they kept their smiles in place for their girls.

"What was that all about?" Sully asked.

"I think we just found the woman in black's disguise," Nate said, low enough so that his daughters couldn't hear him.

"A wig and veil?" Sully asked.

"So it would seem," Nate said. He looked at his wife and then back at Sully. "I can't imagine why she'd want to hide it here. Why not burn it or throw it in a bag to Goodwill?"

"She probably thought it would be untraceable coming from a public trash can," Sully said.

"It seems like a move someone in a panic would make," Lindsey added.

"Yeah, or someone who is overwhelmed with guilt and wants to escape from what they've done," Sully said.

Nate clapped him on the shoulder in understanding. He was clearly thinking the same thing. Had guilt driven whoever the woman in black was to do this? If so, then could it be safely assumed that she was feeling so much guilt because she was the murderer? It seemed likely.

"That's quite a bit of luck, isn't it?" Robbie asked Lindsey as he joined them.

"Is it really, though?" she asked. She turned away from the group and studied Robbie's face. "It just seems reckless. Too reckless, somehow."

"Maybe whoever did it thought the trash would be picked up before tonight," Robbie said. "Maybe she thought she was going to get away with it."

Lindsey searched the crowd, looking for Sam Rubenstein. He was the head of the town facilities crew, and as such, oversaw trash pickup for all the town's public garbage cans, including the ones at the park.

With his bald head covered by his New York Giants knit hat, Sam was standing with his wife, Gloria, by the short stone wall that separated the park from the beach below. Lindsey waved to Robbie to come with her as she approached. Sometimes Robbie's star status worked in her favor.

"Sam, Gloria," she greeted them. "How are you?"

Sam smiled at Lindsey. They had bonded over the lack of quality snacks at the weekly department head meetings at the town hall. The mayor had been on a health kick and only allowed carrot and celery sticks—dry, no dressing—at his meetings. And no coffee, only water. Lindsey had gotten into the habit of bringing her own coffee and hitting the vending machine for a candy bar on her way into the meeting. When Sam had openly coveted her Milky Way, she'd started bringing an extra for him, too.

"Hey, Lindsey," Sam said. "You remember my wife, Gloria?"

"Hi, Gloria," Lindsey shook her hand. "Have you met my friend Robbie Vine?"

Gloria immediately went all aflutter, which Robbie encouraged by bowing over her hand and telling her what a pretty smile she had.

Sam rolled his eyes and said, "I'm going to be hearing about this for the rest of the year."

Lindsey grinned. "You're welcome."

Sam laughed and then nodded to where Emma stood with an officer as they bagged up the trash can and hauled it away. "What's going on over there?"

"Looks like they might have found some evidence tied to the Briggs murder."

"Whoa." Sam's eyes went wide.

"Yeah." Lindsey glanced back at the gazebo, where the mayor droned on. She glanced at Ms. Cole, whose smile looked frozen in place. She wondered how much longer she could hold on. Thankfully, her yogi boyfriend, Milton, was by her side, and it looked like he was advising her to keep breathing. "Tell me, what day is garbage pickup for the park?"

"Usually midday Monday," Sam said.

"So whoever threw out their things did it in the last thirty-two hours," Lindsey said. "Are there any security cameras that cover the park?"

"No," Sam shook his head. "We asked for it in the last budget to help combat the vandals, but the mayor shot it down as an unnecessary expense."

Lindsey made a mental note to mention that to Ms. Cole. Sam's attention was suddenly snagged by his wife as she was handing Robbie a marker and unzipping her coat so he could sign her chest.

"Hey, now, that's enough," Sam said. He reached into his pocket and handed Robbie a receipt from the grocery store. "Autographs are for paper."

"Spoilsport," Gloria grumped.

"You'll thank me when you don't have to explain that ink to your mother," he retorted. With a grunt, Gloria zipped up her coat. Robbie signed the receipt with a flourish and handed both the pen and paper back to her. She pressed it to her chest and sighed.

At that moment, the mayor stopped speaking and hit the switch for the lights. The tall tree lit up and sent a multicolored glow over the crowd. The children's choir burst into song, and for a few moments, the discovery in the trash can took second place in the interest of the town.

Lindsey waved to Sam and made her way back to Sully and his family. Sully was standing with Nate, who was now holding baby Matilda snuggled under his coat. He looked upset, and Lindsey could only imagine that he must be surveying the crowd, wondering if the woman in black was here and if she had, in fact, murdered his brother.

It was a somber group that left the tree-lighting ceremony. As Lindsey and Sully drove home from the park, she told him what she'd learned from Sam.

"What do you make of that?" she asked.

"I think that whoever threw the wig and veil away did it during the tree-lighting ceremony," he said.

"That's a bold maneuver," she said. "They could have been seen so easily."

"She might have been desperate, and if her plan had worked, then no one would ever know," he said. He parked in their driveway and switched off the engine. Together they climbed out of the truck and walked to the front door.

"We're making a few assumptions here," Lindsey said. "One, that it was a woman. A man could have dressed up in a black wig and veil."

"Oh, that's even creepier," he said. He unlocked the door, and Lindsey smiled as she heard their dog, Heathcliff, barking in greeting.

"But an excellent disguise," she said. Sully opened the door, and Lindsey braced herself as her big, black, hairy dog shot out of the house toward her. Heathcliff was a hugger, and he barked at her, telling her all about his day as he wrapped his front paws around her knees while she rubbed him down with both hands in their standard welcome home.

"True." Sully agreed. He had his turn with the dog, and then Heathcliff bolted down the steps and out into the yard to run three crazy-fast laps before he took care of his business.

"The other thing is that we're assuming this person murdered Briggs," she said. "While it looks suspicious, I keep going back to what Molly said. She said Steve sounded excited to meet with the woman in black. That means he knew who she was and he was expecting her or, at least, was happy to see her."

"Maybe he was having an affair," Sully said. "But then why not divorce Jamie? Ugh, this is making my head hurt."

"Me, too," she said. She patted her leg, and Heathcliff finished his patrolling and loped up the stairs and into the house.

"On to a more pressing problem then," Sully said. "Charlie says he has a guy who can marry us."

"Charlie? Rock-and-roll wannabe Charlie? Nancy's nephew?"

"The one and only, mercifully," he said. Charlie worked the high season for him, and despite the teasing, Sully was very fond of him.

"Please tell me the guy isn't a musician," Lindsey said. She kicked off her boots in the small foyer, putting them on the mat where the snow could melt off them.

"Don't know, but Charlie is arranging for us to meet him tomorrow," he said. He reached for her coat and hung it up beside his own.

"Well, no matter who it is, we'll have to be open-minded," she said. "My family is arriving tomorrow, and it would be really nice to have this locked down when they get here."

* * *

Lindsey was only working half days leading up to the wedding. With her parents driving down from New Hampshire and her brother coming in from Boston, she wanted to spend as much time as she could with them before the ceremony.

She was just finishing up her work when her parents and her brother appeared at her office door.

"There she is," Jack said. "Not surprisingly, buried behind a pile of books."

Lindsey glanced up over the stack of titles she was deleting from the catalog. They were old reference books whose newer editions had come in, replacing them.

"Hey," she cried as she jumped up. "You're early."

She hurried around the desk to hug her parents and her brother.

"Couldn't help it," her father said. "We're excited."

He hugged her exuberantly and then handed her to her mother, who cupped her face and studied her. "Are you sleeping enough? I know it's exciting, but you want to be well rested for your big day now that there are going to be a lot more people and all."

Lindsey laughed. "Thanks for reminding me."

Her mother hugged her and then said, "Sorry. It's going to be a beautiful wedding, and you'll be a lovely bride."

Jack swooped in and hugged her next. "Hey, sis."

"Hey, yourself," she said as she hugged him back. She felt so happy to have her family here. Truly, she couldn't imagine getting married without them. She glanced over her brother's shoulder and then leaned back and asked, "Where's Stella?"

Stella was his girlfriend of the past two years and a favorite of Lindsey's.

"She can't come until Friday," he said. "She's taking the train down, and I'll pick her up at the station."

"That works," Lindsey said. She grabbed her coat and her handbag and said, "Sully is waiting over at the pier to take you all out to his parents' house. Are you ready?"

"Can't wait," her dad said. "Too bad it's too cold to go fishing."

The Sullivans and the Norrises had become fast friends since they'd met a few months ago. Christine and John Norris enjoyed spending time on Bell Island and had even had Mike and Joan come up to New Hampshire for a visit in the fall. Lindsey thought it boded well for all of their future holidays and other family-centric ventures.

After stopping to say hello to the various staff members, they made their way out into the cold, stopping by their cars to get their suitcases, and headed across the town green to the pier. Lindsey noted that the trash can that had been taken away the night before was still missing. She wondered what, if anything, Emma had discovered about the wig and the veil.

When her mom looped her arm through Lindsey's and began to talk about the wedding details, she forgot all about the mysterious woman in black. Despite keeping the wedding as simple as possible, there were still things that needed to be managed.

The flowers, the cake, the food, the tent that had been

rented for the communal lawn, the photographer and the music. There was much of it that was out of Lindsey's hands. So many people in the community wanted to contribute to the wedding that they'd taken on significant wedding duties, most either for free or at a discount. Charlie and his band were providing the music, local florist Kelsey Kincaid had been hired to do the flowers, Ian and Mary were providing the food. In a way, it felt all so seamless. Just like Steve had volunteered to be the one to marry them. It had all come together as if the universe really wanted Sully and her to get married.

Of course, she didn't want to look at it like that, because with Steve being murdered, she'd hate to consider *that* a sign of things to come.

"Lindsey, what do you think?" her mother asked.

"Uh," Lindsey had stopped listening and had no idea what her mother was talking about.

"She thinks having her wedding pictures taken on the pier is an amazing idea," Jack said. He was looking over their mom's head at Lindsey. His eyes were wide as if he knew she hadn't been listening and was trying to bail her out. Brother to the rescue again.

"Yes, amazing," Lindsey said. "Although, I'm not sure when—"

"Just before the ceremony," Christine said. "Or maybe after so Sully doesn't see you first. We'll have to see how the day goes."

"True," Lindsey said. "It might snow."

Christine clapped her hands over her chest. "So romantic."

"I was thinking cold, but I suppose it could be considered romantic, too."

Sully must have seen them coming, because he opened the door to his office as soon as they arrived. His octogenarian assistant, Ronnie, was seated at her desk, wearing her chunky plastic lime green jewelry over a vivid purple-and-green-argyle sweater topped by her cranberry-colored updo. She waved a cheerful hello at everyone and continued filing her raspberry-colored nails. To say Ronnie was colorful was an understatement.

Lindsey's parents hugged Sully, who told Ronnie he'd be back, before leading them all out to his water taxi. He and Jack loaded all the suitcases while John helped Christine into the boat, leaving Lindsey to untie the ropes and shove off while Sully started the engine.

She moved to stand beside Sully while her brother took the seat beside them and her parents took the bench seat at the back. Because there was a no-wake zone enforced around the islands, the boat moved at a sedate speed, keeping the wind down, which was a good thing, given that the temperature dropped out over the water and it was already plenty cold.

"It feels like it's getting more and more real," Sully said. Lindsey glanced at him as they rounded one of the larger rocks.

"Our wedding?" she asked.

"Yeah," he said. He looked at her. "You're going to be my missus."

"And you'll be my mister." She grinned. "I like that."

"Me, too."

"Um, hey, Sully." Jack's voice broke into their moment. "I know my memory of the islands is sketchy and full of terrified panic from being held at gunpoint and all, but I don't think that's supposed to be there."

Lindsey's brother had been kidnapped aboard a yacht in these very islands a few years ago, and while he swore he was fine, Lindsey noticed that when he visited, he did not seem eager to go out on any of the boats. She couldn't blame him. She wondered if he was having a little post-traumatic stress at the moment.

She and Sully both glanced toward what he was pointing at. Sully swore and grabbed a pair of binoculars from a cupboard below his control panel. He held them up to his face, and Lindsey saw him visibly pale.

"What is it?" she asked as he handed her the glasses.

"I think your brother just found Steve Briggs's boat," he said.

CHAPTER

13

BRIAR CREEK
PUBLIC LIBRARY

What?" Lindsey cried. She held the binoculars up to her eyes, moving the wheel with her gloved fingers to focus on the white blob in the distance. It came into sharper focus, and it was definitely a boat, a really nice boat, seemingly adrift on the outskirts of the islands. "Are you sure it's his?"

"I was with him when he bought it," Sully said. "I'm sure." He glanced back at her parents and raised his voice to be heard over the hum of the engine. "I'm sorry, folks, but we're going to have to take a detour."

"Is something wrong?" Christine asked.

Sully and Lindsey exchanged a look. She hadn't mentioned that the man officiating their ceremony had been murdered, not wanting to cause them any stress. Now she had to explain that they'd found his boat, which had been missing and which everyone believed he might have taken out on the night of his death. Oh, boy.

"Not wrong so much as complicated," Lindsey said.

Her parents exchanged a look and stood up, coming to join them in the front of the boat.

"Explain," her mother said.

Lindsey did. It began with the party and then the next day out at the Sullivans', where they'd found Steve Briggs. She told them all about Jamie Briggs, Tony Mancusi and the woman in black.

When she was finished, her father adjusted his hat and said, "Well, it seems to me we need to call this in to the police."

"I was just thinking the same thing," Sully said. "Also, I need to catch that boat before it hits the current. Otherwise we're going to be chasing it out to the Race."

"Isn't that all the way over by Fisher's Island?" Jack asked.

"At the mouth of the Sound," Sully said. "But if that boat gets out into the middle of the Sound, anything is possible." He glanced behind him and said, "You all may want to grab a seat. This might get bumpy."

Jack moved to the back to sit with his parents, giving Lindsey the seat next to Sully's. He maneuvered through the remainder of the islands, and soon they were out past the last big red buoy and headed for the boat that was clearly adrift, seemingly with no one on board. At least no one that Lindsey could see with her binoculars.

Sully called Emma and told her what was happening.

He listened as she spoke, his mouth drawing down in the corners.

"Emma, I don't think you want me to wait until the police boat can get out here," he said. "This boat is soon to be on the move in the current. We could lose it. Also, I have the horsepower to tow a boat and the ropes if need be. Your police boat doesn't."

Sully held the phone away from his ear as Emma lectured. No one could lecture quite like the chief of police. When she finally wound down, he said, "I have Lindsey's parents on the boat. I am not going to do anything that would put them in harm's way."

"Of course, if there is anyone on the boat, I'll get out of there immediately," he said.

Lindsey raised her eyebrows. It hadn't occurred to her that someone might be on the boat. She lifted the binoculars and studied the boat as they drew closer.

"Yes, I'll call you as soon as I have it secured," Sully said. Then he ended the call and focused on catching up to the larger vessel.

The wind was whipping at her hair, and she pulled a hat out of her pocket and yanked it on to hold it in place. Then she raised the binoculars back up to her eyes. She scanned the boat. She didn't see anyone. As they got closer, Sully switched on a searchlight that was mounted on the bow of his boat. He trained it on the other vessel, illuminating it beneath the cloudy gray sky. There were no immediate signs of life.

Using his VHF radio, he switched it to channel sixteen

and spoke into the microphone. "This is Captain Mike Sullivan, requesting permission to board."

There was no response.

"Now what?" Lindsey asked.

"I'm going to board," he said. He glanced at Lindsey. "How do you feel about taking the controls?"

"I can do it," she said. She hoped she sounded more confident than she felt. Her nose was cold. The sight of Steve's boat filled her with the worst sort of dread. And she didn't like deep dark water on her best days, never mind when her groom-to-be was going to step onto an abandoned boat, putting himself at all sorts of risk.

"I'll go with him," Jack said. This did not make Lindsey feel any better.

"Why you?" she asked. "I should go."

"I don't know how to drive this boat," Jack said. He shrugged as if to say, *So sad, too bad.*

As Sully slowed the boat down, he used his radio to call for permission to board again. As before, there was no reply. He switched off the searchlight and cruised up to the boat. Lindsey studied it through the binoculars. The interior was dark. It looked abandoned.

"I'm going to pull up alongside it," he said. "Normally we'd maintain speed side by side, but it's drifting, so Jack and I may have to jump for it. Just try to keep us close."

Lindsey took over the controls as the two men climbed up on the side of the boat. Her hands were shaking, and she was desperately afraid of dumping them both into the water. It would take no time at all to develop hypothermia out here, and even with the heat the boat was kicking out, she didn't think they'd make it back to shore without losing a few fingers or toes.

She swallowed. Then she felt her parents come to stand, one on each side of her.

"You've got this," her father said. "Steady as she goes."

His voice was just the right amount of calm, and Lindsey remembered being nine years old and completely paralyzed in a haunted house. Then her dad had appeared beside her and talked her through the whole zombie-infested, screaming nightmare. That was the thing about dads, they could talk a girl through the scariest of moments. She kept the boat within feet of the bigger one without hitting it. Like two big cats, both Sully and Jack stealthily jumped onto the drifting vessel. Sully gave her a thumbs-up while Lindsey felt her heart pound in her chest.

She waited for shouts, gunshots, the boat's engine to fire to life as it zoomed off with her fiancé and her brother. None of that happened. The boat kept drifting. She kept pace with it. Sully and Jack circled the outside, and then they disappeared into the lower decks. After a few tense minutes in which she was certain her heart would stop, Jack reappeared, followed by Sully.

Sully gestured that he was going to the bridge, and she nodded. While she kept pace with the boat, he fired up the engine, which started with a churning noise before slowly coming back to life. The lights switched on in the interior, and Jack gave a shout of triumph.

Lindsey felt her phone vibrate in her pocket, and she pulled it out. It was Sully.

"I'm going to drive the boat in," he said. "It appears to

be in working condition, and this will be easier than trying to tow it."

"All right," she said. "I'll follow you since I'm not as good at navigating the islands."

"All right," he said.

She could see him studying his surroundings.

"Are you okay?" she asked.

"I'm not sure," he said. "Jack and I spotted what appears to be blood on the bow. I'm no forensic expert, but the blood looks like spatter, as if it came from someone dripping blood, not from whacking their head on the bow. I think Steve might have been murdered on his own boat."

Lindsey gasped. She knew that for a sailor like Sully, that was the worst possible thing that could happen on a boat. His boats were his life. She knew that if his theory proved true, it would haunt him forever.

"Let's just get it back to the pier, where the police and the crime scene unit can determine what happened," she said.

"Right," he agreed. "Stay close, but not too close."

"Got it." She waited for him to pull ahead, and then she followed in his wake all the way back to the islands. When they passed the big red buoy, Sully cut his speed to a no-wake crawl and Lindsey felt all the tension in her shoulders and back release. Being this close to shore again filled her with such relief. All they needed to do was turn the boat over, and they were done. She couldn't wait.

Navigating the islands was a painstaking process, but she followed Sully exactly, and in no time they were pulling up to the pier, where Emma and a crime scene unit were waiting for them.

Lindsey docked the boat, grateful when her dad scrambled out to tie up. Sully took the larger vessel to a different dock on the pier, the one he used for his larger tour boat. She switched off the engine and followed her parents out of the boat and up the ladder to the pier above to see what was happening with the Briggs boat.

Sully and Jack were already there, talking to the chief of police. Sully described Jack's spotting the boat and then their adventure in catching up to it. He praised Lindsey for being able to maintain his boat while he and Jack climbed aboard, then he lowered his voice to tell Emma about the bloodstain. Lindsey directed her parents' attention toward the view of town, hoping they didn't hear about the grisly findings. This was supposed to be her wedding weekend, and she didn't want her parents to have to worry about anything more than whether or not to have seconds on wedding cake, assuming there was enough cake.

"It's all right, Linds," her father said. He put an arm around her and pulled her into his side. "We know what's happening. We saw the blood."

"You did?"

"Yes, and in full disclosure, we already knew about Briggs's murder. Joan and Mike called us from the bed-and-breakfast they were staying at," Christine said. "They weren't sure if they'd be allowed home in time to host us, so they wanted to let us know what was happening and that there was room at the bed-and-breakfast if need be."

"Oh. Why didn't you say anything?"

"We didn't want to upset you by mentioning it," John said. "We figured if you wanted to talk about it, you would."

"Now can we talk about it?" Jack asked. He left Sully with Emma to join them. "I have so many questions."

"You and me both," Lindsey said. She glanced at her brother. "Hey, off the subject but still relevant—you haven't been ordained as a minister, become a justice of the peace, or a notary public have you?"

"Sorry, still just an economist," he said. "Why?"

"We're sort of lacking a person qualified to marry us," Lindsey said. At the interested looks on her parents' faces, she added, "But we have a line on someone, so I'm sure it will be fine, perfectly fine."

"Joan did mention her uncle Carl," Christine said.

"So, you knew about this, too?" Lindsey asked.

They nodded.

"Well, I don't even know what to say here," she said. Honestly, what was the point of trying to protect her family from bad news if they were just going to hear it from someone else?

"We could call your cousin Alice. She's a minister in upstate New York, but I'm sure she'd come down and officiate," John said. There was a pause. "Of course, you'd have to apologize for pushing her into the creek when you were kids."

"I didn't push her. She fell," Lindsey said. Her parents didn't say anything, while Jack stood there, clearly trying not to laugh. Lindsey felt compelled to repeat herself. "She did fall, I swear."

"As you have sworn for thirty years," Christine said.

"Which should lend veracity to my side of the story," Lindsey said.

"And it would if Alice hadn't been holding the book you were reading when she fell into the creek," Jack said. "If you'd tried to save her like you did the book, she might have let go of her grudge."

"If she hadn't snatched my book in a fit of mean, she might not have lost her balance and fallen," Lindsey said.

"So, that's a hard pass on Cousin Alice?" her father asked.

"Yes."

"Lindsey, can I have a word?" Emma called to her from across the pier where she stood with Sully.

Lindsey excused herself and hurried across the pier. Emma was dressed in uniform, with her thick coat on over her navy blue dress shirt and slacks. Her fleece-lined hat covered her head, but the tip of her nose was pink, and she sniffed against the cold. Lindsey realized she couldn't feel her toes and stomped her feet a few times, trying to get the feeling back.

"I won't keep you long," Emma said.

"It's fine."

"Can you just tell me everything as you remember it?" Emma said. "I've got Sully's description, but I'm thinking maybe you saw or heard something else."

"All right." Lindsey told Emma everything she remembered about seeing the boat and bringing it ashore. She knew she didn't have much more to say than Sully—less actually, since he'd gone aboard the vessel and she hadn't.

When she finished, Emma interviewed Jack and her parents. Once they were done, they were all half-frozen, and as the crime scene unit towed away the Briggs boat into the marina for safekeeping, Lindsey and Sully took her family out to Bell Island. With an advance call from Sully, Joan had a spread of food and hot cider at the ready.

As they told Sully's parents about the events of the day, Lindsey noticed the frown on Mike's forehead. She nudged Sully in the side with her elbow and tipped her chin in his father's direction.

"What is it, Dad?" he asked.

Mike turned toward Sully and said, "It just seems awfully convenient, doesn't it? That you just happened to be coming out to the island when Briggs's boat was drifting by?"

"Possibly, which means that whoever killed Steve and took his boat was hoping we'd find the boat and assume it was an accident," Lindsey said.

No one said anything. They didn't have to. It was clear that Mike was right. Someone wanted them to find the boat. Just like someone wanted the wig and veil to be found. The question was who? And why?

CHAPTER

14

BRIAR CREEK
PUBLIC LIBRARY

Lindsey was still thinking about finding Steve's boat and the blood on the bow when they met up with Charlie and the man he said could officiate their wedding at the Blue Anchor.

"I've officiated several weddings," Marcus said. "Of course, they have all taken place in the sanctity of a church, and I am a stickler for the vows."

"A stickler?" Lindsey asked. She forced herself to focus on the matter at hand, namely finding someone to marry them.

"I believe in the traditional service where a woman vows to obey her husband in all things," he said.

"Obey?" Lindsey felt herself begin to choke.

"Yes." Marcus pushed his glasses up on his nose. "I'm certain that's why our Mr. Briggs met his unfortunate end.

Clearly, he had little control over his wife. It's being rumored that she had him killed."

"Really?" Charlie asked. "I'd have thought it was his drunken business partner for sure."

"No, it's the wife," Marcus said. "I've seen her about town, flaunting herself without respect for her husband. That's why we have so many divorces these days. Women need a firm hand—"

"And we're done," Sully said. He sent Charlie a pointed look.

"So, this was really great," Charlie said. He bounced up from his seat, grabbing Marcus by the elbow as he went, and physically hauling him toward the door. "We'll be in touch if your services are required."

"Oh, well, all right," Marcus said. "Nice to meet you—"

Charlie didn't slow down long enough for him to finish, which was all to the good in Lindsey's opinion, because her vision had gone red and she'd started to see spots.

"You okay?" Sully asked her.

"Why? Do I look like I'm having an aneurysm?" she asked.

"You're clenching your glass so hard, I'm afraid it might shatter," he said. He reached over and began to pry her fingers off the glass. "Easy does it. There you go. Okay, shake it out."

Lindsey shook her hand out, inviting the blood back into her fingertips.

"Didn't you say we needed to keep an open mind?" he teased.

"I'm sorry. My mind is just not that open," she retorted. "It slammed shut at the word *obey*."

"I figured," he said. "How do you suppose Charlie even knows that guy? They don't even look like they're from the same planet."

Lindsey glanced at the doorway where Charlie stood with Marcus. Charlie was whip thin, wearing torn jeans and a Rolling Stones T-shirt over a thermal shirt. His long black hair flowed well below his shoulders and was parted in the middle in the way of the rock gods he emulated. Marcus, on the other hand, was clean-cut, bespectacled and looked like he was wrapped as tight as a ham sandwich in cellophane.

"No idea," she said.

Marcus departed and Charlie returned to their table. "First, let me start with I'm sorry," he said. "And second, let me add, I'm really, really sorry."

"It's okay," Lindsey said. "I know you were trying to help, but I have to ask, how do you know him? It just doesn't seem likely that your paths would cross . . . ever."

Charlie grinned and tipped his head to the side. His long hair fell around his face, obscuring his features, but not before Lindsey noticed that he looked a teeny bit embarrassed.

"So, the music thing, you know, it's like feast or starvation," Charlie said. "And in winter, when the tour boat is docked, my income is even less dependable."

"Charlie, you should have told me," Sully said. "I can always put you to work in the office."

Charlie looked pained. "I know, and I appreciate it."

"Not your jam, eh?"

"Not even close," he said. "But I was telling my sister about my lack of abundance, and she said I should share my knowledge about music, so I put out an offer of music lessons on the old social media waves, and what do you know? There are a lot of people like Marcus who want to rock."

"So, he's taking guitar lessons from you?" Lindsey asked.

"Yup," Charlie said. "That dude is a Metallica freak."

"No way," Lindsey said.

"Way."

"I have to say, I can't see that," Sully said.

"Me either," Lindsey agreed.

"Yeah, for a guy with great taste in music, he sure doesn't get women," Charlie said. "Not surprised he's single, you know?"

"Yeah, not a shock," Sully agreed.

"I don't think he's alone in his opinion of Jamie Briggs, however," Lindsey said. "It seems like the town is split in its opinion. Half the town thinks Tony Mancusi killed Steve, and the other half thinks it's Jamie."

"There are a few who think he fell off the wagon, drank too much and took off on his boat for a midnight joyride," Sully said. "But I know that's not true, because I did get Emma to admit that the medical examiner said his blood test was clean. No alcohol. And second, he knew the islands. There was no way he'd have crashed, even in the dark of night."

"So it really comes down to which of them, his ex-partner or his wife, wanted him dead the most," Charlie said. "Unless it was the mysterious woman in black."

Despite the warmth of the restaurant, Lindsey felt her skin prickle.

How can there not be anyone who is not a Druid or a day-napper or a chauvinist available to perform a wedding ceremony?" Lindsey muttered to herself as she checked her voice mail for the umpteenth time that morning. "Are we really asking for so much?"

She thought about her cousin Alice and the apology she would have to make in order to get her here for the wedding. Nope. She wasn't going to apologize for something she hadn't done. Alice had swiped her book, *Anne of Green Gables*, right out of her hands while she'd been reading by the creek that flowed through her parents' backyard. The banks of the creek had been slippery, and Alice had wind-milled her arms a bit, almost flinging Lindsey's book into the water, but Lindsey had made a dive and caught the book, saving it from ruin. She had not bothered to save Alice, how-ever, who had landed on her bum in the icy cold foot-deep water. Nope, she still didn't feel bad about it either.

She was not going to apologize to Alice. Period.

"The bride is talking to herself," a voice said from her doorway. "That can't be good."

Lindsey glanced up to see Robbie standing there. He was bundled up in a long wool coat with a plaid scarf wrapped around his neck.

"The bride doesn't have a person to marry her to her groom yet," Lindsey said. "And we're down to the final hours. It's making her crazed."

"And she's talking about herself in third person, which is never a good sign. You know you're overlooking a solution that's right in front of you," he said.

Lindsey sank back into her chair with a groan. "Probably. But I can't think about it anymore or I'm going to have a mental episode."

"Okay," he said. He gave her a reassuring smile. "I'm sure you'll figure it out."

Lindsey frowned at him. Was he being sarcastic? It was not appreciated.

"So I've been thinking since the tree-lighting ceremony that the key to Briggs's murder must be the identity of the woman in black," Robbie said.

There she was again. Lindsey didn't know whether it was because her identity was unknown or because she was a woman, but it felt as if everyone was obsessed with the woman in black. Did the idea of a female murderer appeal that much? Why weren't they as obsessed with Jamie Briggs then? She was the spouse. She seemed the most likely, but she didn't have the alluring element of wearing a long black veil and being a mystery.

"Maybe," Lindsey said. "She could have just been some crazy relative who likes to dress all in black."

"Nate and Steve didn't have any other relatives," Robbie said. "And Jamie didn't have anyone visiting either."

"You've been busy," Lindsey said.

He shrugged. "I don't have much else going on other

than rehearsals at the community theater for *A Christmas Carol*, which I have to leave for in a few minutes."

"Well, how do you propose we go about unveiling the woman in black?"

"I see what you did there," he said.

Lindsey smiled.

"It seems to me, she would have chosen a black wig and veil because her hair is a different color," Robbie said. "Maybe it's red or blond."

"Short?" Lindsey suggested. "Making it different from the long black wig?"

"Precisely," he said. "We don't know her height or build, do we?"

"No one has mentioned anything that stands out," Lindsey said. "I'm assuming average height and weight."

"Hmm," Robbie hummed.

"It's all just speculation," Lindsey said. "We don't even know if she ever saw Steve. Molly said that Steve looked excited and went to find her, but we don't know if they ever caught up to each other."

"Oh, we know," Robbie said. He leaned back, looking very self-satisfied. "I happened to overhear Emma talking to the medical examiner, and he pulled a long black hair off Steve's body that matches the wig."

"No." Lindsey gasped.

"Yes," he said. "I think Steve was having an affair, and this was a rendezvous gone bad."

"You think he went out on the boat with the woman in black and she killed him?"

"Maybe they got into a fight and she pushed him," he

said. "Emma did admit that there was blood found on the boat. No idea if it matches Steve's yet, but it seems likely."

"But that leaves a million more questions," Lindsey said. "Steve was hit in the head with something, but what was it? How did he end up on the island? Why was his boat adrift? If she killed him and pushed him overboard with a head injury, he would have drowned, don't you think? But cause of death was from the head injury. Also, I saw the wig and veil recovered from the garbage can. They didn't look wet. They looked dry. If this woman jumped from the boat and swam for it, the wig and veil would have been wet, and they wouldn't have had time to dry out before they were found."

"Maybe she hit him before they left the dock. Sully verified that Steve's boat was still being kept at his private boathouse. It could be that she pushed a wounded Steve onto his boat and took him for a ride. While out there, maybe he fell overboard and swam to Bell Island," he said.

"It just seems so unlikely," Lindsey said. "Sully could look at the charts and tell us if that was even possible. I'm not sure the currents would have brought Steve to Bell Island. And with a head injury, would he have been strong enough to swim that far in the cold? There are other islands closer to his house than Bell Island."

"You still think someone else killed him?" Robbie asked.

"Mancusi is still missing," she said. "From what I saw, he had the strongest motive to murder Steve, or at least he thought he did."

Robbie glanced at his watch and sighed. "I have to go.

I'll look for you later, and we can discuss it more. In the meantime, keep an eye out for any shifty-looking women with short hair who have a penchant for wearing black."

"Will do," Lindsey said. "And you look out for any enraged ex-lawyers who might have killed their former partner."

"One thing," Robbie said as he stood and moved toward the doorway. "If the woman in black wasn't guilty of something, why did she hide her wig and veil in the park? She could have left them in her house under a floorboard, burned them in her barbecue or taken them to the town dump. Why put them in a public trash bin where one of the biggest events of the season was about to take place? Did she really think hiding them in plain sight was a great idea?"

Lindsey blinked at him. "You do what you have to do for your babies."

"That makes no sense," he said.

Lindsey glanced up at him and forced herself to smile even as she heard Naomi Briggs's voice in her head after Lindsey had seen her hide the dreidel in plain sight for her daughter. She was freaking out, but she contained it, not wanting to say anything until she knew for certain.

"Sorry. I think I've strained my brain," she said.

Robbie seemed satisfied. He gave her a small bow and said, "Let me know when you've figured out who the perfect person is to marry you and sailor boy."

"You'll be the first," she said.

He grinned at that and disappeared through her door and out into the library. Lindsey reached for her phone. She wanted to call Sully and get his opinion. Okay, no, what she wanted was to call Sully and tell him the crazy thought she was having about Naomi being the woman in black, and then she wanted him to talk her out of it. Completely out of it. With logic and reason.

She was about to press call when she stopped herself. They were getting married in just a few days. She did not need to be thinking about who murdered Steve, but rather about who was going to marry them. She knew that Sully wanted to find Steve's murderer. She did, too. But did she really want to bring Naomi into it? Hadn't Nate suffered enough by losing his brother? To have his wife tied to his brother's death, even peripherally? No, she couldn't do that to them. If Naomi was the woman in black, it was up to Emma to figure that out.

At least that's what she told herself. Lindsey had the afternoon off, and she was headed over to the town hall to see if the woman who worked in the mayor's office who acted as the town's notary was willing to marry her and Sully. It was a last-ditch idea that she was hoping would work out. She didn't know Ellen Stein very well, but she thought if they offered to pay her, she'd be willing to give up a portion of her Saturday to go out to Bell Island and officiate.

She bundled up in her long wool coat, hat, scarf and gloves. She stopped by the circulation desk to let Ms. Cole know that she was taking her break and going to the town hall but that she'd be back. Ms. Cole smiled and said, "Say hi to the mayor for me."

Lindsey grinned. Deciding to run for mayor had really channeled the lemon's spunk. She wondered what the next year would look like when the campaigns took on heat. Things could get pretty dicey between the library and the town hall. No matter. She was firmly Team Lemon—or, rather, Team Cole.

"Will do," she said. She crossed the lobby and stepped on the mat that activated the automatic doors. A blast of cold hit her as she stepped outside, and she huddled into her coat.

The town hall was just down the street, and she walked briskly, hoping that it would keep her warm. It wouldn't. She'd lived in New England long enough to know that she'd shiver all the way to the town hall, and then once she stepped inside, she'd start sweating profusely. And when she pulled off her hat, her hair would have a static festival, making it stick to her face and fly up in the air, giving her the very chic recently electrocuted look. The joys of winter.

She was just rounding the corner when she saw Nate Briggs's tow truck parked on the far side of the road. He was loading a BMW onto the back while the owner watched. The owner looked underdressed and half-frozen, while Nate had on insulated coveralls and a wool cap.

Lindsey raised her hand in greeting, and Nate waved back. She was about to keep going when a squad car pulled up behind Nate. She paused, knowing it was none of her business but wanting to see what happened anyway. While she watched, Emma Plewicki and Officer Kirkland got out of the car. Emma approached Nate with a stride that was all business, and the next thing Lindsey knew, Nate had his hands in the air while Emma patted him down. In seconds, she had his hands behind his back, and he was cuffed.

Shock had Lindsey rooted to the spot. She wanted to yell "Hey!" but no words came out.

Instead, the owner of the BMW started to shout. "Wait! You can't arrest him now! What about my car?"

Emma shrugged as she led Nate to the police car and protected his head while she helped him into the back seat.

The owner of the BMW started to pitch a real fit. He kicked the ground, demanded Emma's badge number and swore that he was going to sue. Emma stood with her arms folded, looking singularly unimpressed.

Lindsey used the ruckus as an opportunity to cross the street. She approached the police car casually, as if she'd just been out walking and come upon the scene. Not a total lie. She sidled up to Kirkland and asked the big redhead, "What's going on?"

He glanced down at her with a look of gentle patience that she would have found patronizing in anyone else, but they had a history, so she let it slide.

"If the chief wants you to know, she'll tell you," he said.

Lindsey realized Kirkland was going to keep up his fair impression of a brick wall, so she left him and moved in closer to Emma and the stranded driver until she was just within eavesdropping range.

"Your car is being towed because it's not working, right?" Emma asked.

"Yes." The car owner said. He was a cranky middle-aged man, looking as if he couldn't believe the run of bad luck that was happening to him. How dare his car break down and his mechanic get arrested?

"Then what difference does it make if it sits on the side

of the road or on the back of a tow truck?" Emma asked. "I'm sure one of Mr. Briggs's mechanics will come by to collect it as soon as they can. In the meantime, why don't you go have a cup of chowder at the Blue Anchor, because it's not like you're going anywhere anytime soon."

With that, Emma turned away from the angry little rooster and approached the car. She saw Lindsey and sighed as if she was the last thing she wanted to deal with.

"Lindsey," she said. She didn't stop moving, like if she stayed in motion, similar to a shark, it would keep Lindsey at bay. Yeah, no such luck.

"Emma," she said. "What's going on?"

"You don't really think I'm going to tell you, do you?"

"Can I at least ask Nate if he needs anything?" Lindsey said. "Come on, have a heart. It's almost Christmas, and he's got a wife and kids."

"I'd like to have a heart, but I'm too busy running a murder investigation," Emma snapped.

Lindsey didn't say anything. She just stood there, not moving, like Dickens's Ghost of Christmas Present.

"All right, fine," Emma said. "Ask him if he needs anything, and you might suggest that he use his one phone call to get in touch with the lawyer Sully recommended instead of his wife, since I'm quite sure you'll be in touch with Naomi in a matter of minutes."

Lindsey nodded. That had been her plan. "Thanks."

She opened the back door, where Nate sat looking miserable.

"Hey," she said. "What can I do?"

"Bust me out?" he asked.

"Besides that," she said.

"Tell Naomi not to worry," he said. "Do not tell her that Emma has arrested me for Steve's murder. It'll just upset her. Tell her I'm being questioned and that I'll call the lawyer Sully recommended and I'll be home in time for dinner."

Lindsey nodded. So he had been arrested for Steve's murder. It made no sense. "I thought you had an alibi. You were driving the baby around."

Nate nodded. "I was, I swear I was, but I can't prove it. And it looks like they found one of my tools on Steve's boat, and it was covered in his blood. Probably the murder weapon."

"That doesn't mean it was you," Lindsey said.

Nate shrugged. "I know. Every now and then, he'd show up to borrow a tool of mine. I always felt like it was an excuse he made just to touch base and ease his conscience for not being around. I mean, come on, it's not like he had the time, skill or interest to do any manual labor he could easily hire someone else to do. Which makes this look especially bad."

"I'll call Sully," she said. "We'll figure this out."

"Thanks." He bowed his head, and Lindsey felt as if she was watching a man slowly being broken by one horrible event after another.

She closed the door and turned to find Emma standing there while Kirkland was on the phone with Nate's Garage, asking one of the mechanics to come and collect the tow truck.

"Doesn't this seem a bit convenient?" Lindsey asked.

Emma's lips tightened. "I'm just following the evidence."

"Nate says Steve borrowed his tools all the time and that there are more at Steve's house," Lindsey said. "The only thing finding the murder weapon proves—assuming it is—is that someone used a tool from Nate's Garage. It could have been anyone. Heck, Kerry Tomlinson was in Nate's auto shop the other day, looking none too happy about what her son did to their car."

"So you're saying Kerry stole a tool from Nate and clobbered Steve with it?" Emma asked, being deliberately obtuse.

"No, I'm saying everyone goes to Nate's for car repairs, and it could have been anyone who took the . . . I'm sorry, what item was it?" Lindsey asked.

"Nice try," Emma said. "You already know more than I'd like, so you won't be getting any more information from me."

"Even so, my point holds," Lindsey insisted. "It could have been anyone."

"I know," Emma said. "I've already thought of that, but this is how we start weeding out suspects. You bring them in and question them. I know you know this is how this works, and right now I need to bring him in and get some fingerprints and see if they match what's on the murder weapon."

Lindsey felt her stomach lurch. Fingerprints? They had fingerprints?

"Lindsey, I don't like it any more than you do," Emma said. "But my job doesn't allow me to play favorites. Nate is a suspect. Full stop."

Emma glanced over at Kirkland, who had ended his call, and jerked her head in the direction of the car. With two pats on the roof, she climbed into the driver's seat while Kirkland got into the passenger side, wrapping himself around the computer monitor and all the gear attached to the dashboard.

Lindsey watched as they drove off, realizing only when they disappeared from sight that she'd lost the feeling in her toes.

CHAPTER

15

BRIAR CREEK
PUBLIC LIBRARY

Sully arrived at the library just after Lindsey called him. Thankfully, he hadn't been out on the water taxi and came right from the pier.

"Jim Britton, my attorney friend, is on his way. He's going to meet us at the police station," he said.

Lindsey was done for the day. She was supposed to spend the afternoon doing last-minute wedding stuff like checking on the centerpieces, making sure the tent and heaters were delivered and that the photographer was on deck, but she had called the moms, and they were on it. She and Sully had both agreed that Nate was more important.

Lindsey had called Naomi but only got her voice mail. She and Sully decided to stop by the Briggses' house, figuring this was news Naomi would rather get in person. Unfortunately, when they got to the house, no one was there. As they passed the garage, Lindsey was relieved to see that

Nate's tow truck was there with the BMW he'd been taking in for repair.

Figuring she'd just keep trying to reach Naomi, they decided to go to the police station to see if they could help Nate. They arrived before Nate's attorney, as Jim was coming from New Haven and it would take him a while to get there.

When they walked into the lobby, it was to find Emma out front. She was on her radio, talking to one of her officers. It sounded like Kirkland.

"So, what Nate said checks out?" she asked. Intent on her phone call, she didn't bother to acknowledge Sully or Lindsey.

"*Yes,*" Kirkland answered. "*There are several tools in the boathouse, all with Nate's name on them, as well as some in the garage, and I found a toolbox in the house that had a wrench with Nate's name on it as well.*"

"Okay, then. Bag 'em and bring them in with you," Emma said.

"*Roger that. Kirkland out,*" he said.

The radio went silent, and Emma turned to face them. "Do you have some news for me? Tell me you know something, found something or have a theory, because I am all ears."

Lindsey and Sully exchanged a look. Emma was never this agreeable about them butting into cases.

"What gives?" Sully asked.

Emma heaved a huge sigh. "He confessed."

Lindsey blinked. The words made no sense. "*He* being Nate?" she asked. She was hoping she'd missed something.

"Yes," Emma said. "Why? Why would he do that?"

"Because you brought him in for questioning," Lindsey suggested.

"That doesn't mean I was going to formally arrest him," Emma said. "I was very clear that it was just for questioning. He wouldn't even let us fingerprint him. He refused. Do you know how bad that looks? And the next thing I knew, he confessed."

"I didn't want to say anything without Nate's attorney here, but when I spoke to Jim, his lawyer, today, he said there's a very good chance that he can verify Nate's alibi," Sully said. "Something about an insurance tracker and proof that he was driving the baby around town at the time of Steve's murder."

Emma visibly sagged in relief. "Thank goodness. He's such a good guy. I hated having to bring him in to begin with, but confessing to a crime he didn't commit is not going to help him. In fact, it's bad. Very bad."

The front doors banged open, and on a gust of cold, bitter air Naomi ran into the lobby. She didn't slow down or break her stride. She made right for Emma. Stopping in front of her while breathing hard, as if she'd run the whole way here, she said, "I confess."

Emma reared back. "Say what?"

"I confess," Naomi panted. "I killed Steve, my brother-in-law. It was me."

Emma, not tall to begin with, drew herself up to her highest height, with her back stiff, her hands on her hips and a steely glint in her eye. "Okay, what the hell is going on here?"

"I don't know what you mean," Naomi said. "I'm confessing. Is there a piece of paper I need to sign? Do you need a mug shot? I'm owning it, all of it. I murdered my brother-in-law."

"Really?" Emma asked. "Because I have your husband cooling his heels in a cell, telling me that he murdered Steve. So which is it? Him or you?"

"Me," Naomi said. "He's just trying to protect me."

"Naomi, you don't have to do this," Lindsey said. "Nate has a lawyer, and it looks like his alibi will stick."

"And what if it doesn't?" Naomi asked. "That's a gamble I'm not willing to take when Steve's death is my fault." She turned back to Emma. "I did it. You have to let Nate go and arrest me."

"That's not how this works," Emma cried. She gestured wildly to the station around them. "That's not how any of this works."

"Naomi, where are the girls?" Lindsey asked.

"They're staying with my mother," she said. "I heard about what happened to Nate from Greg, our mechanic, and I took the girls to my mom's so that I could come here." She held up her wrists in front of Emma. "Go ahead. Take me away."

Emma shook her head, and with a look of disgust, she lifted her radio off her shoulder and spoke into it. "Wilcox, bring Nate Briggs up to the front."

"*Roger that,*" a voice said.

Emma switched off her radio and frowned at Naomi. "You still have a chance to rethink this."

"No."

The door from the back of the jail opened, and Officer Wilcox came in with Nate, who was no longer in handcuffs but still in his work coveralls, which looked like a navy blue version of the standard orange prison onesie.

"Naomi, what are you doing here?" he asked. He looked at Lindsey. "You weren't supposed to bring her here."

"I didn't," she said. She stepped closer to Sully, wanting to feel his strength as they watched what happened.

"Nate, I've confessed," Naomi said. She turned to Emma. "You can let him go now, right?"

"You what?!" Nate cried. "No!"

"Yes," Naomi insisted. She turned to Emma. "I killed Steve."

"No, she didn't. I did," Nate said.

Emma pressed a hand to her forehead. "I'm getting a migraine. Why are you two doing this?"

"Wild guess here," Sully said. "But I think it's because they both think the other murdered Steve."

Emma gave him a confused look. "Why?"

"That I can't say," he said. He looked at Nate and Naomi. "Care to tell us what's going on?"

"I killed him," they said together. They looked at each other in frustration and again spoke in unison. "No, you didn't. I did."

"I feel like this is O. Henry's 'The Gift of the Magi,'" Lindsey said.

"Yeah, only with two murder confessions instead of a watch chain and a set of hair combs," Sully agreed.

"Naomi, this isn't helping," Nate said. "I understand what you're trying to do, but the girls need you. Go home to them. I'll be fine."

"No, they need you just as much as they need me," Naomi said. "And I won't leave you confessing to a crime, the murder of your own brother, when everyone knows you could never have done such a thing."

"I'm more likely to have done it than you," he cried. He raised his arms in exasperation. "What are you even thinking, confessing to something like this? You don't have it in you."

Naomi tossed her hair and stared him down. "Oh, don't I?" she asked. Her voice was bitter and full of self-loathing.

They stared at each other as if there were a million things they wanted to say but couldn't. It occurred to Lindsey that there was a reason that they were confessing, trying to clear each other. Something had happened between them and Steve that was causing them to believe that they each could have been driven to murder.

Naomi turned to Emma. "I did murder Steve, and I can prove it."

Emma's eyes went wide, and she said, "Go on."

"I'm the woman in black," Naomi said.

The entire room went still, and even though Lindsey had suspected as much, she was still shocked to hear Naomi admit it.

"The baby did have croup; Nate did drive her around to help her settle back to sleep. When he left, I knew I had an hour to get back to Steve's party and demand that he leave us alone," she said.

"But you were the one who pointed out the wig in the trash can at the tree-lighting ceremony," Emma said. "Why would you do that?"

"To make it look like it wasn't me," Naomi said with a shrug. "I figured if something happened, my defense would be to argue exactly that. It couldn't be me because why would I point out my own disguise? But it was me. Now you have to let Nate go and take me in."

"No, she's lying," Nate said. His voice was rough. He sounded desperate. "I did take the baby, because I knew it would give me an alibi. The truth is I doubled back, and I killed my brother."

The words stuck in his throat, and Lindsey knew she wasn't the only one who didn't believe him. He just couldn't sell it. Of course, she didn't believe Naomi either, not about the murder at any rate. She did believe she was the woman in black, but why she felt she needed to be in a disguise and demand that Steve leave them alone, that was the question that needed an answer.

As if reading Lindsey's mind, Emma turned to Naomi. "Why did you feel the need to tell Steve to leave you alone? What was happening?"

"Nothing," Nate said. He gave Naomi a look. She opened her mouth to answer, but he shook his head furiously back and forth.

"Just family stuff," Naomi said. "But while he and I were talking, it got out of hand, and I . . . I killed him."

"No, you didn't," Nate snapped.

"Yes, I did."

"No, I did."

"Please," Naomi said. "No one believes that."

Nate glanced at Emma. He stared her right in the eye and said, "I did it."

Emma glanced at Nate and then at Naomi. "Yeah, someone's lying, or more likely both of you are. I don't know why, but I will figure it out unless you want to make it easy on me and just tell me now."

The couple stood staring at each other. They looked angry and anguished, but neither of them spoke.

"Fine," Emma snapped. "I'll give you both some time to cool off in a cell, and you can sit and think about what you're going to say in front of a judge."

Lindsey had a feeling she was trying to scare them. Judging by the way both Nate and Naomi paled, it worked.

Emma gestured for Wilcox to take Nate while she took Naomi. She glanced over her shoulder at Sully and Lindsey and said, "Unless you have more information for me, you're free to go."

They nodded, watching as the husband and wife were led away.

"What do you make of that?" Sully asked.

"Something was going down in the Briggs family that was significant enough that both Naomi and Nate thought the other might have been pushed to murder Steve," Lindsey said. "That's not a small thing."

"Yeah, that's my take, too," he agreed. "But what could it have been? Nate admitted that they weren't as close as they once were, but to be estranged to the point of being a suspect for murder? I didn't think things had gotten that bad."

"Naomi said something about Steve being jealous of all that Nate had. The family, the kids—you know, the things his money couldn't buy," Lindsey said. "Do you think that was a part of the rift between them?"

"I don't know," he said. He reached out and pulled her into a hug. "Is it selfish of me to admit that I just want Steve's murder solved so that I can feel at peace about the whole thing? I feel like a jerk even saying this, but this was not how I saw the week before our wedding going."

"You're not a jerk," she said. "It's been hard to get caught up in the wedding, not only because we don't have someone to marry us but also because there's a murderer out there and we don't know who or why."

"Exactly," he said. "Come on, let's go to the Anchor and meet our parents for dinner. At least that will feel somewhat normal."

They joined their parents, Ian, Mary, Jack and his girlfriend, Stella, for dinner. It was a boisterous affair as the moms recounted their day, talking to the florist, the caterer and the guy with the portable heaters, tables and chairs. The island was now fully equipped to host one hundred people on the island, and Lindsey was so relieved that she hugged and kissed both of the moms.

"Don't you worry," her mom said as she patted Lindsey's hand. "It's going to be a beautiful wedding."

"Any luck finding someone to officiate?" her father asked.

"I have a line on a public notary," Lindsey said. "She works at the town hall, and I'm going to try and catch up with her tomorrow."

"The day before the wedding?" Jack asked. "This last-minute lack of planning is so not like you."

"In my defense, there are extenuating circumstances," she said.

"Noted," her brother acknowledged.

The conversation veered to Steve Briggs and his unfortunate demise. Lindsey glanced at Sully to see how he was handling it. He looked resigned, as if the truth was slowly becoming a reality. One that he didn't like but was less shocking as time went on. Just as they realized that despite Steve's gregarious facade, he hadn't really been a happy man.

They were finishing dinner when Emma stopped by their table. She greeted everyone and then asked to talk to Lindsey in private.

"Sure," Lindsey put her napkin on the table and rose from her seat. She followed Emma to the bar and asked, "What's up?"

"I know you're busy with the wedding, and I hate to ask, but"—Emma paused and studied Lindsey's face with a look that said she knew she was asking a lot, but she was going to ask anyway—"is there any way you could bring some books and magazines by the jail tomorrow morning and use that visit as an opportunity to talk to Naomi?"

"She's going to be there overnight?" Lindsey asked.

"Both she and Nate," Emma said. "Neither one will recant their confession. Frankly, I'd like to knock their heads together, but that would be wrong, so . . ."

"You want me to see if I can get Naomi to tell me what's going on?"

"You have a way about you," Emma said. "People tell you things."

"It's the librarian in me."

"I don't care what it is," Emma said. "There are five little girls at their grandmother's house, which is fine, but they're not with their parents, which is not fine, because their parents are being thick. Any info you can get out of Naomi would be much appreciated."

"I'll be there first thing in the morning," she said.

"Excellent," Emma said. "I owe you one. Next parking ticket you get, you let me know."

"I don't own a car," Lindsey said.

"I know." Emma grinned.

Lindsey laughed and shook her head. When she returned to her table, it was to find everyone getting ready to leave. The Sullivans would take Lindsey's parents, her brother and his girlfriend back to Bell Island in their boat, while Ian and Mary would get back to work and Sully and Lindsey would head home. She couldn't wait.

She wanted to be in front of the fire with her dog and her book. Not fretting about the wedding or their friends, but escaping into a nice Southern magical realism book, her favorite author of the genre being Sarah Addison Allen.

They were almost out the door, almost home and tucked cozily under a thick blanket with a cup of Sully's hot chocolate and a novel, when Jamie arrived at the Blue Anchor looking for Emma. Dressed dramatically in a long black patent leather trench coat with a vibrant red scarf and leopard-print boots, Jamie banged through the door and stood on the threshold with one foot in front of the other, looking like she expected the paparazzi to descend upon her. Instead, everyone turned back to what they were doing without showing any interest in her.

This did not sit well with Jamie. She tugged off her coat and threw it behind her to be caught by the man everyone believed she was having an affair with, who was also her attorney. He looked chagrined.

"You!" Jamie cried. She pointed at Emma. "I've been looking for you."

Emma spun on her swivel bar stool, holding her pilsner of beer up to her lips as she took in Jamie.

"Yeah?" Emma asked. "Looks like you found me."

Jamie sauntered across the room like it was a catwalk. Lindsey's hips hurt just watching her. Emma calmly sipped her beer as if bracing for whatever Jamie was about to unleash upon her.

"My attorney, Blaise Anderson"—she paused to gesture to the man carrying her coat—"and I have information for you," Jamie said. She didn't whisper, clearly wanting everyone in the restaurant to hear her.

"I'm listening," Emma said.

"I have just learned that Steve had an affair with Naomi a little over a year ago, and he believed that the baby, the sickly one—what's her name? Marjorie? Margarine?"

"Matilda," her lawyer said.

"Yes, that's it," Jamie said. "Steve believed that she was actually his."

CHAPTER

16

BRIAR CREEK
PUBLIC LIBRARY

I f she had detonated a bomb, Jamie couldn't have shocked the entire restaurant more. No one moved. In fact, the head of the post office, Mr. Tinsdale, was so stunned his clam fritter fell out of his open mouth, landing with a splat.

"I think this is a conversation best had in private," Emma said. She looked furious. Lindsey couldn't blame her. This dramatic reveal was devastating and also not super helpful in the middle of an investigation.

Emma put down her beer and began to stride to the door. Jamie didn't follow. Instead, she leaned up against the bar and said, "No."

Blaise glanced at his watch. He opened his mouth to speak, but Jamie shook her head. She snapped her fingers at Ian, who was behind the bar, and said, "Dirty martini, heavy on the olives."

Ian gave her a side-eye and set to work.

"Jamie, unless you want to be arrested for compromising an investigation—" Emma began, but Jamie cut her off.

"Is that a thing?" Jamie asked Blaise.

He shrugged. "It's hard to prove."

"But not impossible," Emma snapped.

Jamie stared her down, scooping up the martini Ian had just poured. She took a sip and then began to walk through the tables, staring at the diners who watched her with a rapt fascination.

"You all thought *I* murdered him, didn't you?" she asked. "Me. The outsider, the person you never liked, the woman who was never good enough for your precious Steve Briggs. Well, how does it feel to know that the murderer was one of your own? Because it's as obvious to me as the pimento in my olive"—she paused to bite an olive off of the cocktail stick before she continued—"that the murderers are Naomi and Nate Briggs, probably working together so that they can inherit everything."

"Jamie, I am warning you—" Emma hissed.

"And do you want to know how I found out about the affair and that the baby might be his?" Jamie asked, ignoring Emma. Her voice was hitting a shrieky pitch in a combination of temper and hysteria. "I was just at the reading of his will, and he left everything to *it* contingent upon a paternity test."

"That's enough." Emma stormed forward, grabbed Jamie by the elbow and hauled her toward the door. When Blaise of the shiny suit and pointy shoes stepped forward, blocking the path, Emma said, "Do not make me pull my gun."

His eyes went wide, and he scuttled back, letting Emma

escort his client to the door. Jamie wasn't done, however. She downed her martini and dropped the glass on a nearby table.

"And as if it isn't enough that he left everything, *everything*, to his bastard spawn, if it proves out that the baby isn't his, then everything goes to his brother, Nate," she said. She glanced around the restaurant, looking for something. Sympathy, maybe. "Do you understand? Do you get it? He left me, his wife, *nothing*!"

Emma pushed her through the door. Blaise followed, still carrying Jamie's coat, while she let loose a verbal tirade on Emma, calling her every name in the book and a few Lindsey had never heard before.

Lindsey sank down onto a nearby barstool. Sully took the one beside her. There was no question that this changed everything.

"Drinks are on me," Ian said. He poured them each a beverage. Wine for Lindsey and beer for Sully.

As their parents left the restaurant to go back to the island, Lindsey forced her lips to curve up so as not to worry them.

"That woman who was here a few minutes ago," Christine said as she hugged Lindsey. "She's not invited to your wedding, is she?"

Lindsey blinked. She had no idea. Steve was supposed to officiate, and she didn't know if he'd been planning to bring his wife or not. She had assumed that Jamie wouldn't come because she rarely participated in any of the local events, but maybe she had planned to come. Still, there was no need to worry her mom.

"No," Lindsey said. "She just lost her husband. She has a lot going on right now."

"Good," Christine said. "Don't mistake me, I feel bad for her loss, but that is a diva if I've ever seen one, and you do not want her at your wedding. She'd find a way to make it about her. Trust me, I know the type."

"Good night, Mom," Lindsey said. She hugged her mom and kissed her cheek and then did the same with the rest of the parents.

"Do you need me to stay in town?" Jack asked. He stood with an arm wrapped around his girlfriend, Stella, who was the only woman who'd ever been able to handle him.

"I don't think so, but thanks for the offer," she said. "I think Sully and I are going to call it an early night."

"Probably the smart choice," Stella said. "Call us if you need us."

Once the families were gone, Lindsey collapsed back in her seat. She turned to face Sully and said, "Emma asked me to talk to Naomi tomorrow. What the heck am I supposed to say to her now?"

"Nothing," Sully said. "If I were you, I'd let her do all the talking." He ran a hand over his face. "I wonder if Nate knows."

Lindsey thought about it. Did Nate know? She thought back to the conversation Robbie had overheard. He'd heard one of them say, "She's not yours." And the other retorted with "She is for the right price." Could they have been arguing about Naomi? Or, rather, was it about the baby? Did Steve think he could buy custody of the baby if she proved to be his? Could he have been that cruel to Naomi, who loved all her girls so much?

If it was true, and Lindsey had the sinking feeling that it was, then it would explain why Naomi thought Nate could have murdered his brother—for having an affair with her and trying to stake a claim on their youngest. It also explained why Nate thought Naomi could have murdered Steve, too. He was threatening her family, and as she'd said, "You do what you've got to do for your babies."

"Well, that was bloody over-the-top, wasn't it?" a British voice spoke from behind them, and Lindsey and Sully both spun around to find Robbie standing there, looking gobsmacked. "I felt like I needed to announce 'And the Emmy goes to . . .'"

Sully snorted. "She was enjoying the limelight a bit."

"She can't be lying though, can she?" Lindsey asked. "I mean, if that was in the will, then it's going to become public record, right?"

"Eventually," Sully said. "In the meantime, she could just be slandering Nate and Naomi to get the heat off herself."

"But that doesn't make any sense," Robbie said. "Sure, it'd work in the meantime, but when the truth comes out, she'd be in worse shape than she is now. Plus, if what she said is true, that Steve left her nothing, then she had no motive to murder him, since she was going to lose everything upon his death."

"That's true," Sully said. "Whoever did murder him cost her a fortune."

"Which is a point she'll be sure to announce as loudly

as possible," Lindsey said. "She'll make Nate and Naomi look like criminals, and there's nothing we can do about it. People tend to believe the most salacious gossip, and then they don't care to hear the facts."

"That's true," Robbie said. "But we don't actually know the facts, do we?"

Sully was quiet. Lindsey studied his face. His usual bright blue eyes were shadowed, and the dimples that always lurked at the ends of his smile were nowhere to be seen.

"What's wrong?" she asked.

"I saw them together once," Sully said. His voice was soft so that no one could overhear their conversation. Both Lindsey and Robbie leaned in. "I was returning from a run in the water taxi, and I took a shortcut past a secluded cove. I saw Steve's boat anchored and paused to go and say hello. When I pulled up, it was just Naomi and Steve on the boat. It was clear from the vibe that I'd interrupted something, but I convinced myself that I was misreading the situation."

"When was that, mate?" Robbie asked.

"About a year and a half ago," Sully said. "About the time a baby the age of Matilda would have been conceived."

Lindsey blew out a breath. "Well, it looks like Naomi may have a lot to talk about tomorrow."

It was the day before her wedding, and Lindsey still didn't have anyone to officiate. The mothers were continuing to oversee the details, and here Lindsey sat, in the jail, waiting with a basket of books for Naomi to appear. She had no idea how to play this when she desperately wanted to ask Naomi if it was true.

She wondered if stories of Jamie's scene at the Anchor had reached Naomi yet. And if they had, would she ask Lindsey about it? What should Lindsey say? Emma had given her no specific instructions, but she knew from stopping at the bakery for a muffin and a coffee that the entire town was talking about the possibility that Matilda was Steve's baby. The poor thing. Six months old and the center of a gossip storm. It wasn't right. It was poorly done of Jamie, and Lindsey found that she had actively begun to dislike the woman.

Naomi came into the lone meeting room in the small town jail. A utilitarian table and two hard chairs were the only furniture in the room. Officer Wilcox unlocked the door and let Naomi in while Lindsey stayed seated at the table.

Naomi looked at her in surprise, and Lindsey gave her a small smile of encouragement. She gestured to the basket of books and said, "I thought you might be bored."

Naomi's shoulders sagged, and she looked like she might cry. "Not bored so much as worried about my girls and my husband. I miss them all so much. I've never been apart from any of them for this long."

A single tear spilled down her cheek, and she brushed it away impatiently. She looked cold and tired and smaller than Lindsey remembered her being. Naomi was always laughing and playing, with her children gathered around her like a mother hen with her chicks. Now, she looked lonely and adrift, as if she had no idea what to do with herself if she wasn't attending to someone else's needs.

"Have you spoken to Sully's friend Jim, the attorney?" Lindsey asked. "He seemed confident he could help you."

"I did," Naomi sighed. She glanced at the basket of books. She thumbed through them, but it was clear she wasn't really seeing them. "There's been new information that's come to light, however, and I'm not sure he can help me anymore."

She glanced up at Lindsey. The dark circles under her eyes made them seem huge, as if they were being swallowed up in her sadness.

"What happened, Naomi?" Lindsey asked. "Do you want to tell me?"

"I . . . I don't want you to hate me," Naomi said. She folded her arms on the table and put her head down and wept. It broke Lindsey's heart.

She moved her chair around the table and sat beside Naomi. She gently put her hand on Naomi's back, letting her know she was there, while Naomi sobbed. "It's all right. There's nothing you could tell me that would make me hate you."

"I slept with Steve," Naomi said. The words were garbled, but Lindsey got the gist. She kept her hand in place, letting Naomi know that she wasn't judging her or pulling away. Lindsey was here, and she wasn't going anywhere.

"What happened?" she asked when Naomi's sobs settled a bit.

Naomi lifted her head and said, "I messed up. I was

scared and desperate, and I was just so damn tired of being afraid."

Lindsey ran her hand over Naomi's back in a gesture of comfort. She didn't say anything, just let Naomi tell her what happened in her own time.

"Our oldest, Maddie, has a condition. It's called pectus excavatum."

Lindsey had never heard of it, but it sounded bad.

"About two years ago, she had a massive growth spurt. She shot up five inches in six months. When it happened, the cartilage in her rib cage slowly collapsed. We had no idea. She didn't tell us until one night she had a sleepover with friends, and when they were changing into pajamas, her friends saw her chest and gasped."

Naomi paused to press the heels of her hands to her eyes. "When she came home and showed me—Ugh, my baby."

Lindsey waited for Naomi to gather herself.

"When you look at her chest, it's as if someone has put their fist right into her rib cage and made a massive dent. We took her to the doctor, and they did X-rays. It's bad. Her ribs are compressing her heart and lungs. The front of her heart is actually flat where it's smashed up against her ribs. She's going to need surgery, otherwise she'll end up with a hunched back, looking like a question mark, and have limited heart and lung capacity."

"Oh, Naomi, I'm so sorry," Lindsey said. "How frightening."

Naomi nodded. "The surgery is prohibitively expensive. We have benefits, but because we own a small business, they're not great, and they won't cover most of the surgery. It can run up to seventy-five thousand dollars or more, as they'll have to insert steel bars into her chest to brace her ribs for the next three years until the cartilage hardens. She'll be in the hospital for about a week. Nate and I have tried everything we can think of to come up with the money, but . . ."

Naomi bent her head. It was clearly painful for her to talk about, but she pressed on. "We tried to get a second mortgage on our house, but we didn't qualify. Nate considered taking on investors or a partner, but no one was interested in the garage. We tried to think of anything we could sell, but we don't own anything that valuable. I begged Nate to talk to Steve about borrowing the money, but he refused. They hadn't been close since Steve married Jamie, and Nate felt awkward asking for help."

Naomi turned to look at Lindsey. "I understood how he felt, but you do what you have to do for your babies."

She was quiet, and Lindsey had a feeling she knew where the story went from here. "You went to Steve on your own?"

Naomi nodded. She looked miserable. "I was desperate."

"I can only imagine," Lindsey said. She gave Naomi a bracing hug. "You were in a terrible position."

Naomi turned and looked at her. Her eyes were troubled, and her voice was soft when she said, "I only spent one night with him. It was a mistake, and I regretted it immediately. I love my husband. My life is with Nate. But for a few seconds, it was just so nice to have someone promise that they were going to take care of things and know that they actually could make my troubles go away. Steve told me that he'd pay for Maddie's surgery. He promised me that she'd be okay, that he'd get her the best care. I was so insanely grateful and relieved that I fell into his arms, and one thing led to another.

"When I got pregnant, he was convinced the baby was his. She isn't. I know it, but he didn't believe me. He was pushing for me to have a paternity test and refused to pay for Maddie's surgery until I had Matilda tested. I didn't know what to do. I dressed up as the woman in black the night of his party so that I could meet with him without anyone knowing who I was. I was going to beg him to go forward with the surgery and to stop insisting on a paternity test, but he refused. In fact, he said if I didn't do as he asked, he planned to have a court-ordered paternity test, and if Matilda was his, he was going to sue me for custody."

Lindsey tried to grasp the kind, jovial Steve she knew being this man who so ruthlessly used his sister-in-law to get what he wanted at any cost. She had no doubt that he manipulated her into sleeping with him when she was terrified for her child and at her most vulnerable. That was not okay.

"Does Nate know about any of this?" Lindsey asked.

"I never told him," Naomi said. "I know I should have, but I just couldn't stand the thought of him looking at me with disgust or hatred. He's my life, Lindsey. He and the girls are everything to me."

"Steve told him, didn't he?"

"He must have. When Matilda woke up coughing that night, Nate got up to take her for a drive. When he was putting her in the car seat, he looked at me and said, 'She's my daughter,' and I just knew that he knew. That's why I dressed up and went to confront Steve."

Naomi started to cry, and Lindsey felt her own heart break a bit. Life could be so complicated and so cruel at times. She patted Naomi's back and said, "Listen, it's going to be okay. The lawyer Sully has helping you, Jim, is a genius. He'll be able to figure this out. I'm sure of it."

Naomi didn't look convinced. Lindsey knew that the only thing she could give her friend at this moment was hope, so she took Naomi's hands in hers and held them tightly. "I promise. It's going to be okay."

"Thank you," Naomi said. "You're a good friend, Lindsey Norris."

"Well, I'm an even better librarian," she said. "Now, pick some books so you can think about something else until we get you out of here. And we will get you out."

"But I confessed," Naomi said. "And I stand by it."

"Are you doing that because you think Nate might have killed Steve because of the affair?"

"No!" Naomi said. But her answer came in quick and hot, letting Lindsey know that was exactly what she was afraid of.

"We're going to prove your innocence," Lindsey said. "And Nate's, too. Trust me."

There must have been something in Lindsey's expression that gave her courage, because Naomi nodded. Then she peeked inside the basket. She chose a British rom-com by Beth O'Leary entitled *The Flatshare* and a mystery, *Hid From Our Eyes* by Julia Spencer-Fleming.

"Good choices," Lindsey said.

Officer Wilcox appeared at the door and announced that the visit was over. Naomi clutched the books to her chest, and Lindsey gave her a quick hug. "Be brave. You'll be home with your girls soon."

Lindsey watched Naomi leave and wondered if she had just told the biggest pack of lies of her entire life. She picked up the basket and made her way to Emma's office, where she knew the chief was waiting for her.

She rapped on the door and walked in. Emma was at her desk, with Sully sitting across from her and Robbie pacing about the room.

"How did it go?" Emma asked.

"Brutal," Lindsey said. She then shared everything Naomi had told her. When she got to the part about Naomi suspecting that Nate had found out about her affair, Sully jumped in. He'd spent the morning talking to Nate and had gotten an even clearer picture of how Steve had used the financial stress of his brother's family to his own advantage.

"Nate knew," he said. "In fact, the argument Robbie overheard, Nate admitted to me, was Steve telling him about his plan to have the baby's paternity tested, then he was going to sue for custody and woo Naomi away from Nate. Steve thought he was in love with her, and he was prepared to do anything he could to win her from his brother, including pay for the surgery for their oldest daughter."

"How did Nate feel about that?" Lindsey asked. "I mean, I assume he was furious."

"Actually, he said he didn't believe Steve," Sully said.

"He thought it was all just some crazy scheme Steve had cooked up in his head because Jamie refused to have kids. He figured Steve would get over it, but when Naomi 'found' the wig and veil in the trash can, he began to wonder if she was the woman in black. And if she was, then he wondered if everything Steve had told him was true."

"Does he think Naomi is guilty?" Lindsey asked.

"He says he doesn't, but I think he doesn't know for sure," Sully said. "He believes the baby is his but said he doesn't care if she isn't biologically his. She's his in every way that counts. He said he knows how charming his brother can be when he wants something, and he doesn't fault Naomi, especially given the circumstances with their oldest daughter, for falling for Steve's promises."

"Wow," Robbie said. "That Steve Briggs was a right manipulative bastard." When they all glanced at him, he said, "Sorry, I know he was a friend of yours, but still."

"No, you're right," Emma said. "That's not the Steve Briggs I knew. He must have become obsessed with having a family of his own at any price."

"And now, between finding out that the murder weapon came from Nate's shop and their mutual confessions, plus the information about the will and the dubious parentage of the baby, it seems the most likely person to have wanted Steve Briggs dead is, in fact, his brother, Nate Briggs."

CHAPTER

17

BRIAR CREEK
PUBLIC LIBRARY

A knock on Emma's door interrupted whatever else she was about to say. Standing in the doorway in a dress shirt and tie, with his briefcase in hand, was Jim Britton, Sully's attorney friend.

"Sorry, I couldn't help but overhear your conversation," he said. "I actually have proof that my client was nowhere near the scene at the time of the murder."

Yes! Lindsey felt her spirits lift. She flashed Sully a relieved smile, which he returned. They were going to get Nate and Naomi out of this.

"I'm listening," Emma said.

Jim walked into the office and closed the door behind him. Tall, thin and dressed in slim-fitting designer clothes, he was the sort of professional who inspired immediate trust with his air of competence and the fact that he seemed to be thinking four steps ahead of everyone else. Lindsey would bet he was an excellent chess player.

"Although my client disagrees, I need his confession to be thrown out," he said. "I discovered prior to his confession that in addition to footage of him driving during the time of the murder gathered from several security cameras in town, he also has a tracker on his car that was installed by his insurance company. It's to monitor how he drives in order to lower the rates. Well, it monitored him the night of the murder and puts him exactly where he said he was with the baby. His story that he drove to his brother's house is a lie."

A collective sigh went through the room. Then Emma glanced at Jim with a shrewd gaze and asked, "Was there a device on Naomi's car, too?"

Jim looked away, clearly not wanting to answer.

"You can either tell me or I can find out for myself. Why don't you save us both some time?"

"There is a device on her car," he said.

Emma waited. He said nothing until she gave him a pointed look. "And?"

"It puts her at the Briggs house an hour before the time of death as determined by the medical examiner," he said.

"So Naomi had motive, opportunity and means," Emma said. She looked sick to her stomach. "I'll have Officer Kirkland release Nate, but I'm going to have to formally arrest Naomi for the murder of Steven Briggs."

"No!" Lindsey cried. "I'm sure she didn't do it. We still don't know where Mancusi is, and isn't he the likeliest suspect?"

"Yes, he is," Emma said. "But Naomi confessed."

"So did Nate," Sully said.

"Yes, but we can place Naomi at the scene around the time of the murder," Emma said. "Listen, I don't like it any more than you do, but what choice do I have? I can only hold her for so long before I have to charge her or let her go. I can't let her go. Not when she confessed and, quite frankly, had plenty of reason to murder her brother-in-law."

"How could she have gotten rid of his body?" Lindsey asked. "That's where it all falls apart. She had to be home within an hour to meet Nate when he got home from driving the baby. There is no way she could have murdered Steve, driven his body around the islands in his boat, dumped his body, gotten back to shore and made it home before Nate and the baby. It's impossible."

Lindsey looked at Sully and asked, "Right?"

He nodded. "She's right." He glanced at Jim. "You could call me as an expert witness. I know the islands, I know his boat, and I know where he was found. To accomplish all that in an hour would be impossible."

"Unless Naomi had an accomplice," Emma said. She glanced at Lindsey. "Thoughts?"

"She didn't."

"Proof?" Emma asked.

"None . . . yet." Lindsey tried to stare her down, but Emma was unflinching. Seconds ticked by and no one moved, like a standoff at high noon in the Old West.

Jim looked chagrined. "Am I to assume I'm representing Mrs. Briggs now?"

"Yes," Sully said, adding, "please."

*   *   *

Sully and Lindsey left the police station feeling as if they'd taken three steps forward and two steps back.

"Naomi didn't kill him," Lindsey said.

"I know."

"He wasn't the man I thought he was," Lindsey said.

Sully sighed. "Agreed. I can't believe he would willingly destroy his brother's life just to get what he wanted when there were so many other ways he could have achieved it."

"Do you think he loved Naomi all these years?" Lindsey asked. "It seems that Steve and Nate grew apart just as Nate was marrying Naomi. Maybe Steve was in love with her, or thought he was, and when the opportunity presented itself, he went for it."

"Well, that's just sad," Sully said.

They were standing outside in the cold. Lindsey tightened the scarf around her neck. She stared out at the islands, thinking about tomorrow. A surge of panic went through her when she realized she'd been so caught up in Nate and Naomi's situation that she still hadn't found anyone to officiate their wedding.

"Tonight is our rehearsal," she said. She looked at Sully with wide eyes.

"I know," he said.

"We don't have anyone to rehearse with." She clapped a hand to her forehead. "We have to call it off. We can't get married. How did this happen? Why can't we find anyone? Do you think it's a sign that we're not supposed to get married? I mean look at Nate and Naomi. I thought they had it nailed down, but their marriage is a mess. And Steve and Jamie. You'd think they'd had it all, wouldn't you? But in the end, they didn't even like each other."

"Darlin', I think you're panicking," Sully said. He put his arm around her and began to lead her to the library, where she was supposed to meet Beth, who had a whole itinerary planned.

"You think?" she asked. "Just because we're supposed to get married in a little over twenty-four hours and we don't even have someone willing to marry us? We're going to have to call your uncle Carl. The cold will probably kill him, and we'll have another death on our hands."

"Steady there, you're going fully sideways now," he said.

"Oh God, I'm going to have to apologize to my cousin Alice," Lindsey moaned. "I swore I would never ever do that. She's a mean girl. She put *Anne of Green Gables* at risk! I'm going to have to be married by a mean girl."

"Breathe, darling, I've actually found someone, and I'm optimistic that it's going to be just fine," he said.

"Who?" she asked. "When? Why didn't you tell me?"

"It's still in the works," he said. "But I'm confident it's going to work out, and if it doesn't and we have to use my uncle Carl, well, that'll be all right, won't it?"

"So long as he doesn't die on us," Lindsey said. "I'm even okay if he takes a nap in the middle of the service. We all could. It might be a nice meditation."

Sully laughed and hugged her. "See? It's going to be just fine. Let me handle getting a person to marry us, and you just focus on saying *yes*."

"Well, that's the easy part," she said.

"I'm glad to hear it."

"What about Nate and Naomi?" she asked.

He looked concerned. "We'll do what we can, but you know they'd both want us to forge ahead with the wedding."

"Right," she said. She looked at him in surprise. "This time tomorrow we'll be almost married."

She had known the day was coming for months. It had consumed hours of her life to plan even the small stripped-down wedding of her dreams. But now that it was here, she felt blindsided, as if it had crept up on her unawares.

"There you are," Beth said as they approached the library. "I was just going to call Emma and ask if she'd seen you. Come on, kiss the groom-to-be goodbye because we have an appointment for mani-pedis in twenty minutes."

"Is this required?" Lindsey asked. "I'm not really a mani-pedi gal."

"It is," Beth said. "You need to relax and be pampered a bit. Don't worry, I loaded up some good listens on my audiobook app. We can listen while we get polished and buffed and discuss during chapter breaks."

"My God, we really are book nerds of the first order," Lindsey said.

"I think it means we're the new cool," Beth said.

Lindsey laughed and hugged her friend. "Only you would see it that way."

"What? Reading is cool," Beth said.

Lindsey turned to Sully. "All right, when do I see you again?"

"At the rehearsal," he said. "I'm going to be taking people to and from the island in the larger boat, but I had the marina guy bring the second water taxi out of storage so that Charlie could have it just for you and Beth when you're done with your girl day. He'll be waiting for you two at five o'clock."

"That's so nice," Lindsey said. "Thank you."

He leaned down and kissed her, lingering for just a bit. When he pulled back and left them with a wave, Beth was staring at Lindsey with her hands clasped over her chest and a delightfully sappy look on her face.

"You two are going to be so happy," she cried. "I just know it."

"Me, too," Lindsey said. "I know it, too." Beth looped her arm through Lindsey's and led her down the street to the only salon in town, Putting on the Glitz. Shanna, the owner, was expecting them, and it didn't do to keep Shanna waiting.

As they walked, Lindsey tried to keep her mind on her wedding and off Nate and Naomi, but it was tough. She was anticipating the best day of her life while friends of hers, good friends, were struggling with their own worst nightmare. It didn't seem right or fair, and she hated that she couldn't do a thing about it.

Lindsey and Beth met Charlie promptly at five. He was waiting for them in Sully's office as promised. Tonight's rehearsal and dinner were just for the people participating in the ceremony. Charlie was going to perform a song, Violet was doing a reading, and Nancy had volunteered to be a greeter, while Ian was Sully's best man and Beth was Lindsey's matron of honor.

Lindsey and Beth had both worn dresses, the better to practice their aisle walking, and while this had seemed liked a good idea at the time, Lindsey's legs were freezing even though she was wearing thick tights and knee-high boots. As they climbed onto the small boat, Charlie took the captain's seat while Lindsey and Beth huddled under a heated blanket on the bench seat behind him.

Beth sniffed the air and frowned. "The tide didn't turn recently, did it?"

Lindsey glanced at the waterline. It appeared to be mid-tide, but even so, in winter the low tide didn't carry the briny fishy smell of a summer low tide. It was just too cold. Still, there was no denying the pungent smell of something really awful in the air.

She glanced over the side of the boat, looking for a dead fish or something that would explain the stench. "Hang on," she said. "I'm going to ask Charlie what it is."

"Please do," Beth said. She looked a bit green. "I'm afraid I might be sick."

Lindsey climbed out from under the warm blanket and joined Charlie at the front of the boat. Even though he was maintaining a no-wake speed, there was enough of a breeze that there was no smell up here at the bow. Lindsey thought that if they couldn't figure out what it was, she and Beth could always stand up here for the duration of the trip.

"Charlie, did anyone use this boat for fishing recently?" she asked.

"No," he said. He glanced at her. "Why?"

"There's a really bad smell back there," she said. "It smells as if something died. It's making Beth sick."

Charlie frowned. He cut the engine and the boat slowed. The small craft bobbed as the short waves rocked it from side to side.

"I'll check it out," he said. He walked toward the back. He smelled the air and made an expression of disgust. "Gah, what is that?"

"It's stronger over here," Beth said. She pointed over the side of the boat. "I keep thinking we're dragging a dead fish or something."

"I think it's below you." Charlie gestured for her to move and Beth rose from her seat, taking the blanket with her. She stood beside Lindsey in the center of the small boat and shared the blanket. Lindsey gratefully wrapped it around herself.

Charlie knelt in front of the padded bench they'd been seated on and undid a latch on the front. Hooking his fingers beneath the top, he lifted the lid and propped it up. The horrible smell that unfurled from inside the bench was like getting punched in the nose repeatedly.

Lindsey gagged and covered her nose with the blanket, and Beth did the same. Only in her case, she turned a deep shade of green and looked as if she was going to vomit for real.

A blue plastic tarp covered whatever was in the bench and Charlie reached in and pulled it aside. "Ah!" he yelled and stumbled back.

"What is it?" Lindsey asked.

Charlie was panting and with a shaking finger he pointed at the bench and said, "Body!"

"What?" Lindsey dropped the blanket and hurried forward.

She glanced past the blue tarp and saw the bloodless face of a man staring up at her with unseeing eyes. She turned to Beth and said, "Call Emma. We found Tony Mancusi."

CHAPTER

18

BRIAR CREEK
PUBLIC LIBRARY

While Beth talked to Emma, Lindsey moved the thick blue plastic, trying to see what might have caused Tony's death. The stab wound, right where his heart was, seemed the most likely cause of death.

"Emma says not to touch him," Beth said.

"I'm not touching him," Lindsey said. "I'm just trying to see what happened to him. It looks like he was stabbed."

"Lindsey says it looks like he was stabbed," Beth spoke into the phone. A screech was emitted from the phone, causing Beth to hold it away from her ear. "She said no touching."

"I can hear her," Lindsey said. "And I'm not touching."

"That's definitely a hole in his chest," Charlie said. "It looks like he's lost a lot of blood." He glanced down into the bench. "Ugh, it's filled the bottom of the boat."

He made a gurgling sound and spun away, looking sick.

"Oh, don't you start," Beth said. She swallowed hard and then thrust her phone at Lindsey. "You talk to her. I'm going to be—"

She rushed to the side of the boat where she and Charlie were both dry heaving. Lindsey turned away and took a deep breath, in through her nose and out her mouth.

"Hi, Emma," she said. "We're turning around and heading back to the pier. We should be there in a few minutes."

"Are you positive it's Mancusi?"

"Yes."

"How did he end up in one of Sully's boats?"

"No, idea, but I do know that Sully just had this boat brought over from the marina today, so it's been there for a few weeks."

"Meaning Mancusi could have been killed over there," Emma said. "You realize what this means?"

"Whoever murdered Steve murdered Mancusi," Lindsey said. She clutched a handrail while Charlie, recovered from his queasiness, took over the controls and turned the boat to the shore.

"Yes, but also we've just lost our prime suspect for Steve's murder," Emma said. She hung up without saying another word. Poor Naomi. Things were not looking good for her.

Lindsey slid Beth's phone into her coat pocket since Beth was still hanging over the side, trying not to puke.

Lindsey glanced down at Mancusi. He was wearing different clothes than he had the night of the party. He was dressed in a dark gray sweater and jeans. The sweater looked to be sodden with what Lindsey assumed was his own blood. The realization made her knees wobble, but she fought it off.

Upon closer inspection, she could see that his sweater was also covered in tufts of brown hair. She glanced at the hair on his head, avoiding looking at his face, and noted that his own brown hair was a couple of shades darker, shot with some gray. Weird.

Feeling like a ghoul, Lindsey pulled the tarp up, covering his face and body as best as she could. She didn't know much about forensics but she knew that the human body started to smell due to the gasses being released and the bacteria beginning to corrode the flesh. She shivered. That was it, she wasn't going to read any police procedurals for a while. In fact, when she and Sully went on their river cruise, she was only packing romantic comedies.

As Charlie headed for the pier, Lindsey called Sully and told him what had happened. He said he'd meet her at the police station while the rest of their people went ahead to the Blue Anchor for their rehearsal dinner since there was no way Beth and Lindsey would make it back out to the island in time to rehearse after meeting with Emma. Lindsey realized she and Beth would just have to wing it during the ceremony the next day. Lindsey tried not to let the thought of that freak her out.

She joined Charlie and Beth at the front of the boat, away from the smell. Beth immediately wrapped the warm blanket around her, for which Lindsey was grateful. She felt as if the cold had gotten into her bones and she'd never get warm. Whether it was the cold or fear, she wasn't sure, because when she glanced up at the town and saw the quaint houses perched along the shore, the only thing she could think was that there was a murderer out there somewhere.

The morning of their wedding dawned clear and cold. A sparklingly beautiful day, with fresh snowfall from the night before coating the town, making it seem clean and bright. Sully and Lindsey shared coffee and pastries before he headed out to the island to check on the details before coming back to pick her up for the wedding.

"I'll be back in a couple of hours," he said. "What will you be doing in the meantime?"

"I'm going to get Heathcliff ready for his ring bearer duties," Lindsey said. "Then I'll go and get my hair and makeup done because Beth insists that only a professional can give me hair that will hold up to the boat ride. Then I'm going to come back here, get my dress and meet you at the pier."

"Excellent," Sully said. "It's all coming together. We're so close to our moment, I'm feeling a little paranoid about letting anything interfere with it."

"Agreed," she said. She put down her coffee mug and hugged him in what she hoped was a reassuring way and not with the desperate clinging feelings she actually had. "In just a few hours we'll be husband and wife."

When his blue eyes met hers, they shone with delight. "I can't wait."

"Me either."

After a prolonged kiss that left Lindsey wondering why they didn't just elope and skip to the honeymoon, Sully headed out, and Lindsey took her coffee and a dog brush into the living room, where Heathcliff had collapsed on his dog bed after a bout of playing in the new-fallen snow. Heathcliff did not love to be brushed—understatement— but he tolerated it from Lindsey because he loved her so much, or at least she thought he put up with it for that reason. Maybe it was the dog biscuit at the end.

She worked on his thick black coat until his fur was soft and shiny. She fastened a white bow tie to his collar and checked him over. He sat in front of her, looking very earnest, so she gave him his biscuit, which he devoured. Yes, it was probably the biscuit.

"It's even better if you eat it slow enough to taste it," she said. He was too busy sniffing her hand, looking for more, to listen. Lindsey smiled and shook her head. She finished her coffee and picked up his brush. She plucked the few stray hairs out of the bristles and went to throw them in the garbage. She paused as she rubbed them between her fingers, noticing how soft they felt.

In a flash, she knew what the hair on Mancusi's coat was. Dog hair. And not just any dog hair but the sort of dog hair that required brushing and clipping, like Heathcliff's, but instead of his black hair, the stuff on Mancusi had been pale brown . . . like Jamie Briggs's dog, Teddy.

Lindsey suspected that Emma had already made the connection, but she called her anyway. The phone rang six, seven, eight times with no answer. Lindsey thought about leaving a message but figured she might sound nuts. She glanced at her watch. Beth would be at the house at any moment to pick her up for the hair salon.

The police station was on the way to the salon, so she decided to stop by and tell Emma about the dog hair. Maybe it was nothing, but it didn't feel like nothing. That way, at least she could let it go, knowing she'd passed the information on.

When Lindsey asked Beth to stop by the police station on the way to Putting on the Glitz, Beth didn't even bat an eyelash. This was what best friends meant, never having to explain your choices even if they seemed crazy.

Lindsey ran inside while Beth waited. Molly was in the front alone since there'd been a call that both Emma and Kirkland had gone to answer, which explained why Emma hadn't answered her phone. Meanwhile Wilcox kept watch over Naomi in the holding cell in back.

Not wanting to make too big a fuss, Lindsey decided to leave a note. In it, she wrote everything she was theorizing about Jamie and her dog, Teddy, which was basically that Jamie killed Mancusi with the very sharp dog shears she carried to groom Teddy with when she was feeling stressed. It would explain the hair on his sweater and the hole in Mancusi's chest.

Of course, Lindsey had no idea why Jamie would murder Mancusi. What could she have gained from his death? Unless Jamie had murdered Steve, or had him murdered, and Mancusi had found out. But that made no sense since Jamie gained nothing from Steve's death. Lindsey paused, remembering Jamie's ugly scene at the Blue Anchor where she announced that she was out of the will and inherited nothing. If Jamie hadn't known she'd been disinherited, then she might have murdered Steve, expecting to inherit it all.

She glanced at the clock. It was time to go. She'd have to leave the details of Mancusi's stab wound and what they meant up to Emma.

"Thanks, Molly," Lindsey said as she left the chief's office after attaching a note to Emma's computer monitor where she'd be sure to see it.

Lindsey dashed back out to the car where Beth was waiting.

"Did I make us late?" she asked.

"No," Beth said. "And even if you did and Shanna pitches a fit, I will just start throwing up."

"You can do that on command now?" Lindsey asked.

"The baby and I are coming to an understanding," Beth said. She put the car in drive and nibbled a saltine, looking perfectly in control. Only Beth.

They parked in a spot on the street in front of the salon. It was empty except for Shanna, who watched them enter with one eyebrow raised. "You're late."

"Bride privilege," Beth said.

"There's no such thing in the salon," Shanna said. She tossed her pink hair over her shoulder. Her eyebrows were drawn with a dark blue line, and her lips were a full raspberry red pout today. Lindsey could never be that colorful. Suddenly, she felt nervous. She hoped Shanna knew she was a less-is-more sort of girl when it came to makeup. Mascara and lip gloss were usually it. Even getting her nails done yesterday had been a stretch for her, and after Shanna had heard that her gown was ice blue with a lace overlay, she'd tried to talk Lindsey into blue nails. That had been a hard pass. She looked down at her shell pink nails. Did she have the stamina to fight over her hair?

"All right," Shanna said. "Judging by your personal style, I'm guessing we want a natural look, with the hair half up, half down?"

She turned Lindsey to the mirror and lifted up her hair, pulling a few curly tendrils to frame her face. "When you get dressed, you can attach your veil to the crown of your head and let it fall down your back. I'll show you how. Very romantic." She glanced at Lindsey. "You do have your veil, don't you?"

Lindsey blanked. Veil?

"I have it," Beth said. She held up a bag.

"Thank you," Lindsey said.

"Being a good matron of honor is all about the details," she said. She glanced at her watch. "All right, let's get to work. We have an hour and a half before we need to be back at the house to get our things."

While Shanna worked, Lindsey kept one eye out the window, looking at the police station down the street. Several cars came and went, but she didn't see Emma return. She would have used her phone to call her again, but she was a bit afraid of Shanna, especially as she was holding a hot curling wand in her hand most of the time. By the time she was finished, Lindsey's butt was numb, but when Shanna finally allowed her to look in the mirror, she was rendered speechless. Using what felt like no makeup, Shanna had made Lindsey's eyes pop, and she looked as if she had cheekbones that she was quite sure she'd never had before. In a word, it was the prettiest she had ever felt. She looked at the stylist in wonder.

"I told you I was good." Shanna laughed. "I bet you wish you'd let me paint your nails blue now."

Lindsey laughed. "No, but given that I don't recognize myself, in a good way, I will bow to your genius."

"That's all I ask," Shanna said. "Well, that and a substantial tip."

"It's yours," Beth said. She was looking at Lindsey in wonder. "Sully is going to keel over when he sees you coming down the aisle toward him."

"I hope not," Lindsey said. "A slight loosening of his knee joints will suffice."

They left the salon and headed back to the house. Lindsey grabbed her dress, as she and Beth were to be picked up at the pier by Ian, since the mothers, in a sudden fit of traditionalism, had texted that Sully could not see Lindsey before the wedding ceremony.

When they got to the pier, carrying their garment bags and duffel bags, Charlie was waiting for them instead of Ian. There had been an issue with the catering, and Ian was on Bell Island sorting it out.

"Do not worry," Charlie said. "Ian said to tell you that everything is under control."

Lindsey looked at Beth. "What do you think? Should I start panicking?"

"Not yet," Beth said. "Wait until there's evidence of a real catastrophe."

"All right," Lindsey agreed. She glanced at the garment

bag in her hand and then at Beth. "Do we have everything?"

"Let's see," she said. "Dress. Shoes. Extra makeup. Veil. No, wait. No veil. Damn it. I left it in the car. Wait here. I'll be right back."

Heathcliff, who had come with them, barked and followed Beth to the car.

"We'll get the boat loaded," Charlie said. He took Beth's bags as she hurried back down the pier toward her car.

"Are you sure you want to take us given the last time we were in a boat together?" Lindsey asked. She was teasing, mostly.

"Sure, it's not like anything like that could possibly happen again, right?" he asked.

Lindsey looked at the boat. It was sleek and new-looking and wasn't one she'd seen before. "Who's boat is this?"

"Sully borrowed it from Josh, the owner of the marina," Charlie said. "He made the case that since his boat was impounded because someone managed to stuff a body in it while under Josh's watch, Josh owed him one."

"Solid argument," Lindsey said. Charlie handed her into the boat, and Lindsey arranged the garment bags and duffels so that they would come to no harm. She also lifted the bench seat to make sure there were no surprises. It was empty except for a few life preservers. She glanced up at the pier to see if Beth was on her way. Suddenly, now that she was headed to her ceremony, she was feeling a little bit nervous.

The pier was empty, but the sound of an engine brought her attention back to Charlie. Was he firing up the boat already? No. Another boat was coming toward them. She squinted against the sun on the water, but the blond woman in a thick fur coat and the man in the shiny suit were instantly recognizable: Jamie Briggs and her attorney-slash-bodyguard, Blaise. Lindsey felt her heart drop into her feet.

Jamie was driving, and their boat was closing in fast. There was no way Lindsey and Charlie could get up to the pier before the boat reached them. She glanced up. There was Beth, hurrying toward them, clutching Lindsey's veil in her hands, with Heathcliff beside her. She was pregnant. There was no way Lindsey was going to let Beth and her baby be put in harm's way. And Heathcliff. What was it Naomi had said? "You do what you have to do for your babies."

"Charlie, get off the boat," Lindsey said.

"What? Why?" he asked.

"Just do it," she ordered as she started untying the boat. "Now."

Charlie glanced from her to the incoming boat. "Trouble?"

"Big trouble," she said. She jumped into the boat. "Now go."

"Hell, no. You can't navigate the islands," he argued. He switched on the engine, and despite the no-wake rule, he gunned it out of their space, turning the boat hard enough to send up a splash in the direction of the incoming craft. A pop sounded, and Lindsey knew it was a gunshot. Jamie and her thug attorney were planning to kill them.

CHAPTER

19

BRIAR CREEK
PUBLIC LIBRARY

Charlie sped out toward the islands, maneuvering his way through the large rocks hidden beneath the surface with the knowledge of a person who had spent his life navigating the water. The boat behind them dropped into Charlie's wake, drafting up behind them and forcing Charlie to duck and weave to avoid the bullets that were randomly shot at them.

Lindsey dug out her phone and tried to reach Emma, but she got cut off when she dropped her phone as Charlie jerked the boat into a hard left to try and ditch their pursuers. It worked, but only for a few seconds. They were cruising past Bell Island, and Lindsey saw Sully and Robbie standing on the dock. As they passed, she could just see Sully's eyes go wide as he took in the scene of his bride bouncing past him as their boat pounded off the waves with another speed boat in hot pursuit.

Lindsey dropped to the floor of the boat, trying to find her phone. It had slid under the control panel and was soaking wet from the spray. With her heart racing and her adrenaline surging, she didn't feel the cold, but her fingers were stiff as she tried to call Sully and tell him what was happening.

"Darlin'," he answered. "Correct me if I'm wrong, but a boat chase was not on the wedding itinerary."

He sounded so at ease. Lindsey instantly felt his calm fall over her like a blanket.

"It's Jamie Briggs," she shouted over the wind and the sound of the engine. "She killed Mancusi. I figured it out and left a note for Emma at the police station. Jamie must have seen it."

"All right, we can handle this," Sully said. The sound of an engine came through the phone, and Lindsey knew he was entering the chase. She hated that he would be in harm's way, but she also knew that if anyone could stop Jamie, it was Sully. "Tell Charlie to lead them to Horseshoe Island. We're going to trap them in the cove. Robbie called Emma. She and Kirkland are coming in the police boat. Don't worry, darlin', it's going to be just fine."

Lindsey shouted Sully's directions to Charlie. He nodded. Another pop sounded, and Lindsey looked back to see that Jamie and her attorney were gaining on them. She didn't want to think poorly of Josh at the marina, but the speed boat coming at them looked like a bullet, while their boat seemed to saw through the waves more like a dull bread knife.

She saw Blaise raise his gun, and another pop sounded,

followed by a splash just off the side of the boat. It occurred to her then that if he ever actually hit the boat, they could sink into the freezing water and likely die of hypothermia without the aid of bullets. Her hair whipped across her face, obscuring her vision. Not a bad thing, she thought as she hunkered down beside Charlie, trying not to be a target.

They whipped around the islands, the spray from the sea drenching them. Lindsey lost the feeling in her fingers and her toes. Her teeth were chattering so hard she was afraid she might crack a tooth, but Charlie drove like a madman, in a good way, and soon they were cruising around what Lindsey recognized as Horseshoe Island. Sully had taken her there on a few boating trips. The beach was one of the finest in the area, and the owner was very generous about sharing it with the locals.

The tricky part here, if Lindsey remembered right, was navigating the barrier of rocks that protected the cove. A boat could scrape along the bottom of one and lose its hull. She assumed Charlie would slow down as a precaution. He didn't.

He whipped the boat in and out of rocks like a needle pulling thread in and out of a cloth. There was a loud bang behind them, and Lindsey glanced back to see that Jamie had scraped the side of her boat against a rock. Blaise lost his balance and dropped his gun over the side of the boat as he flailed his arms, trying to regain his footing.

Jamie was screeching at him, with Teddy clutched in one of her arms. Blaise turned his head to yell back at her, and their boat hit another rock, sending both of them to their knees. Jamie released Teddy, who bounded to the bow and began to bark. Lindsey was certain it was a cry for help. With no one at the controls, their boat maintained its speed, slamming into the jagged ring of rocks repeatedly until there was a terrific crack and their boat split clean in two, dropping them both into the water and sending Teddy forward until he was perched on the tip of the bow.

"Let's save the dog," Lindsey said, grabbing Charlie's arm and pointing. He was already on it, turning their boat and gently cruising up alongside that half of the boat, which was rapidly sinking.

"Take the wheel. Keep it steady," Charlie ordered as he draped himself out over the side and snatched the little dog up by the sweater. Teddy began to lick his face immediately, and Charlie smiled as he clutched him close and moved back to the controls.

Lindsey saw Jamie and Blaise clinging to the back end of their boat just as Sully and Robbie arrived, with Emma in the police boat right behind them. Sully navigated the rocks, arriving just in time to grab the two before they went under. Once inside the treacherous rocks, he pulled up alongside Emma's police boat and handed over Jamie and Blaise, who were wet and shivering and immediately started blaming each other for the crimes they had just committed.

"It was all his idea!" Jamie cried. She snatched the heated blanket Emma handed to her. Glancing at Lindsey and Charlie, she shrieked, "Teddy! Give me my Teddy!"

"Like hell," Charlie muttered. He opened his coat and zippered Teddy inside so that just his round little head poked out.

"My idea?" Blaise roared. "You're the one who found her note to the chief," he pointed to Lindsey before he continued, "and decided we had to kill her because she figured out that you had stabbed Mancusi to death with those stupid dog shears you carry."

"They're not stupid, they're essential," she argued. "And he had it coming. He was blackmailing me. I had to stop him before he could talk. He ruined everything."

"So you stabbed him," Blaise snapped. "I told you when we hid his body in the boat at the marina that it was going to ruin us."

"How was I supposed to know they'd find him? It's winter. No one is boating right now," she said. "Besides, that wouldn't have happened if you'd taken out the boat and dumped him like I asked."

"I told you I don't know how to drive a boat," he argued.

And so it went, back and forth.

"And once trapped, the rats turn on each other," Robbie observed. He and Sully were coming alongside Lindsey and Charlie.

Sully gestured to Robbie to take the controls. Without a word of warning, Sully jumped from his boat to theirs, snatched Lindsey into his arms and held her tight.

"I think I died a thousand deaths when you went speeding past," he said. His voice was gruff. He cupped her face and looked her in the eye while he ran his hands over her as if to reassure himself that there were no bullet holes.

"I'm okay," she said. He kissed her cheek, her forehead, her nose. "I'm all right." He kissed her again and again until she started laughing, trying to kiss him back. He hugged her tightly, as if he never planned to let go.

"Boss, not to interrupt the moment," Charlie said. "But don't you have a wedding to get to?"

Sully and Lindsey looked at each other and grinned.

"Oh, yeah, that," Lindsey said. She reached up to push her hair out of her face. It was a snarled mess, and she was certain that the tears and snot she'd leaked from the cold had ruined her makeup. She wondered if Shanna was coming to the wedding—because she still had no idea who was actually going to be there—and if so, was the stylist going to have an episode when she caught sight of Lindsey?

The absurdity of it all struck her as funny, and she started to laugh. So much for a small, easy-to-manage wedding. Sully looked at her as if reading her mind, and he started to laugh, too.

Emma pulled alongside in her police boat. "Get yourselves to Bell Island, pronto," she said. "People are freaking out. We can take statements later. I have to lock these two up, but don't you dare start that wedding without me." She turned to glare at her boyfriend. "Robbie Vine, you have some explaining to do."

"Explaining?" he cried. "Did you not see how I was riding shotgun, getting ready to heave our anchor at them if need be? I felt like bloody James Bond. It was thrilling!"

"Thrilling?" Emma cried. "You could have gotten killed!"

"But I didn't."

"But you could've."

"I'm just going to hop over there and try to save him

from himself," Charlie said. He was still holding Teddy, who looked delighted with the change in ownership. "Why don't you lead us all out, boss?"

"With pleasure," Sully said. He kept an arm around Lindsey as he picked up speed and steered them safely through the rocks and out of the cove.

Helpfully, Shanna was one of the guests at the wedding. One look at Lindsey and she closed her eyes for just a second as if centering herself, then she grabbed her emergency beautician's kit and attended to the rat's nest that had become Lindsey's hair.

Beth, who'd been abandoned on the pier with Heathcliff, had been picked up by her husband, Aidan, when he'd realized what had happened. She met Lindsey in the master bedroom of Sully's parents' house, which had become command central for the wedding.

The moms popped in and out. Lindsey's brother, Jack, dropped by with Stella. The crafternooners all visited. Nancy reported that Brendan had outdone himself on the cake and there was definitely more than enough for everyone. Because most of the guests had seen the boat chase, there was much explaining to be done. In fact, so much of her preparation was telling everyone about Jamie's confession—that Tony Mancusi had killed Steve and that she'd killed Mancusi—that Lindsey didn't have any time to think about the wedding or how many people were down there or whether she should be nervous.

In fact, before she knew it, her mother was handing her

a bouquet of white anemones, red poinsettias, and eucalyptus fronds, all tied together with a white ribbon. She looked like she wanted to say something but was too choked up to speak.

Lindsey hugged her close and said, "I love you, Mom."

"I love you, too. So much," Christine whispered, tears already starting as she kissed Lindsey's cheek and then turned to let Jack escort her into the ceremony.

Beth dabbed at her own eyes with a handkerchief. "Shoot, I was really going to try not to cry today."

Lindsey smiled at her and said, "Come here." She hugged her close and said, "Thanks for being my best friend all these years. I couldn't do this without you."

"Oh, now you've done it," Beth said with a sob. She cried and then dabbed at her face with a tissue from the pocket of her dark green dress, cut in an A-line to accommodate her expanding belly. She clutched Lindsey's hand in hers and said, "Without you, well, my life certainly wouldn't have turned out as amazing as it has, so if anyone should be thanking someone, I'm thanking you."

She hugged Lindsey again and then turned away with another sob.

"Is she going to be all right?" John asked.

Lindsey looked at her father, all buttoned-down in his tuxedo. She'd never seen him in formal wear before. "Yeah, she'll be all right eventually. You look very dapper, Dad."

"Thank you," her father said. He adjusted his bow tie. Then he turned to her, and his gaze softened. "You look beautiful, Linds. Your mother and I . . ." He put his fist to his lips as if he had to cough, but Lindsey saw the sheen of tears in his eyes. He cleared his throat and continued, "We love you so much, and we hope . . . well, we hope that you and Sully have as happy a marriage as we've had."

Lindsey felt her own throat get tight. Her parents and Sully's parents were amazing examples of doing it right. She nodded and said, "I love you, too, and don't worry. We will. We have your lead to follow for a long and happy life together." She took a quick breath, trying to maintain her composure. "Thank you for that."

Her father kissed her forehead and then held out his arm. Lindsey tucked her hand around his elbow, and together they headed down the stairs and through the house. The photographer surreptitiously snapped pictures as they went.

It had been decided that the service and the reception would be held in the big tent outside. In her green tea-length dress, with her hair done up and fastened with pearl-tipped hair pins, Beth stepped up to the entrance of the tent. As Milton Duffy held open the thick cloth curtain, Beth gave Lindsey one last glance. Her smile was quick and bright, pure Beth, and she gave a little wave and disappeared.

The sides were tied down, keeping the heat in, and a path of flower petals had been dropped in the snow. Music was playing, and as they stepped up to the entrance, which Milton had closed after Beth, Lindsey appreciated the cold bite in the air. It was like a gentle slap in the face, making her present in the moment.

She took a second to center herself, taking in the faint scent of woodsmoke on the air, the cry of a seagull in the distance, the gentle breeze that tugged at her restored hair and her long veil, the feel of her father's strong arm beneath her fingertips and the swish of her beautiful ice blue gown with the delicate lace overlay at her feet. She was filled with gratitude for every single bit of this quiet moment.

Just then, Milton pushed aside the heavy curtain and gestured them forward. Lindsey and her father exchanged a look, and taking a deep breath, they entered the tent. Lindsey's breath caught when she saw what the moms had achieved over the past few days. Twinkling lights shone down from above while thick garlands of holly and ivy and poinsettias were strung all around the tent, making it seem like an outdoor garden. It was breathtaking.

Charlie played his acoustic guitar, a beautiful melody, and Lindsey saw the guests rising to their feet as she and her father began their walk down the aisle, also strewn with flower petals. She saw so many faces she recognized: the library staff, the crafternooners, their friends and neighbors in Briar Creek, people who had come to mean so much to her over the past few years. Suddenly, she was immensely grateful that she'd given the stationer the wrong list. She couldn't imagine getting married without all their nearest and dearest here.

She glanced up ahead and saw Sully. He looked devastatingly handsome in his black tuxedo and bow tie. His mahogany curls shone in the overhead lights, and his wide-eyed look at the sight of her more than made up for having to be at the mercy of Shanna's curling iron twice in one day. The love in his eyes made her heart beat at triple time, and when he grinned at her and coupled it with a wink, she felt the same dizziness she always felt when he looked at her in just that way. She returned his grin and his wink, and his smile grew even brighter.

Just beyond Sully, she glimpsed the man who was officiating their wedding, wearing a thick white robe and deep green and gold vestments. She wondered if it was Sully's uncle Carl after all, but no. She actually missed a step when she recognized . . . *Robbie?*

Grasping the reason for her stumble, her father steadied her, leaned close and said, "Turns out he didn't just play a vicar on television. He's actually ordained."

Lindsey glanced from Robbie to Sully, whose eyes were twinkling, and she burst out laughing. This was perfect!

When her father handed her off to her groom, Heathcliff appeared from behind Sully and sat down between their feet like a perfect gentleman. Lindsey was certain her heart had never been fuller.

Robbie grinned at the three of them, and then in the voice of a very proper vicar, he said, "Dearly beloved, we are gathered here today in the presence of . . . this dog." He paused, and Heathcliff barked. The guests laughed, which encouraged Heathcliff to bark again. Robbie raised one eyebrow and looked at him and said, "I suppose you think you could do a better job." Heathcliff wagged, which set the crowd off again.

Lindsey took the opportunity to lean into Sully as she whispered, "If this ceremony is any indicator, I think we're going to live happily ever after."

Sully grinned at her and said, "Of that you can be sure, darlin'." And she knew he spoke the truth.

CHAPTER

Epilogue

BRIAR CREEK
PUBLIC LIBRARY

The library was only open for a half day on Christmas Eve. Of course, in the years since Lindsey had been head librarian, it had become a sort of open house for the community, with everyone popping in to wish their friends and neighbors a happy holiday, snag a cookie from Nancy, do a calming yoga meditation with Milton, make a last-minute crafty gift with Paula or listen to Beth read "A Visit from St. Nicholas" during one of the many times she read it while dressed in her Mrs. Claus outfit.

It was one of Lindsey's favorite days of the year because they didn't even pretend to try and work other than to empty the book drop, check in the books that were returned and answer any pressing reference questions, which usually consisted of "What present can I buy my wife last minute?" or "Will Nancy give me the recipe for her ginger-snaps?" That was a *maybe*, if she liked you.

The crafternooners were all there having an impromptu meeting. They had just agreed that the next book they were going to read would be *Where the Crawdads Sing* by Delia Owens. Nancy and Violet had lobbied hard for the book, since Owens, the author, was a debut novelist at age seventy, and they felt they needed to support her.

Lindsey was walking to the break room to refill the punch bowl when Naomi and Nate came in with all five of their girls. The girls, especially the middles, were practically vibrating with excitement. The oldest gave her parents a put-upon look but took a cookie and dutifully walked her sisters to Beth's reading.

Nate, who was wearing the baby in a sling, and Naomi saw Lindsey and walked toward her.

"Hi." She greeted them with a smile. "The girls look excited."

"Completely bonkers, more like," Nate said, but he was smiling. "Lindsey, we wanted to thank you and Sully. Is he here?"

"He will be soon," she said. "He's my ride home."

"I'll make sure I thank him then, too," Nate said. "What you did for us, well, we'll never forget it."

Lindsey glanced between them. Now that she was married, she felt a new understanding of what a lifetime commitment meant. She knew that she and Sully were still in the salad days and that there would be inevitable struggles ahead, but when she looked at Nate and Naomi, who were clearly going to give it another go, she felt a surge of optimism that no matter what life threw at a couple, they could try and make it.

"It was nothing," Lindsey said. "Right place at the right time and all that."

He gave her a look. Then he waved one of the baby's chubby fists at her. "Librarian for the win, then."

Lindsey laughed.

"I'll go keep an eye on the girls," he said to Naomi, and kissed her cheek.

"I'll be right there," she said. She watched him go with a look of love in her eyes that was so tender, it made Lindsey sigh.

"Things are good?" Lindsey asked tentatively.

"As good as they can be," Naomi said. "Because of Steve's will, we felt we had to have Matilda tested. She's Nate's." She looked weak with relief when she said it, and Lindsey knew that it had been important to her that the baby be her husband's.

"And you're staying together?" Lindsey asked. She pushed open the door to the break room and put the punch bowl on the counter. Naomi joined her.

"We're going to try," Naomi said. She started to fill the bowl with ice from the freezer while Lindsey poured in a bottle of cranberry juice. "We're in counseling, and I think we'll be able to put the past behind us. The counselor says the fact that we both were willing to sacrifice ourselves for the other shows how much we love each other."

Lindsey handed her a bottle of sparkling cider, while she poured in a bottle of ginger ale. The punch began to fizz.

"Of course, she also said that our ability to believe each other capable of murder meant we have some communication issues." Naomi's tone was wry, and Lindsey laughed.

"What about Maddie?" she asked. "Will she be able to have the surgery?"

Naomi looked up at her, and her eyes filled with tears. She nodded and said, "With Nate's inheritance, we can afford it. It's still terrifying, but there's a surgeon at Phoenix Children's Hospital in Arizona who is supposed to be the best in the country."

Lindsey put down the bottle and hugged Naomi. She felt her own eyes get watery. "I'm so glad."

"Me, too," Naomi said. "It's hard for Nate, though. He's got a lot of conflicting feelings toward his brother, which my affair didn't help. I know if he was given the choice, he'd give it all back to have his brother back, and I feel for him. I really do."

"'. . . the two most powerful warriors are patience and time,' Leo Tolstoy from *War and Peace*," Lindsey said.

"Oh, I like that," Naomi said. "I think we're going to need both."

"From what I've seen, you have them," Lindsey said. "You're going to be all right."

"Thanks," Naomi said. "Like Nate said, we can never thank you enough. If you hadn't left that note for Emma, and if Jamie hadn't seen it—"

"We would have had a very boring wedding," Lindsey said. She lifted up the punch bowl and followed Naomi, who led the way to the door. "It was purely selfish what we did."

Naomi laughed, and it was wonderful to see her smile again. "Well, when you put it like that."

They returned to the main room in the library, and

Lindsey was delighted to see that her husband had arrived. It had been a week since they'd been married, but Lindsey still wasn't used to saying *my husband*. They had postponed their honeymoon until after the holiday, knowing that Emma might need them as she put together the pieces of Steve Briggs's murder and then Tony Mancusi's.

According to Jamie's full confession, she'd wanted out of the marriage so that she could be with Blaise, so she had hired Mancusi to take Steve out on his boat after the holiday party, saying that he wanted to talk. He was supposed to push Steve off the boat and leave him to drown or freeze, whichever killed him first. Jamie hadn't known about the will leaving her nothing and had assumed that she would inherit everything as a widow, which was substantially more than she'd get as a divorcée.

The murder didn't go as planned, and when Steve put up a fight, Tony grabbed the first thing he could find, Nate's wrench, and clobbered Steve in the head, killing him instantly, or so he thought.

In a panic, Mancusi decided he needed to dump the body. He shoved Steve overboard, then he set Steve's boat adrift, hoping people would think Steve had taken out his boat by himself and had an accident. He had no idea that when he pushed Steve overboard, he was still alive, and Steve somehow managed to swim to Bell Island, where the head injury and hypothermia finished him off.

According to plan, Mancusi went into hiding in one of the stored boats at the marina, but when he realized there would be no payout because Jamie had been disinherited, he confronted her, demanding his money, saying otherwise he'd go to the police and confess that she'd engineered the whole thing.

In a fit of rage, Jamie stabbed Tony with the dog-grooming shears she had in hand, as she was grooming Teddy at the time. Then she and Blaise tried to hide Mancusi in a boat, planning to dump him after either Nate or Naomi was arrested, giving Jamie an opportunity to contest the will.

Everything changed when Lindsey found the dog hair on Mancusi and left a note for Emma, which Jamie found when she stopped by the police station to see how the case was going. Of course, now that the truth was out, Jamie was denying that she'd hired Tony and was trying to change the narrative, saying that she killed Tony as revenge, out of love for her husband. Lindsey didn't think anyone was going to buy that.

The doors to the library opened, and Emma and Robbie appeared, with Charlie right behind them. He was carrying Teddy, whom he now called Theodore, in a baby sling much like Nate's. Lindsey elbowed Sully and pointed with her thumb. He glanced up from handing a cup of punch to Violet and grinned.

"I think they're perfect for each other," he said.

"Agreed," she said.

They handed out more punch to the newcomers, and when everyone had a cup, Robbie stood up on a chair, because of course he did, and cleared his throat.

"I believe a holiday toast is in order," he said. "And since I've been doing readings of *A Christmas Carol* for two weeks, let's take it from the master."

And then in his best Dickensian voice, Robbie said, "'Then all the Cratchit family drew around the hearth in what Bob Cratchit called a circle, meaning half a one; and at Bob Cratchit's elbow stood the family display of glass. Two tumblers and a custard cup without a handle. These held the hot stuff from the jug, however, as well as golden goblets would have done; and Bob served it out with beaming looks, while the chestnuts on the fire sputtered and crackled noisily. Then Bob proposed, "A Merry Christmas to us all, my dears. God bless us!" Which the family re-echoed. "God bless us every one!" said Tiny Tim, the last of all.'"

"Merry Christmas, wife," Sully said as he clinked his plastic cup with Lindsey's.

She smiled and said, "Merry Christmas, husband." And she knew that it was going to be the first of many in what she hoped was a long life together.

The Briar Creek Library Guide to Crafternoons

What is a crafternoon? It's an afternoon (or whenever) gathering of friends who do a craft and share a meal or snacks while discussing a book they've recently read. It's a great way for friends to come together and reconnect when it seems life just gets busier and busier! To get you started, here is a readers guide, some recipes and a craft! Enjoy!

Readers Guide for
A Christmas Carol

by Charles Dickens

1. What do you think of Ebenezer Scrooge? Do you know anyone in real life who reminds you of him?

2. At its heart, *A Christmas Carol* is about family. How did Ebenezer's family life shape him into the man he became? What do you think of the Cratchits as a family?

3. It is an act of great generosity by Scrooge to give his clerk a goose for Christmas dinner. How has Christmas dinner changed since Dickens wrote the story in 1843?

4. Which of the three ghosts—Christmas Past, Christmas Present or Christmas Future—is most important to the story? Why do you think they helped reform Mr. Scrooge?

5. What do you think is the main theme of *A Christmas Carol*? That it's never too late to change or that it's important to give back to the community?

6. The disparity of wealth is a common theme in Dickens's work. How did he view the wealthy? What contribution to society do you believe his work made, and why has it lasted over time?

Craft:
Fire-starter Pine Cones

pine cones (dry)
wax (enough to dip a pine cone in)
old crayons or candle dye
essential oil—peppermint
cotton string
double boiler
waxed paper
tongs
scissors
wooden paint stirrer

Melt the wax in the double boiler. If you want to add color, you can add a few crayons of the desired color or use a candle dye. Add a few drops of essential oil, too. Use a wooden paint stirrer to mix in the color and scent. Twine your string around the pine cone in a spiral from bottom to top, leaving ½ inch to act as a wick at the top. Using tongs, dip the pine cone, topside down, into the wax and coat thoroughly. Carefully lift the pine cone out, and let it drip the excess wax back into the boiler. Carefully place the pine cone, bottom side down, on the wax paper to cool.

Recipes

CRANBERRY-GINGER PUNCH

1 liter apple juice
1 liter ginger ale
¼ cup lemon juice
½ liter unsweetened cranberry juice
¼ cup sugar
4 cups crushed ice
1 cup fresh cranberries

Pour all the liquids into a large punch bowl, stir in the sugar until fully dissolved, and top with ice and cranberries.

SCOTTISH SHORTBREAD

2 cups butter, softened
1 cup packed brown sugar
4 ½ cups all-purpose flour

Preheat oven to 325°. Cream together butter and sugar until fluffy. Add 4 cups of flour, mixing until blended. Turn onto a floured surface and knead for several minutes, adding the remaining flour until a soft dough forms. Use a floured rolling pin to roll the dough until it is ½-inch thick. Cut into 3x1-inch rectangles. Place cookies 1 inch apart on an ungreased cookie sheet and bake until cookies are golden brown, about 20–25 minutes. Makes 48 cookies.

Acknowledgments

Big thanks to my editor, Kate Seaver, and my agent, Christina Hogrebe, for their enthusiasm and encouragement. You make my books sparkle and shine, and I am ever grateful. Also, I am so pleased to have such a tremendous team at Berkley—Jessica Mangicaro and Brittanie Black—you are amazing. And, as always, I am thrilled to have cover artist Julia Green use her tremendous talent to make my book covers so breathtakingly beautiful.

Special thanks to the Pectus Excavatum team at Phoenix Children's Hospital, especially Dr. Notrica and Jackie Hurley, and all of the staff on the ninth floor. You took amazing care of our boy, and we are ever grateful.

And, as always, big thanks to my family and friends, who put up with my inability to remember what day it is while on deadline. I love you all—most especially, Chris Hansen Orf, Beckett Orf and Wyatt Orf, who are my very favorite people.

I 'm getting married."

"Huh?"

"We've already picked our colors, pink and gray."

"Um . . . pink and what?"

"Gray. What do you think, Chelsea? I want your honest opinion. Is that too retro?"

I stared at my middle-aged widowed father. We were standing in a bridal store in central Boston on the corner of Boylston and Berkeley Streets, and he was talking to me about wedding colors. *His* wedding colors.

"I'm sorry—I need a sec," I said. I held up my hand and blinked hard while trying to figure out just what the hell was happening.

I had raced here from my apartment in Cambridge after receiving a text from my dad, asking me to meet him at this address because it was an emergency. I was prepared for heart surgery, not wedding colors!

Suddenly, I couldn't breathe. I wrestled the constricting wool scarf from around my neck, yanked the beanie off my head, and stuffed them in my pockets. I scrubbed my scalp with my fingers in an attempt to make the blood flow to my brain. It didn't help. *Come on, Martin*, I coached myself. *Pull it together.* I unzipped my puffy winter jacket to let some air in, then I focused on my father.

"What did you say?" I asked.

"Pink and gray, too retro?" Glen Martin, a.k.a. Dad, asked. He pushed his wire-frame glasses up on his nose and looked at me as if he was asking a perfectly reasonable question.

"No, before that." I waved my hand in a circular motion to indicate he needed to back it all the way up.

"I'm getting married!" His voice went up when he said it, and I decided my normally staid fifty-five-year-old dad was somehow currently possessed by a twenty-something bridezilla.

"You okay, Dad?" I asked. Not for nothing, because the last time I checked, he hadn't even been dating anyone, never mind thinking about marriage. "Have you recently slipped on some ice and whacked your head? I ask because you don't seem to be yourself."

"Sorry," he said. He reached out and wrapped me in an impulsive hug, another indicator that he was not his usual buttoned-down mathematician self. "I'm just . . . I'm just so happy. What do you think about being a flower girl?"

"Um . . . I'm almost thirty." I tried not to look as bewildered as I felt. What was happening here?

"Yes, but we already have a full wedding party, and you and your sister would be really cute in matching dresses, maybe something sparkly."

"Matching dresses? Sparkly?" I repeated. I struggled to make sense of his words. I couldn't. It was clear. My father had lost his ever-lovin' mind. I should probably call my sister.

I studied his face, trying to determine just how crazy he was. The same hazel eyes I saw in my own mirror every morning held mine, but where my eyes frequently looked flat with a matte finish, his positively glowed. He really looked happy.

"You're serious," I gasped. I glanced around the bridal store, which was stuffed to the rafters with big fluffy white dresses. None of this made any sense, and yet here I was. "You're not pranking me?"

"Nope." He grinned again. "Congratulate me, peanut. I'm getting married."

I felt as if my chest were collapsing into itself. Never, not once, in the past seven years had I ever considered the possibility that my father would remarry.

"To who?" I asked. It couldn't be . . . nah. That would be *insane.*

"Really, Chels?" Dad straightened up. The smile slid from his face, and he cocked his head to the side—his go-to disappointed-parent look.

I had not been on the receiving end of this look very often in life. Not like my younger sister, Annabelle, who seemed to thrive on "the look." Usually, it made me fall right in line, but not today.

"Sheri? You're marrying Sheri?" I tried to keep my voice neutral. Major failure, as I stepped backward, tripped on the trailing end of my scarf, and gracelessly sprawled onto one of the cream-colored velvet chairs that were scattered around the ultrafeminine store. I thought it was a good thing I was sitting, because if he answered in the affirmative, I might faint.

"Yes, I asked her to marry me, and to my delight she accepted," he said. Another happy, silly grin spread across his lips as if he just couldn't help it.

"But . . . but . . . she won you in a bachelor auction two weeks ago!" I cried. I closed my mouth before I said more, like pointing out that this was hasty in the extreme.

The store seamstress, who was assisting a bride up on the dais in front of a huge trifold mirror, turned to look at us. Her dark hair was scraped up into a knot on top of her head, and her face was contoured to perfection. She made me feel like a frump in my Sunday no-makeup face. Which, in my defense, was not my fault, because when I'd left the house to meet Dad, I'd had no idea the address he'd sent was for Brianna's Bridal. I'd been expecting an urgent care; in fact, I wasn't sure yet that we didn't need one.

Glen Martin, Harvard mathematician and all-around nerd dad, had been coerced into participating in a silver-fox bachelor auction for prominent Bostonians by my sister, Annabelle, to help raise funds for Boston Children's Hospital. I had gone, of course, to support my sister and my dad, and it had mostly been a total snooze fest.

The highlight of the event was when two socialites got into a bidding war over a surgeon, and the loser slapped the winner across the face with her cardboard paddle. Good thing the guy was a cosmetic surgeon, because there was most definitely some repair work needed on that paper cut.

But my father had not been anywhere near that popular with the ladies. No one wanted a mathematician. No one. After several minutes of excruciating silence, following the MC trying to sell the lonely gals on my dad's attempts to solve the Riemann hypothesis, I had been about to bid on him myself, when Sheri, a petite brunette, had raised her paddle with an initial offer. The smile of gratitude Dad had sent Sheri had been blinding, and the next thing we knew, a flurry of numbered paddles popped up in the air, but Sheri stuck in there and landed the win for $435.50.

"Two weeks is all it took," Dad said. He shrugged and held out his hands like a blackjack dealer showing he had no hidden cards, chips, or cash.

I stared at him with a look that I'm sure was equal parts shock and horror.

"I know it's a surprise, Chels, but when—" he began, but I interrupted him.

"Dad, I don't think a bachelor auction is the basis for a stable, long-lasting relationship."

"You have to admit it makes a great story," he said.

"Um . . . no." I tried to sound reasonable, as if this were a math problem about fitting sixty watermelons into a small car. I spread my hands wide and asked, "What do you even know about Sheri? What's her favorite color?"

"Pink, duh." He looked at me with a know-it-all expression more commonly seen on a teenager than a grown-ass man. Hmm.

"All right, who are you, and what have you done with my father?" I wanted to check him for a fever; maybe he had the flu and he was hallucinating.

"I'm still me, Chels," he said. He gazed at me gently. "I'm just a happy me, for a change."

Was that it? Was that what was so different about him? He was happy? How could he be happy with a woman he hardly knew? Maybe . . . oh dear. My dad hadn't circulated much after my mom's death. Maybe he was finally getting a little something-something, and he had it confused with love. Oh god, how was I supposed to talk about this with him?

I closed my eyes. I took a deep breath. Parents did this all the time. Surely I could manage it. Heck, it would be great practice if I ever popped out a kid. I opened my eyes. Three women were standing in the far corner in the ugliest chartreuse dresses I had ever seen. Clearly, they were the attendants of a bride who hated them. And that might be me in sparkly pink or gray if I didn't put a stop to this madness.

"Sit down, Dad," I said. "I think we need to have a talk."

He took the seat beside mine and looked at me with the same patience he had when he'd taught me to tie my shoes. I looked away. Ugh, this was more awkward than when my gynecologist told me to scoot down, repeatedly. It's like they don't know a woman's ass needs some purchase during an annual. *Focus, Martin!*

"I know that you've been living alone for several years."

I cleared my throat. "And I imagine you've had some needs that have gone unmet."

"Chels, no—" he said. "It isn't about that."

I ignored him, forging on while not making eye contact, because, lordy, if I had to have this conversation with him, I absolutely could not look at him.

"And I understand that after such a long dry spell, you might be confused about what you feel, and that's okay," I said. Jeebus, this sounded like a sex talk by Mr. Rogers. "The thing is, you don't have to marry the first person you sleep with after Mom."

There, I said it. And my wise advice and counsel were met with complete silence. I waited for him to express relief that he didn't have to get married. And I waited. Finally, I glanced up at my father, who was staring at me in the same way he had when I discovered *he* was actually the tooth fairy. Chagrin.

"Sheri is not the first," he said.

"She's not?" I was shocked. Shocked, I tell you.

"No."

"But you never told me about anyone before," I said.

"You didn't need to know," he replied. "They were companions, not relationships."

"They?!" I shouted. I didn't mean to. The seamstress sent me another critical look, and I coughed, trying to get it together.

Dad shifted in his seat, sending me a small smile of understanding. "Maybe meeting here wasn't the best idea. I thought you'd be excited to help plan the wedding, but perhaps you're not ready."

"Of course I'm not ready," I said. "But you're not either."

"Yes, I am."

"Oh, really? Answer me this: Does Sheri prefer dogs or cats?"

"I don't—" He blinked.

"Yes, because it's only been two weeks," I said. "You remember that lump on your forehead? It took longer than two weeks to get that biopsied, but you're prepared to marry a woman you haven't even known long enough for a biopsy."

My voice was getting higher, and Dad put his hands out in an *inside voice, please* gesture. I would have tried, but I felt as if I was hitting my stride in making my point. I went for the crushing blow.

"Dad, do you even know whether she's a pie or cake sort of person?"

"I . . . um . . ."

"Do you realize you're contemplating spending the rest of your life with a person who might celebrate birthdays with pie?"

"Chels, I know this is coming at you pretty fast," he said. "I do, but I don't think Sheri liking pie or cake is really that big of a deal. Who knows, she might be an ice cream person, and ice cream goes with everything."

"Mom was a cake person," I said. There. I'd done it. I'd brought in the biggest argument against this whole rushed matrimonial insanity. Mom.

My father's smile vanished as if I'd snuffed it out between my fingers like a match flame. I felt lousy about it, but not quite as lousy as I did at the thought of Sheri—oh, but no—becoming my stepmother.

"Your mother's been gone for seven years, Chels," he said. "That's a long time for a person to be alone."

"But you haven't been alone . . . apparently," I protested. "Besides, you have me and Annabelle."

"I do."

"So why do you need to get married?" I pressed.

Dad sighed. "Because I love Sheri and I want to make her my wife."

I gasped. I felt as if he'd slapped me across the face. Yes, I knew I was reacting badly, but this was my father. The man who had sworn to love my mother until death do them part. But that was the problem, wasn't it? Mom had passed away, and Dad had been alone ever since, right up until he met Sheri Armstrong two weeks ago when she just kept raising her auction paddle for the marginally hot mathematician.

I got it. Really, I did. I'd been known to have bidding fever when a mint pair of Jimmy Choos showed up on eBay. It was hard to let go of something when it was in your grasp, especially when another bidder kept raising the stakes. But this was my dad, not shoes.

One of the bridal salon employees came by with a tray of mimosas. I grabbed two, double fisting the sparkling beverage. Sweet baby Jesus, I hoped there was more fizz than pulp in them. The bubbles hit the roof of my mouth, and I wished they could wash away the taste of my father's startling news, but they didn't.

"Listen, I know that being the object of desire for a crowd of single, horny women is heady stuff—"

"Really, you know this?" Dad propped his chin in his hand as he studied me with his eyebrows raised and a twinkle in his eye.

"Okay, not exactly, but my point—and I have one—is that you and Sheri aren't operating in the real world here," I said. "I understand that Sheri is feeling quite victorious, having won you, but that doesn't mean she should wed you. I mean, why do you have to marry her? Why can't you just live in sin like other old people?"

"Because we love each other and we want to be married."

"You can't know this so soon," I argued. "It's not possible. Her representative hasn't even left yet."

My dad frowned, clearly not understanding.

"The first six months to a year, you're not really dating a person," I explained. "You're dating their representative. The real person, the one who leaves the seat up and can't find the ketchup in the fridge even when it's right in front of him, doesn't show up until months into the relationship. Trust me."

"What are you talking about? Of course I'm dating a person. I can assure you, Sheri is very much a woman," he said. "Boy howdy, is she." The tips of his ears turned red, and I felt my own face get hot with embarrassment. I forged on.

"Dad, first, *ew*," I said. "And second, a person's representative is their best self. After two weeks, you haven't seen the real Sheri yet. The real Sheri is hiding behind the twenty-four-seven perfect hair and makeup, the placid temper, the woman who thinks your dad jokes are funny. They're not."

"No, no, no." He shook his head. "I've seen her without makeup. She's still beautiful. And she does have a temper—just drive with her sometime. I've learned some new words. Very educational. And my dad jokes are too funny."

I rolled my eyes. I was going to have to do some tough love here. I was going to have to be blunt.

"Dad, I hate to be rude, but you're giving me no choice. She's probably only marrying you for your money," I said. Ugh, I felt like a horrible person for pointing it out, but he needed protection from gold diggers. It was a kindness, really.

To my surprise, he actually laughed. "Sheri is more well off than I am by quite a lot. I'm the charity case in this relationship."

"Then why on earth does she want to marry *you*?" I asked.

The words flew out before I had the brains to stifle them. It was a nasty thing to say. I knew that, but I was freaked out and frantic and not processing very well.

"I didn't mean that the way it sounded—" I began but he cut me off.

"Despite what you think, I'm quite a catch in middle-aged circles."

He stood, retrieving his coat from a nearby coatrack. As he shrugged into it, a flash of hurt crossed his face that made my stomach ache. I loved my father. I wouldn't inflict pain upon him for anything, and yet I had. I'd hurt him very much. I felt lower than sludge.

"I'm sorry, Dad. Really, I didn't mean—" I began, but he cut me off again.

"You did mean it, and, sadly, I'm not even surprised," he said. "Listen, I have mourned the loss of your mother every day since she passed, and I will mourn her every day for the rest of my life, but I have found someone who makes me happy, and I want to spend my life with her. That doesn't take away what I had with your mother."

"Doesn't it?" I argued. This. This was what had been bothering me since his announcement. How could he not see that by replacing my mother, he was absolutely diminishing what they'd had? "Sheri's going to take your name, isn't she? And she's going to move into our house, right? So everything that was once Mom's—the title of Mrs. Glen Martin and the house where she loved and raised her family— you're just giving to another woman. The next thing I know, you'll tell me I have to call her Mom."

A guilty expression flitted across his face.

"No." I shook my head. "Absolutely not."

"I'm not saying you have to call her that. It's just Sheri's never had a family of her own, and she mentioned in passing how much she was looking forward to having daughters. It would be nice if you could think about how good it would be to have a mother figure in your life again."

"I am not her daughter, and I never will be," I said. My chest heaved with indignation. "How can you pretend that all of that isn't erasing Mom?"

Dad stared down at me with his head to the side and his right eyebrow arched, a double whammy of parental disappointment. He wrapped his scarf about his neck and pulled on his gloves.

"You know what? I don't know if Sheri will take my

name. We haven't talked about it," he said. "As for the house, I am planning to sell it so we can start our life together somewhere new."

I sucked in a breath. My childhood home. Gone? Sold? To strangers? I thought I might throw up. Instead, I polished off one of the mimosas.

"Sheri and I are getting married in three months," he said. "We're planning a nice June wedding, and we very much want you to be a part of it."

"As a flower girl?" I scoffed. "Whose crazy idea was that?"

"It was Sheri's," he said. His mouth tightened. "She's never been married before, and she's a little excited. It's actually quite lovely to see."

"A thirty-year-old flower girl," I replied, as tenacious as a tailgater in traffic. I just couldn't let it go.

"All right, I get it. Come as anything you want, then," he said. "You can give me away, be my best man, be a bridesmaid, or officiate the damn thing. I don't care. I just want you there. It would mean everything to Sheri and me to have your blessing."

I stared at him. The mild-mannered Harvard math professor who had taught me to throw a curveball, ride a bike, and knee a boy in the junk if he got too fresh had never looked so determined. He meant it. He was going to marry Sheri Armstrong, and there wasn't a damn thing I could do about it.

"I . . . I." My words stalled out. I wanted to say that it was okay, that he deserved to be happy, and that I'd be there in any capacity he wanted, but I choked. I sat there with my mouth opening and closing like a fish on dry land, trying to figure out how to mouth breathe.

My father turned up his collar, bracing for the cold March air. He looked equal parts disappointed and frustrated. "Don't strain yourself."

He turned away as I sat frozen. I hated this. I didn't want us to part company like this, but I was so shocked by this sudden turn of events, I was practically catatonic. I waited, feeling miserable, for him to walk away, but instead he turned back toward me. Rather than being furious with me, which might have caused me to dig in my heels and push back, he looked sad.

"What happened to you, peanut?" he asked. "You used to be the girl with the big heart who was going to save the world."

I didn't say anything. His disappointment and confusion washed over me like a bath of sour milk.

"I grew up," I said. But even to my own ears I sounded defensive.

He shook his head. "No, you didn't. Quite the opposite. You stopped growing at all."

"Are you kidding me? In the past seven years, I've raised millions to help the fight against cancer. How can you say I haven't grown?" I asked. I was working up a nice froth of indignation. "I'm trying to make a difference in the world."

"That's your career," he said. "Being great at your profession doesn't mean you've grown personally. Chels, look at your life. You work seven days a week. You never take time off. You don't date. You have no friends. Heck, if we didn't have a standing brunch date, I doubt I'd ever see you except on holidays. Since your mother passed, you've barricaded yourself emotionally from all of us. What kind of life is that?"

I turned my head to stare out the window at Boylston Street. I couldn't believe my father was dismissing how hard I worked for the American Cancer Coalition. I had busted my butt to become the top corporate fundraiser in the organization, and with the exception of one annoying coworker, my status was unquestioned.

He sighed. I couldn't look at him. "Chels, I'm not saying what you've accomplished isn't important. It's just that you've changed over the past few years. I can't remember the last time you brought someone special home for me to meet. It's as if you've sealed yourself off since your mother—"

I whipped my head in his direction, daring him to talk about my mother in the same conversation in which he'd announced he was remarrying.

"Chels, you're here!" a voice cried from the fitting room entrance on the opposite side of the store. I glanced away from my dad to see my younger sister, Annabelle, standing there in an explosion of hot-pink satin and tulle trimmed with a wide swath of glittering crystals.

"*What. Is. That?*" I looked from Annabelle to our father and back. The crystals reflected the fluorescent light overhead, making me see spots, or perhaps I was having a stroke. Hard to say.

"It's our dress!" Annabelle squealed. Then she twirled toward us. The long tulle skirt fanned out from the formfitting satin bodice, and Annabelle's long dark curls streamed out around her. She looked like a demented fairy princess. "Do you love it or do you love it?"

"No, I don't love it. It's too pink, too poofy, and too much!" I cried. The seamstress glared at me, looking as if she were going to take some of the pins out of the pin cushion strapped to her wrist and come stab me a few hundred times. I lowered my voice a little. "Have you both gone insane? Seriously, what the hell is happening?"

Annabelle staggered to a stop. The spinning caused her to wobble a bit as she walked toward us, looking more like a drunk princess than a fey one.

"How can you be happy about this?" I snapped at her. I gestured to the dress. "Have you not known me for all of your twenty-seven years? How could you possibly think I would be okay with this?"

Annabelle grabbed the back of a chair to steady herself. "By 'this' do you mean the dress or the whole wedding thing?"

"Of course I mean the whole wedding thing," I growled. "Dad is clearly having some midlife crisis, and there's you just going along with it. Honestly, Annabelle, can't you recognize an emergency when we're having one?"

Annabelle blinked at me, looking perplexed. "What emergency? Dad's getting married. It's awesome. Besides, I feel like I have a vested interest given that it was my auction that brought Dad and Sheri together."

"Because you, like Dad, have gone completely nuts!" I declared. "Two weeks is not long enough to determine whether you should marry someone or not. My god, it takes longer to get a passport. What are you thinking supporting this craziness?"

"Chels, that's not fair and you know it," Dad said.

My expression must have been full-on angry bear, because he changed tack immediately, his expression softening.

"When did you stop letting love into your heart?" he asked. His voice was gentler, full of parental concern that pinched like shoes that were too small, but I ignored the hurt. He didn't get to judge me when he was marrying a person he barely knew. "Is this really how you want to live your life, Chels, with no one special to share it with? Because I don't."

I turned back to the window, refusing to answer. With a sigh weighty with disappointment, he left. I watched his reflection in the glass grow smaller and smaller as he departed. I couldn't remember the last time we had argued, leaving harsh words between us festering like a canker sore. Ever since Mom had died, the awareness of how precious life was had remained ever present, and we always, always, said *I love you* at the end of a conversation, even when we weren't getting along.

I thought about running after him and saying I was sorry, that I was happy for him and Sheri, but it would be a lie, and I knew I wasn't a good enough actress to pull it off. I just couldn't make myself do it. Instead, I tossed back my second mimosa, because mimosas, unlike family, were always reliable.